"Are you suggesting we pick up where we left off?"

She might have been flustered, but he'd give her credit—she could turn on the freeze when she needed to. While something sharp and needy filled him, he was more than aware this task force was a huge opportunity for him. For both of them, no doubt.

Was he even remotely considering muddying the waters with sex?

His body screamed a resounding yes, but the control he was known for somehow managed to prevail at the last minute.

"I'm suggesting we both deserve to go into this partnership fully acknowledging what came before. This is a major step in my career. I have to believe it is for you, too. Not addressing the past is foolish in the extreme." He leaned forward slightly over the table, the incredibly small space ensuring he could see her as clearly as if she were sitting beside him. "Don't you agree?"

That flutter of pulse at her throat never faded, and if he were a fanciful man, he'd say he could practically hear her heartbeat.

Dear Reader,

The New York Harbor Patrol team has just caught a unique case when a cache of deliberately dumped guns is discovered on one of their dives. What does it mean? And who's hiding evidence they don't want found?

Gavin Hayes is one of the harbor team's finest. He's strong, dependable and driven to succeed—in and out of the water. A point his captain supports with Gavin's appointment to a major interjurisdictional task force. But when his New Year's Eve one-night stand shows up on the first day, Gavin's stunned.

Serafina Forte never expected to see the guy she welcomed in the New Year with, but there he was! She's sick to her stomach over seeing him again— and not just because of nerves. Sera's pregnant and hasn't had any way of finding Gavin to tell him.

Only now they're partners on the task force, all while trying to fight their attraction *and* figure out how to co-parent. But that mysterious cache of guns is suddenly causing a lot of chaos for the harbor team. And when cops' family members become targets, the consequences are dire.

I've had so much fun spending more time sailing around New York Harbor with my NYPD divers. I hope you fall in love with Gavin and Sera just like I did.

Best,

Addison Fox

THREATS IN THE DEEP

ADDISON FOX

ROMANTIC SUSPENSE

ROMANTIC SUSPENSE™

Recycling programs for this product may not exist in your area.

ISBN-13: 978-1-335-50242-1

Threats in the Deep

Harlequin Enterprises ULC
22 Adelaide St. West, 41st Floor
Toronto, Ontario M5H 4E3, Canada
www.Harlequin.com

Printed in Lithuania

MIX
Paper | Supporting responsible forestry
FSC® C021394

Addison Fox is a lifelong romance reader, addicted to happily-ever-afters. After discovering she found as much joy writing about romance as she did reading it, she's never looked back. Addison lives in New York with an apartment full of books, a laptop that's rarely out of sight and a wily beagle who keeps her running. You can find her at her home on the web at addisonfox.com or on Facebook (Facebook.com/addisonfoxauthor) and Twitter (@addisonfox).

Visit the Author Profile
page at Harlequin.com.

For everyone who believes their past dictates their future. There's more joy and wonder and beauty awaiting you than you can ever know.
Reach for it—always!

Chapter 1

Special task force.

Those words swirled through Gavin Hayes's mind as he prepared himself for a morning in the waters around New York City.

He stared up at the beautiful stretch of the majestic Verrazzano-Narrows Bridge as his police boat moved through the tidal strait that separated Brooklyn and Staten Island on their way toward the Statue of Liberty. The bridge's arches speared toward the bright blue early spring sky, a testament to man's ingenuity and sheer prowess at building over, around and *through* nature.

He was on a patrol shift, and while they had no overt mission at the moment, he had no doubt something would come in before the day was out. He'd worked two recovery jobs yesterday and had done structural checks the day before that. So it was a nice change of pace to just be out on the water, focused on the city that rose up as majestically as the bridge.

The quiet moments were also just low-key enough that he had plenty of time to think through Captain Reed's invitation to join a special task force in collaboration with the Feds, the Coast Guard and the DA's office.

It was a welcome change from the endlessly roiling

thoughts that hadn't left him since welcoming in the new year with a gorgeous redhead who'd fled on New Year's Day never to be seen or heard from again.

Put it in the past, Hayes. Firmly in the past.

There were bigger challenges ahead. Ones that he had some control over. Unlike the reality of being left all alone around three in the afternoon after the most incredible sex of his life.

Which was only a small portion of the problem. The bigger issue was that the sex—amazing as it was—had only been the physical outcome of the most extraordinary eighteen hours he'd ever spent with another person.

Sera.

He could still feel her name on his lips and could still picture the way a lock of her deep auburn hair lay over her cheek as she slept.

Damn, he needed to let this go.

Because all he had were the memories of those eighteen hours and her first name.

He caught the light spray of water as it foamed up from the boat's wake and imagined it as a cool slap in the face.

Let.

It.

Go.

It was time. He had an exciting new opportunity in front of him and recognized it would be a challenge. A task force full of large governmental entities was a big deal. But the moment you mixed local and federal jurisdictions, things could get sticky quickly.

As much as that was true, he also recognized that New York was different. And while everyone liked returning to their own corners at the end of the day, everyone also understood that governance and security in the largest city in America was unique.

Which only added to his excitement. He'd worked his tail off to make the Harbor team, and he loved what he did in the water, but he also saw it as a path toward his future. The men and women who worked the Harbor team might have expertise in diving, but they were NYPD cops, and as such, he wanted to make detective and continue his progression up the ranks.

The task force would go a long way toward supporting those ambitions.

It was also an opportunity to show what Harbor could do. While he'd felt respected from day one, the uniqueness of his job and the work they did wasn't as well understood by outsiders. Joining a team with federal as well as local government resources would give him an opportunity to raise the profile of their diving work, too.

While there was a lot of overlap between the Coast Guard's responsibilities and the Harbor team's, there were significant differences, as well. The Coast Guard's remit was far broader, including search and rescue, marine safety and fisheries law enforcement. Gavin and his team supported search and rescue in extreme circumstances, but their work was far more narrowly defined in the realm of public safety and police work, and specific to the waters surrounding the city.

As such, there was clear sharing of jurisdiction in a way that provided minimal friction and maximum benefit to the city of New York.

Especially because once a problem hit Atlantic waters, the Coast Guard took over.

He understood it, Gavin thought as he looked out over

the harbor, the Statue of Liberty growing larger as they narrowed the distance. The work. The jurisdictions. Even the politics.

And when you understood something, you could influence the good and help support change of the not-so-good.

"Gav!"

He turned to find their dive lead for the day, Detective Wyatt Trumball. Wyatt had been a force for change on the Harbor team, leading several cases over the past few years that had been both high-profile and well-executed to ultimately help reduce crime in the city.

It had also led him to his new wife, Marlowe McCoy. Granddaughter of one of the 86th Precinct's most respected detectives, Anderson McCoy, Marlowe was practically a legend in her own right in their Sunset Bay neighborhood. She was the precinct's favorite lock-and-vault technician and was frequently pulled in on jobs to help open recovered items in the course of casework.

A series of safes, strapped to bodies, that Gavin and Wyatt had pulled up early last fall had been a huge case for the Harbor team.

One that had also created the unexpected proximity for Marlowe and Wyatt to fall in love. Sadly, the case also brought the disturbing news that her grandfather had used his well-respected position of authority in the precinct to hide Marlowe's father's misdeeds decades ago.

They'd all reeled from that unsettling revelation, and the lingering fallout hadn't fully subsided, but Wyatt had held up well under it and so had his new wife. Anderson had come clean and, while not fully exonerated, had been able to avoid jail time due to his overarchingly positive contribution to the NYPD. Now working off his remaining debt in volunteer service, the man was doing some great things with an at-risk youth program several days a week.

Was it justice?

Gavin knew there were several around the 86th who didn't think so. But others who had already seen some improvements in those at-risk youth thought the tradeoffs were more than fair.

"Hey." They shook hands in greeting.

Wyatt had already been in the wheelhouse when Gavin boarded, so they'd missed initial hellos as they'd started their shift. Wyatt settled in against the rail as the boat steadily navigated through the harbor.

"Heard the good news about the task force."

"Word travels fast."

Wyatt smiled before shrugging. "When the captain asked for recommendations, there was no one else who came to my mind. I couldn't put you forward fast enough."

Although they'd always had a good relationship, the endorsement went a long way.

"Thank you."

"You're going to knock this one out of the park."

"It'll reduce my time on Harbor for the next few months."

It was the only fly in the ointment of the opportunity, and Gavin had weighed that aspect when Captain Reed first approached him.

"Which will be a loss for us," Wyatt acknowledged, "—but you have to do this. The opportunity's too big, and frankly, it's time to spread your wings a bit. Good things happen here, but the only way we keep getting better is to expand perspective and grow our talent."

This mindset was a key element of Wyatt's management. Even bigger than that, it was the ethos of the entire 86th Precinct they were part of in Brooklyn. Under Captain Dwayne Reed's leadership, those who showed promise were given opportunity.

And, in a virtuous cycle, because people knew there was opportunity, they worked harder and smarter and more collaboratively for it.

"I do think I can make a difference." Gavin said it because he believed it. Way down deep.

"I know you can."

"Speaking of different, how's married life treating you?"

Wyatt had only returned from his honeymoon a few weeks before. "Married life is amazing. Marlowe is incredible. And she proved just how awesome she is by indulging me in a honeymoon full of diving in Grand Cayman."

It was good to see his friend so happy. More, Gavin admitted, it was encouraging to see him come out the other side. The case that had pulled him and Marlowe together had been difficult, for the work itself, the impact on the precinct and the fact that Marlowe's father was murdered in the process.

He was well aware that sort of grief didn't just vanish, but it was good to see people he cared about showing signs of moving past it with the right partner to make it through.

Sometimes the right people did find each other.

It was a sobering thought, especially when all it did was bring to his own mind images of deep blue eyes and lush auburn hair.

Shaking it off, Gavin gave Wyatt a hearty slap on the back. "So you spent two weeks with an amazing woman and crystal-blue water, and now you're back here."

He and Wyatt turned to look over the other side of the railing. Although the Hudson had improved considerably over the past decade, the river still surrounded a major city, in a shade of blue that bordered on gray. Along with the less-than-appealing color, they regularly dived through all manner of undesirable things.

Wyatt nodded, his grin broad and most definitely sincere. "A dream all its own."

Gavin recognized those words for truth just as a shout went out from the wheelhouse. They were heading up toward the George Washington Bridge for evidence recovery after an accident.

And as he slipped into the cold, late March water under the bridge ten minutes later, clad head-to-toe in his gear, Gavin couldn't help but grin. He really was living the dream. Wide awake, full of the sweetest adrenaline, every damn day.

Now if he could only get a certain redhead out of his nighttime ones.

Serafina Forte reached for the clean tissue she'd had the foresight to stuff into her suit jacket pocket and wiped her mouth as she got up from the floor beside the toilet. She'd gotten lucky this afternoon. The ladies' room at the courthouse was empty, and she hadn't had to worry about being overheard.

A fate she had failed to escape several times over the past few months. A woman could only claim a winter stomach bug or a "touch of food poisoning" so many times.

The only upside to her daily visit to the ladies' room—and really, what idiot called it *morning* sickness when her visits could happen at any time?—was that she hadn't put on much weight. Her body was still changing, though, and she could see that in the fit of her work suits.

A fate that was going to catch up with her before she knew it.

With a sigh, she laid her head against the cool tiles of the wall, grateful she'd chosen the last stall so she could give the misery in her stomach time to settle a bit.

What was she going to do?

The question had been her constant companion for the past two months since she'd discovered her pregnancy and, as of yet, she hadn't come up with much beyond *take it one day at a time*.

Perhaps the advice she should have taken was *don't have amazing sex with a man you've known five hours as a way to ring in the new year*.

It seemed sound and eminently smart now, but was nowhere near as loud as the clanging voice in her head—one that had echoed through her body—on New Year's Eve. That night, all she wanted to do was get as close to Gavin as possible.

Gavin.

That was all she knew. His name was Gavin, and he was a cop. They'd met at a local bar in Brooklyn and had struck up a conversation so engrossing it had taken a while for them to realize their friends had moved on to another party down the street.

Neither one of them had cared.

They'd agreed to only discuss who they were in broad strokes, which is why she'd only told him she was a lawyer, not an ADA with the city. And all she knew was that he was a cop. Since the NYPD employed roughly 36,000 people, it was a bit of a needle in a haystack.

Even if he'd wanted to get a hold of her, she hadn't made

that easy, fleeing his apartment after a bout of lovemaking that had left her breathless.

And scared.

Because people didn't feel this way about each other— or have this sort of reaction to one another—that quickly after meeting.

Hadn't she learned that young?

And hadn't she been paying the price ever since?

Since that thought only produced profound misery, pregnant or not, Sera shook it off and pondered, yet again, how she could have played this differently.

They'd gone to his apartment, and it had been full of boxes. When she'd teased him on his decorating skills, he'd confirmed that he was moving in a few weeks. It was the perfect segue into a congenial conversation about why he was moving and did he like his building and where was he going?

Only their need for each other had taken over and they'd ended up kissing against said boxes, evaporating any questions she might have asked about where he was moving *to*.

Which now only left her with one dead end and absolutely zero lines to tug.

She had no last name. No cell phone. No known address.

And she was pregnant with his child.

On a sigh, she pushed off the wall and fixed her skirt. She slipped a breath mint out of the package she'd taken to carrying in her other jacket pocket and smoothed her hair.

Between her crushing workload, her random acts of morning sickness and her endless mooning over Gavin, she'd sort of drifted through her days—and nights. She needed to get her head back in the game.

Today's case was big, and it meant they could get a solid

handful of thugs out of the local drug trade. She'd prepped well, and she had a strong case. It was time to put her focus back on that and *off* her memories.

Off her worries.

Off her stupidity.

After all, crime in the city didn't stop. And she'd be damned if she was going to let her current lapse in judgment stop her from her work.

She would figure this out. And while it wasn't what she'd planned, in a relatively few short months, she'd have a child. One she was already beyond excited to meet. That was her reality, and her child needed to be her full focus.

Not the child's father.

And not the way she'd become pregnant.

Even if she did look for him every time she walked the neighborhood. She'd even tried going back to their bar a few times, although once she'd realized she was pregnant, she'd switched to club soda instead of her usual wine spritzer as she'd sat alone in the bar, her breath catching in her throat each time the door opened.

But to no avail.

Gavin was a memory, and whether she liked it or not, he was going to stay there.

Their child was her future.

Gathering her things along with her renewed focus, Sera headed for the door and the waiting courtroom. Which made the presence of her boss in the hallway something of a surprise.

"Sera?"

"David. Hello."

David Esposito was a formidable presence in the Brooklyn courts, their district attorney as adept at his job as he was at working the media. Tall and dashing, he had just the right amount of gray in his dark hair to make people feel he had the necessary gravitas to prosecute the criminals of the city and his broad shoulders filled out his suits to perfection. The media loved him, and lucky for her, his ADAs loved him, too.

He had an agile, exemplary legal mind, *and* he was a champion of his people. She loved working for him.

"Do you have a minute?"

"Of course." She moved to take a seat on one of the benches that lined the hallway, but he gestured toward a small meeting room.

"Let's go in there. I want to discuss something with you."

"About the Landers case?"

He smiled as he waited for her to enter the room before him. "I read your brief. You've got it more than well in hand."

Although she appreciated the compliment, it only added to her confusion. But he was the boss, which gave him the right to be a bit mysterious. Resolved to let him tell her in his own time, she took a seat at the small table that filled most of the room.

"I know how hard you've been working, Sera."

"It's the job." She gave a light shrug, knowing that for the truth. "And I love the work."

"Which is what I want to talk to you about."

Although all lawyers were subject to scrutiny and the highest of expectations as to their behavior, the bar was set infinitely higher for the district attorney's office. They were scrutinized, evaluated and, ultimately, held to a standard that was beyond the beyond. She'd always believed herself up to the task, but she knew there would be raised eyebrows as her pregnancy became widely known. She wouldn't be fired for it—she had full confidence on that front—but she would get knowing glances. A fact that would only be further exacerbated by the reality that she wasn't dating anyone.

Was that why David had pulled her into this discussion? Had her bathroom retch sessions somehow tipped someone off?

Her mind raced, and she nearly missed his words until she finally keyed back into what he was saying.

"I'm proud of all my ADAs, but you have to know, Sera, just how much your work stands out. Your dedication and your passion for the law is something to see. Our city is better for it, and my office is better for it."

"Thank you."

"It's why I'm willing to give you time away to take advantage of this opportunity."

"Away?"

He smiled at that, his expression lighting his normally serious face. "I've put you in for a borough-wide task force. It'll be members from my office, the NYPD, the Coast Guard and several federal agencies."

"A task force on what?"

"The drug trade is out of control. The governor and the mayor have been in talks with the Feds, and we want to put a team together to evaluate what can be done with the situation."

"But I'm not a cop. I have no real knowledge of how to apprehend or take down criminals."

"That's why your contributions are so valuable. This is a problem we want to attack from every angle. From the jurisdiction to those running the ops to the way we prosecute. We need every mind on this and all the effort we can muster to get ahead of the enterprising criminals who make New York their home."

It was a huge ask, and her pregnancy flashed quickly through her thoughts as a reason to decline. In fact, she nearly came out with it before Sera stopped herself.

Why say no?

What example did that set for her child? More, what did it say to herself? She was pregnant, not dead. And motherhood aside, she fully expected to have a long career in front of her.

Now would be the worst time to say no.

"I feel like I should ask you a few more questions, but you know I'm in, David."

"I hoped so. Which is why you need to be at the 86th bright and early Monday morning." David leaned forward and laid a hand over the back of hers folded on the table. "I'm going to miss having you in the office, but we'll get your caseload redistributed. I want to keep you on the Landers case as well as the discovery on the Nicholson murders, but everything else will be shared out."

Sera mentally calculated the workload. While both of those were huge cases, the reprieve from her other work would be welcome.

"It's an amazing opportunity, David. I won't let you down."

He gave her hand a quick squeeze before he stood up, effectively ending their meeting. "That thought never crossed my mind."

Sera walked the last few blocks from the subway, her umbrella up, albeit ineffectively, against the howling spring rain overhead. April had come in with a vengeance, and the city felt like it was practically underwater as she dodged puddles and what looked like a small lake at the intersection just shy of the 86th Precinct.

She'd opted for one of her pantsuits, but the thick rain boots pulled up over her calves, her slacks firmly tucked inside, were the height of frump. A fact she'd willingly overlooked as she anticipated dry feet for the day. The boots could be stowed in a corner of whatever conference room they'd be stuffed in this morning, so the fashion faux pas wasn't permanent.

She hadn't spent much time at the 86th, but she'd been here before. Captain Dwayne Reed ran an outstanding team, and she always enjoyed working with his officers when it was necessary for a case.

Captain Reed's style of leadership—and his belief in his people—had caught on, and there had been clear winds of change blowing through the other neighborhoods in an effort to emulate the precinct.

We need every mind on this and all the effort we can muster to get ahead of the enterprising criminals who make New York their home.

David's pitch for the task force had lingered in her mind all weekend as she prepared for this morning. She wanted to start off strong and make a good impression, meeting the other professionals she'd work with for the next several months.

Could they get ahead of the criminal element?

While she wasn't an inherently negative person, she would admit to moments of frustration and disillusionment with the system. Too many criminals flooding the streets. Too few people to catch them and ultimately prosecute them. And a bad life for the ones who were caught, locked up in a system that, while often full of well-intentioned people, was home to many who weren't.

She'd always understood it, but had also believed the work she did to serve the goal of justice would result in good outcomes. Even if her pregnancy had made her start to question some of those things and the reality of the world she was bringing her child into.

Her parents had never set a very good example, and she'd had to forge a path forward on her own. It was only recently that she'd begun to wonder if her dogged pursuit of justice was more because of them than in spite of them.

"Sera!"

Saved from her own maudlin musings by the loud shout, she glanced up to see a former law school classmate waving to her from down the hall. Picking up her pace, Sera headed his way.

"Sam, how are you?" They quickly exchanged hugs. "It's great to see you, but what are the odds we're here on the same day?"

"Pretty good if we're both on the new task force starting up this morning."

"You're a part of it?"

He smiled before pointing toward the conference room a few feet away. "I am and will confess to getting here early *and* seeing your name badge on the sideboard. I'm glad we're working together again. I'm representing the local FBI office."

"I'd heard the Feds snapped you up. Lucky for them."

"Lucky for me, too. I love the work."

Although she'd always known she wanted the DA's office, Sera was happy for him. His agile mind and love of complex cases likely made him a huge asset to the government.

"I love it, too, but I do have to say I'm disappointed in us."

"Oh?" His blue eyes widened.

"We're both guilty of that dreaded post-law school sin of spending most of our waking hours together for three years and then abandoning one another for the work after getting out."

"Proof they didn't lie about the work."

She shook her head but couldn't hold back the smile. "I wouldn't have it any other way."

"Me, either."

They found seats at the table and, after settling their things, wandered over to the sideboard to pick up their badges and get some breakfast. Sera eyed the pastries with a bit of caution, but was pleased to also see a selection of hard-boiled eggs and some dry toast waiting for toppings.

She hadn't been able to stomach anything that morning, but recognized the breakfast foods as a gift of fate. The protein from the egg and the bland toast with a bit of honey on top would go a long way toward keeping her level throughout the introductory meeting. A bit of tepid tea and she'd have a breakfast trifecta that would hopefully stave off morning sickness.

"You always were a healthy eater," Sam whispered, leaning in conspiratorially.

"Not everyone can eat sugared cereals and donuts for breakfast." She eyed his plate, a match for her own. "What happened?"

Although he'd always been a good-natured person, even in the throes of the most difficult exam periods, Sam lit up in a way she'd never seen before. "I'm a man with a fitness plan. And a wedding in three months."

"Sam! That's wonderful." Sera put her plate down and pulled him in for a hug. "Tell me all about her."

"Her name's Alexandra. Alex." He smiled, his gaze going hazy with love. "We met at the Bureau my second week on the job. She held out for a long time, saying we shouldn't mix personal with work and that it was a bad idea."

Although it wasn't forbidden in the Bureau, Sera could understand the reticence. But she also knew Sam Baxter and figured the woman was a goner when faced with such an earnest and truly wonderful man.

"Is she a lawyer, too?"

"Nope, a field agent. Which puts us in the same office, but not working directly together most of the time."

His happiness was electric, and Sera tried to tamp down the small shot of sadness that filled her as she pictured Gavin's face in her mind's eye.

Would it ever fade?

Even as she considered it, she knew the truth. Did she want it to?

And then she pushed it all away and gave Sam another hug. She could be sad in her own time, but there was no call for anything but joy in the face of such good news for a friend.

Which made the hard cough and rough "excuse me" a bit jarring as she pulled back from Sam's embrace.

And turned to find the one man she hadn't been able to forget standing two feet away.

Chapter 2

*S*era.

She was here—actually *here*—with her arms full of another man.

As he tried to maneuver around the hugging couple, Gavin wasn't sure what was more embarrassing. That his heart was exploding in his chest or something worse.

Something that felt a lot like jealousy.

It's just a hug.

With some dude who looked like he'd walked out of the pages of a men's magazine in his perfect suit, crisp red tie and artfully sculpted hair.

Bastard.

Especially since Gavin had forgotten an umbrella and currently felt like a wet junkyard dog after the run from the subway to the precinct entrance.

The perfect specimen of law and order turned and extended a hand. "Hello. I'm Sam Baxter. Local FBI bureau."

"Gavin Hayes. NYPD." He then turned to Sera, his expression carefully neutral. "I'm Gavin."

"Serafina Forte. Brooklyn DA's office."

Her hand slipped into his, and while it was a cordial handshake, he immediately had the memory of their fingers linking together on New Year's Eve as they walked to his apartment.

Something raw and elemental sparked between them, and Gavin purposely pushed it down. Whatever sparks had flared between them three months ago—and obviously still flashed and burned now based on their touch—had no place here. This was his shot. His appointment to the task force was an essential step in matching his ambitions to the outcomes he wanted at work. And in a span of two minutes, he'd raced through jealousy, envy and embarrassment.

Not the way he'd envisioned his first day on this all-important next step in his career. Yet here they were.

While he'd known she was a lawyer, he hadn't known she was with the district attorney's office. They'd avoided talk of what they did beyond the basics. It had seemed intriguing at the time, the "who do you know" and "what do you do" conversations too mundane for them. Too pedestrian to interfere with the passion that arced between them.

It was only now, face-to-face, that he realized a bit more conversation might have helped in the months that had passed since.

If he'd known she was in the DA's office, he could have…

Could have what?

Gone after her?

Tried to talk to her?

Asked her why she left him?

None of those questions led to good outcomes. Especially because of one, outstanding truth: if she'd wanted to see him again, she'd have found a way.

And she hadn't.

Even with that disappointment, he couldn't fight the

bone-deep interest that filled him. That vivid color of her hair was even richer in person than his memories. The sweep of her heavy lower lip still intrigued him, leaving him with the raw, damn near elemental need to draw it between his teeth.

And those eyes.

It was idiotically poetic, but those liquid blue eyes were fathoms deep, full of knowledge and secrets and something that looked a lot like forever.

Which only added to the bad mood that punched holes in his gut.

He'd wondered about her every damn day since the first of the year, and now she showed up on the most important morning of his professional life?

"We were just getting some breakfast." Sera gestured toward the table along the wall lined with breakfast and coffee carafes. "Please, help yourself."

Her voice was low, professional and incredibly polite. Something in it made Gavin wish he could smudge a little bit of that perfection that had gotten under his skin and made him ache.

It was hardly rational. Or fair.

But what about this situation was fair?

Before he had a chance to consider it further, the room was brought to attention, and they were all instructed to get breakfast, pick up their badges and find a spot at the conference room table.

"Looks like the bell for round one," Sam said with a chuckle.

Sera's answering laugh had Gavin crumpling the edge of the notebook he'd grabbed from his locker on the way in, but it *was* enough to pull him out of his thoughts.

Time to get coffee and take a seat as far away from *Serafina Forte* as he could. He had his future to focus on.

And he needed to get his mind the hell off his tempting past.

Gavin was here.

In the room. In the building. And *on* her freaking task force.

Gavin *Hayes*.

He was a cop, and in a twist that she should have seen coming, he worked in the precinct that covered her Brooklyn neighborhood.

What were the odds?

Even as that question drifted in and out of her mind, she had to admit, they were pretty darn good. They had met at a local bar, after all. On some level it was a bit of surprise she hadn't seen him sooner.

Only...

He was here. Now. Back in her life as she embarked on one of the most important opportunities of her career. A three-month task force, the lead had told them during introductory remarks, with a possible extension to a fourth month.

And she was pregnant with Gavin's child.

She'd complete the work, of that she had no doubt. But there was no way she'd complete it without everyone knowing she was pregnant.

Which meant Gavin would know.

Hadn't she wanted that?

She'd gone to their bar several times in hopes of seeing him so she could tell him the news. So she could...

Could what?

Apologize for running out? Apologize for getting scared

because she didn't do relationships and she wasn't cut out for the emotional commitment required to be with another person? Even as she'd thought, more than a few times, that emotional commitment might be worth the risk with Gavin.

"The purpose of this task force is to ensure cooperation and collaboration." The moderator's voice cut back into her thoughts, and Sera knew she needed to focus.

She could obsess over next steps later. Right now she had to pay attention and find a way forward.

"We're fortunate in a city this size that there's a strong base of support across federal, state and local agencies, but it needs to be stronger. Tighter. It's the only way we'll maximize our strengths. One and one will make three."

Sera nearly choked on the small sip of herbal tea she'd taken as the moderator's words hung over the room. Unbidden, her gaze drifted to Gavin. He'd taken a seat at the opposite end of the room, but since he was on the other side of the table, she could still see him easily enough.

His dark gaze seemed to see through her, and she had the most absurd impulse to laugh.

Because one and one *had* made three.

The moderator pointed toward a screen at the front of the room and a slideshow presentation she'd used to frame the launch meeting. As the woman flipped to a new slide, Sera directed her attention back to her words.

The first week of the task force would focus on getting to know one another and creating an action plan. Every team would build out ideas on how to address crime, expand a plan for social services and address the legal ins and outs of their ideas. One team would be fully local, one fully federal and then two would be a mix, having one federal team member and one local member. It was, their moderator explained, a chance to collectively review how collaborations could grow and how they would look different with varied perspectives.

Sera had already begun to envision the work she could do if she was paired with Sam. They knew each other and had worked well together all the way through law school, and she had every confidence their collaboration would be strong. She was doing this work so she could improve her relationships with federal jurisdictions in the region. Wasn't that the whole point?

"Serafina Forte, DA's office. Gavin Hayes, NYPD Harbor. You're a team."

Of course we are.

The urge to drop her head to the table was strong, but she kept her gaze straight ahead and didn't dare glance Gavin's way again. Just like she wouldn't lift a fist to the sky and rant and rail that this was all some cosmic mistake.

She did offer a small smile and nod for the moderator in a show of gratitude for the assignment.

Nothing in her life had been normal or usual for three months now. Why should that change?

She jotted down the conference room where she and Gavin would be paired for the day to begin work on their project before gathering her things from where she'd stowed them beneath the table.

But as she glanced down and saw the thick rain boots still wrapped around her calves and her slacks, Sera was sorely tempted to lift that fist.

Could she look any worse?

Since the room was already in motion, there was no time to slip them off and change into the heels buried at

the bottom of her bag, so she picked up her things and proceeded toward the door.

Gavin waited for her just outside, and she lifted a hand
in a small waving motion. "Let's go, local team."

"Sure."

Ooooh-kay.

What was that joke Sam had made about the bell for
round one?

She followed Gavin down the hall and toward an elevator. Several other task force members were with them and
their nervous small talk to the others ensured she could avoid
talking to Gavin for a few more minutes.

Until they were the only ones left, heading toward the
top floor of the precinct.

"Serafina, is it?"

"Sera. I mean, I go by Sera." Damn it, she would *not*
stammer before this man. "Serafina is my given name, but
I go by Sera." When he only nodded, she pressed for a bit
more from him. "And you're on Harbor patrol? Diving?"

The elevator stopped, the doors swishing open on a quiet
floor. "That's what I do."

"But you're a cop?"

"Yep."

He was already heading down the hall, and she clomped
behind him in the damn boots, each step a sort of squeaky
thwap on the ground.

Irritation spiked at the quick dismissal and the feeling
of following him. They hadn't followed each other three
months ago. Instead, there'd been a sort of *entwining*. An
equal footing that had engaged them both and pulled them
forward with an elemental tug she'd never felt before.

But this?

He had a cold, almost military demeanor. His back was so straight and his gaze deliberately held straight ahead.

Well, fine. She could give as good as she got.

Even as she nearly slipped over her squeaky boots when a terrible, awful thought filled her.

What if he didn't remember her?

Gavin caught her just as she reached out to grip the door frame to their small conference room. She straightened herself, unwilling to read too much into the fire radiating up and down her arm where he'd held her, firm yet gentle, just above the elbow.

"Thank you."

He dropped his hand and just nodded.

God, why did she feel so clumsy? And so off her game?

She hadn't felt this way three months ago. Sure, she'd been a bit nervous, but their time together had seemed to melt away any nerves or concerns. They'd just been Sera and Gavin, and it had been...

Well, it had been wonderful.

And now they were here, and they both had to make the best of it.

But how had she managed to forget just how good he smelled? And exactly how broad his shoulders were? And...

And she needed to get her damn head in the game because there was no way she was going to let a single bit of whatever happened to them three months ago ruin this. She was highly competent, and this task force was a shot at her future.

Mooning over Gavin was *not* the way to start it off right.

So she marched into the room, her head held high, her bearing damn near regal.

She could *do* this, she thought, a fierce sort of righteousness welling up inside of her. She *would* do this.

The conference room might be roughly the size of a broom closet, but she deliberately selected a spot on the far side, settling her things on the scarred table. Gavin still stood by the door, his gaze on her when she finally glanced up after carefully placing each of her personal items.

"Serafina?"

"I told you, I go by Sera."

"Fine. Sera."

"Is this room okay?"

"It'll do just fine."

She stared at him, suddenly realizing her mistake in taking the far corner. The windows might be at her back, but she suddenly felt her lack of escape. Or, more to the point, the need to move past him in order to escape.

One more sign she was flustered and off her game. Worse, that she suddenly felt like his quarry, his deep brown gaze seeming to size her up.

Where was that man she'd met on New Year's? The one with the kind eyes and broad smile and caring touch? Had he been an illusion?

She'd lived with the reality of her momentary lapse in judgment for three months now, but she'd never felt that she'd shared herself with a jerk.

A stranger, maybe. But never a jerk.

Resolving to worry about it later, she tapped the folder she'd settled on the desk, on top of the legal pad she'd used to make notes during the initial briefing. "Let's get down to it. We're the local team. Between the police perspective you bring and the legal perspective I bring, we should be able to put together a solid plan of local cross-collaboration."

"I'm sure we will."

Heat filled that dark gaze at her reference to collaboration, but Sera ignored it and soldiered on. "We've all seen the challenges to both our teams with budget allocations, staffing constraints and the overall volume of what runs the streets of the city." She realized her potential misstep and added, "Or fills the waters around it."

"Day in and day out."

"So where should we start?"

He finally took a seat, but never touched the folder that had been handed to them during the briefing. Instead, his attention was fully focused on her, nearly pinning her to her seat. "I think the first place we start is with the past."

"Oh?" She dimly sensed a trap closing around her, but had no idea why. The city had a legacy of crime—that sort of underbelly was impossible to separate from a place so large—but so much work had been done over the years to make New York not only livable, but a truly thriving, positive place to live for its ever-growing population.

"The city does have a history," she agreed. "But this task force really is about the future."

"The task force is, sure. But I'm talking about you and me. And why you walked out on New Year's Day without so much as a goodbye."

Gavin took the slightest measure of satisfaction at the way Sera's throat worked around whatever words she was trying to come up with.

What he couldn't figure out was why the satisfaction was so short-lived. And why this desperate need to question her seemed to live inside of him like some wide-open, gaping maw. They were here—as she'd said—to focus on the future. Why tread through a past that had happened months ago and realistically should mean nothing to him?

He wasn't generally interested in one-night stands, but he could hardly say he'd never had sex with a woman he didn't know well. And since his life up to now had been suspiciously devoid of successful long-term relationships, he couldn't understand the weird, swirling emotions this woman churned up in him.

And yet, she did. From the unceasing thoughts of her these past several months to the spears of jealousy at seeing her hug another man, he clearly hadn't moved on the way he should have.

The way he *needed* to.

So maybe just putting it all out on the table would help him get past it.

"Why I walked out?"

"Yes. We had a pretty amazing night. I don't think I gave any suggestion you needed to leave so quickly, but if I did, I'm sorry."

His apology clearly flustered her, her hand coming up to smooth her blouse.

"We were two consenting adults who welcomed the year in, Gavin. It was great, but all good things have to come to an end, right?"

If he weren't looking so hard, he'd have taken her words at face value. He'd likely have believed her, too.

But the heavy pulse at her throat was evident, as was the barely-there quaver in her voice.

"And now?" he finally asked.

"Now what?"

"Now we're working together. So our good thing hasn't actually come to an end after all."

"Are you suggesting we pick up where we left off?"

She might have been flustered, but he'd give her credit, she could turn on the freeze when she needed to. While something sharp and needy filled him, he was more than aware this task force was a huge opportunity for him. For both of them, no doubt.

Was he even remotely considering muddying the waters with sex?

His body screamed a resounding yes, but the control he was known for somehow managed to prevail at the last minute.

"I'm suggesting we both deserve to go into this partnership fully acknowledging what came before. This is a major step in my career. I have to believe it is for you, too. Not addressing the past is foolish in the extreme." He leaned forward slightly over the table, the incredibly small space ensuring he could see her as clearly as if she were sitting beside him. "Don't you agree?"

That flutter of pulse at her throat never faded, and if he were a fanciful man, he'd say he could practically hear her heartbeat.

But he wasn't given to whimsy. And he had zero illusions about life anymore.

What he didn't expect was her to capitulate so easily. He figured her for a bit more bravado. Maybe even a few excuses. Not the warming of her freeze ray. Or a raw sort of truth that settled hard in his gut.

"We had a lovely night together, Gavin. One I don't regret in any way. But the new day had dawned." She shook her head. "The new *year* had dawned, and it suddenly struck me that sitting around the apartment of my one-night stand wasn't a good look. For either of us, but certainly not for me."

He was tempted to ask again if he'd given her any hint she needed to leave, but opted for a slightly different tack. "Did you want to leave?"

"It was time for me to leave."

It was hardly an answer, but it was the one she was willing to give. He could keep pressing and probing, in hopes he'd get a different reply, but why? Worse, why was he hoping for a different answer?

The knock on the door pulled him out of the question without an actual answer, and he turned to find Wyatt Trumball in the doorway.

"Detective." Gavin nodded as he stood. "How are you?"

"Good. I wanted to talk to you about the dive tomorrow morning. I'm sorry I'm interrupting." Wyatt glanced over at Sera, his smile broad. "The task force started today."

"It did."

Wyatt stepped into the small conference room, extending a hand toward Sera who'd already stood to say hello. "Wyatt Trumball, NYPD."

"Sera Forte. I'm with the DA's office."

"So you two are representing the local team."

Since there was little that got past the seasoned detective, Gavin shouldn't have been surprised by the man's ready knowledge of the work, but it still stunned him how much Wyatt actually *knew*.

"We are. We'll present solutions on how the city's resources can work together," Sera said. "I know everyone thinks the solution to this is working with the Feds, and I don't think that's wrong, but I am excited to show what we can do right here, too."

"Everyone thinks bigger's better. But some of the best work I've ever seen has been local teams who know their neighborhoods, working together to get it done."

"Fewer egos?" Gavin asked, his sole intention to make a joke.

Which made it a surprise when Wyatt's demeanor changed. "The Feds have a lot to offer, but they get in the way, too. They think we're rubes who can't see past the end of the block, or they want to run the show."

Coming from a man who was a quintessential team player, Wyatt's words struck hard. But if he were being fair, Gavin had already seen a bit of that posturing that morning. Hell, they were all posturing, trying to prove their worth to be a part of the team. But that tension was there, all the same.

"We'll be sure to keep our guard up," Sera cut in smoothly. "I happen to like my block quite a bit. I think I've got a rather sophisticated approach to the work, too."

Wyatt's smile returned, his grin broad. "Then I say, go get 'em. I know you two will do great. Let me know if you need anything from me."

Gavin nearly let Wyatt walk away before he remembered. "And tomorrow's dive?"

"I just came to give you the oh-so-happy news that we're diving up at Hell Gate tomorrow."

Gavin sensed Sera's attention to the matter, but didn't want to give Wyatt any indication anything was off. So he went with his usual good-natured humor. "Lucky us. With all this rain, it'll be sure to be churned up and extra gross."

"Which is why the team can't dive it today. Weather's expected to clear up tonight, and we should have a grand time running evidence recovery. Criminals really do love tossing weapons off the city's bridges."

"Only trains run over Hell Gate," Gavin said. "Someone was dumb enough to try to cross electrified train tracks on foot?"

"Not quite that bad, but not much better. Someone ran across the RFK Bridge on foot."

"In the middle of traffic?"

"Yep. Slammed on the brakes when he realized the cops in pursuit were getting close. He jumped out of his car, then raced through traffic to the first break in fencing he could find. Tossed the weapon as hard as he could north." Wyatt smiled, his hands up in the air in a what-can-you-do gesture. "We're the ones who get to go find it."

Wyatt made his goodbyes, and it was only as Gavin took his seat again that he caught Sera's gaze.

"It's really called Hell Gate?" she asked, a small furrow lining her otherwise smooth brow.

"Yep. The upper portion of the East River. We'll be in the area underneath the RFK Bridge and a little farther north probably."

"Wow. I—"

"What?"

"It sounds dangerous, is all."

"It's one of the tougher waterways, but that's why we dive in pairs and have a team working around us, also keeping close watch."

"Sure. Of course. It's just that I…" She stopped again, seeming to gather her thoughts. "I didn't realize just how difficult your job was. Anyone who works in law enforcement has a challenging job with obvious risks. But this sounds like a whole other level."

Although he appreciated the concern and her obvious bother at the work, he wasn't entirely clear where it was coming from. "It's a job I'm trained for. And something I continue to train for regularly. We don't rest on our laurels or ignore our conditioning."

"No, of course not."

"Wow. Be careful there." He gave the warning as he opened his folder, pulling out the briefing sheet they would work against for the next week. He nearly cursed himself for saying anything, but now that it was out, he realized his emotions had about as much finesse as that criminal who'd run out in the middle of traffic.

Emotions he had no business even having.

Way to be an ass, Hayes. You might as well see it through now.

"Be careful of what?"

"All that concern. You keep talking like that, and I might start to think you care."

Chapter 3

I might start to think you care.

That rather dismissive brush-off had remained in the back of her mind all day, through her walk home and on through the preparation of dinner.

And damn it—Sera tossed a potholder on the counter after dumping a pot of cooked pasta and boiling water into a waiting colander in her sink—he'd gotten to her. Yes, it was unexpected to walk into the conference room that morning and see him. And yes, she was fully aware that she was nervous and off her game when the two of them had broken off for their committee work.

But that line? Seriously?

I might start to think you care.

Start to?

What an ass.

Only he wasn't. Despite the tense working conditions and the subtle threads of irritation he wove around her all day, he wasn't a jerk.

She would bet quite a lot on that fact.

The man she'd spent the night with wasn't a jerk. The man the NYPD had selected to represent them on a multi-jurisdictional task force wasn't a jerk. The man who'd *fathered her child* wasn't a jerk.

Unable to pivot well with her reentry into his life? Yeah, she'd give him that one. But he wasn't a bad person. No amount of conference-room bravado was going to change her mind on that point.

Which meant she needed to double down. Leave her irritation at home and focus on the good that would come of working together.

And oh yeah…tell him she was pregnant with his child. But how?

While it was incredibly easy to put their night together firmly in the column of sexual attraction, part of why it had been so incendiary had nothing to do with the sex. It had been the connection between them.

They'd spoken freely and easily after meeting in the bar. It was the only way she'd have actually gone home with him, if she were honest. She needed that connection in order to feel it was worth taking things further.

And oh, they had a connection.

She'd laughed easily, and they'd talked of so many things. Their work in broad strokes, yes, but more *why* they were drawn to what they did. How they'd found their paths in life. And what drove them as people.

It had been wonderful to speak freely about her ambition and not feel it was either being judged as too work-focused or worse, threatening somehow that she had goals for herself. Instead, he'd asked her questions and seemed genuinely interested in her answers.

And for her, Sera knew, there was no greater aphrodisiac.

She shook the colander of any excess water before scooping out a portion for herself and the waiting sauce she'd made for it. Although she still struggled with food, especially in the morning, by the time dinner rolled around, she was always hungry and had seemingly gotten rid of that day's roiling stomach acid.

Pasta had been one of her steady cravings over the past few weeks, so she'd taken to making extra and preparing a cold salad with it for the next day's lunch. It wasn't perfect, but it seemed to be working, and her doctor hadn't felt the food was problematic, especially when she'd assured her ob-gyn that she was adding vegetables to the mix.

With dinner in hand, she headed for the small kitchen nook to eat just as a heavy knock came on her front door.

Sera set her plate down on the drop-leaf table nestled in the corner of her kitchen and headed for the foyer. Her apartment wasn't huge, but she had some space in her over-size one-bedroom corner unit, courtesy of an uncle who owned the building and had given her a good deal since she'd graduated from college.

Anyone defending my city deserves to live in a good, safe space while doing it, Uncle Enzo had intoned as he handed over her rental contract.

She half expected it would be him and Aunt Robin at the door, their occasional drop-ins always welcome.

Only to find Gavin on the other side.

"Hi."

He stood there in her doorway, his shoulders set, and her stomach gave an involuntary flip. Damn, why was he so attractive? Tall, broad and extremely fit from the work he did.

All of which was appealing, but had nothing on the smile that lifted the edges of his lips. A small bouquet filled his hands, and despite his solid bearing, she could see the slightest hint of nerves in the way his foot tapped lightly on the ground.

"Hey." She fought the small smile of her own that threatened to undermine her attempts at being aloof.

"I'm sorry to bother you."

"It's no bother." She stepped back, extending a hand to allow him in. "Though I am curious how you found me. I work for the DA's office. I don't keep my address in public databases."

"I live in the eternally up-to-date database that is Sunset Bay, Brooklyn." When she must have given him a curious look, Gavin added, "Once I knew your last name, I put two and two together. Your uncle, Enzo Forte, is my landlord. I saw him coming into my building this evening with your aunt and some of their friends and mentioned we were working together."

"My uncle gave you my address?"

"I told him I was a pompous jerk during our first meeting, and I owed you an apology. Your aunt couldn't rush fast enough to give me your address." He held out a hand. "She told me you like Gerbera daisies, too."

"I do."

She took the bouquet—a solid peace offering yet not so large as to appear pompous or as if the flowers could solve everything—and gestured toward the kitchen. "I was about to eat some dinner. Would you care to join me?"

"You don't mind?"

Since she'd already invited him, she just shot him a look and headed for the kitchen and the small pitcher she kept on her windowsill. In a matter of minutes, she had the colorful daisies in the pitcher, settled on the edge of the table where they sat across from each other.

He'd taken the portion of pasta she was going to use for tomorrow's lunch, and as she saw him settle his napkin on his lap, Sera had to admit to herself she didn't mind.

She didn't mind at all.

The pasta wasn't much, but Gavin dug into it like a starving man. If she expected him to complain that her vegetable and herb-filled sauce was missing meat, she soon realized she wasn't going to get it.

Instead, she got the opposite.

"This is really good."

"Thanks." She took a sip of her club soda before returning to their earlier topic. "My aunt and uncle really told you where I live?"

"I'll admit to some surprise on that front as well, but I guess I ooze trust." He grinned at her, that bright flash broad and wide. "It also helps I rented right out of the academy in their building over on Eleventh. They have my credit score, my phone number *and* my address. You know, basically it's like they know how to hunt me down."

"I suppose they could."

And while she did get the local connection, it was clear she needed to give her aunt Robin a bit of a drubbing on sharing personal information like that.

"The moment I saw them I made the connection with their last name. And then once I mentioned us working together on the task force, that clinched the deal."

Since Sera could also imagine the twinkle that no doubt had lit up her aunt's eyes, she opted to shift the conversation.

"Is your pasta hot enough?"

Although she'd intended the question as a kindness, all it really served to do was show her extreme nerves at his presence in her kitchen. One that had felt a heck of a lot larger before he arrived than it did now.

"The temperature is fine. It's not really why I'm here, though I'll never turn down dinner with a beautiful woman."

"Flattery?"

"Is it working?"

She didn't want to be flattered by the compliment. Even worse, she didn't want to be caught up in him again or the cute banter that was stamped full of notes of appreciation and…*notice.*

Wasn't that how all this had started? That compelling gaze and ability to make her feel as if she was the only woman in the world?

"I also didn't come here to give you a line," he continued, smoothly shifting gears. "I came to give you the apology you most definitely deserve."

"Oh."

"I wasn't the best version of myself today. I knew it, even as it was happening, but I couldn't seem to see past myself, and I am sorry." He set down his fork. "I'm truly sorry for it."

For all that the apology was a surprise, Sera had to admit it fit the man she remembered. What she'd sensed of his character, even after only spending less than a day together. And with that memory came a resolution of her own.

"If we're being honest—" her gaze drifted to the small bouquet "—I'm not above saying the flowers weren't a smooth touch."

"I'm glad you like them."

"But I wasn't my best self, either. I was surprised to see you this morning. And then we were put together for the duration of the task force and—" She couldn't fully hold back the sigh. "It was like my personal life slammed right into my professional life, and I didn't like it."

"Same."

"This task force is an important step in my career growth. I'm sure it's equally important for you."

"It is," he agreed.

"Then we're going to have to find a way to put what happened between us at the holidays firmly in the past."

"Is it?"

His comment sort of hung there between them, like a pulsing question mark hovering over them in blinking neon.

"Is it what?"

"Is it behind us?"

The irrational urge to laugh hysterically at his question suddenly gripped her and she had one terrifying moment where she thought she actually might break down in laughter. Because that night might be over, but nothing about it was behind them. In fact, in six more months the consequence of their choice would be right there in *front* of them.

She'd had their one night together expressly for the lack of strings. Attachments. Or any consequence other than pure, unadulterated need. She wasn't particularly well-versed in doing that, and it had felt good—better than good, actually—to take something just for herself.

Her life had been about studying and remaining focused and living with a strict, almost rigid, code of behavior. She wasn't going to be her mother. And she had no interest in throwing her life away to listlessness or to excess.

And yet, Gavin had somehow found a way beneath that. In the moment, he'd felt like impulse, but never excess.

So she took a long, deliberate moment to stare at her

fork before lifting it to toy with a few pieces of pasta. "It's all behind us. Of course it is."

"Things ended a bit abruptly."

Whatever distraction her dinner had provided faded as she stared at him head on. "We had a one-night stand, Gavin. By their very definition, they have a short shelf life. A point I've thought was pretty clear based on how neither of us has found the other these past several months."

"Did you try to find me?"

Just like that morning, it was a neat, verbal trap and one she'd walked straight into. Yet even as a part of her wanted to wrap herself up in emotional tinfoil, deflecting the truth with all that she was, she found she couldn't.

"I went to that bar several evenings in hopes I'd see you again. When you never showed, I figured I wasn't meant to see you."

A series of emotions flashed across his face, telling in that he obviously felt *something*, but maddening in that she couldn't actually read a damn thing.

Did he think her needy? Hopeful? Was he glad she'd tried to find him? Or was it more proof what they'd had was only meant to last a few hours?

Which made his quiet, scratchy tone a bit of a surprise when he finally spoke. "If you wanted to see me again, why'd you leave?"

Had she been wrong?

Since there was no way of knowing, she pressed on, willing him to understand her explanation.

"Again, Gavin. New Year's Day. One-night stand. Two strangers. It's sort of the exact definition of awkward."

"It didn't feel awkward."

"No, it didn't."

And when his dark gaze met hers, she had to admit that even now, it still wasn't awkward at all. It was freeing. This strange connection between them that had no reason for existing yet did all the same.

"I wanted to see you again, Sera. I looked for you every time I went out. Each time I walked the neighborhood. Each time I got on the subway."

He'd looked for her? Hoped to see her again?

All those lonely moments, practically willing him to show up at the bar hadn't actually been for naught. Even if they really didn't have a shot at a future, there was a special sort of joy in knowing that he hadn't been unaffected.

And with that knowledge, she couldn't hold back the small smile that she suspected held the slightest notes of sorrow for what could have been. "And here all you really needed to do was call my aunt and uncle. Keep that in mind next time you go hunting for a one-night stand."

"Why would I go hunt for anyone else?"

Whatever humor had pulled at her faded, and something sharp speared through her at the earnest expression that set his face in serious lines.

"This can't go anywhere," Sera finally said, even if she wished she were wrong. "Especially with the task force. It's a conflict now."

"How?"

Whatever outcome he was considering wasn't readily apparent, but the fact he was considering any outcome other than the path they'd been on—going their separate ways—needed to be squelched.

"What do you mean, how? We're partnered on an important work project."

"One that won't last forever. We don't work in the same

department. We don't even work for the same entity. Last time I checked, employees of the City of New York can date each other."

"We're not—" She stopped abruptly, catching herself before trying again. "What we had isn't dating. Let's not pretend there's more between us then there actually is."

Sera wasn't quite sure who she was trying to convince, but knew she needed to hold her ground. Because she *had* wanted to see him again. And once she'd gotten over the shock of seeing him again that morning, it had felt so good to be in his presence once more. To look across the table and see that face that had been emblazoned on her mind as if every feature had been captured in indelible ink.

But she couldn't give in to this.

Nor could she delude herself into thinking somehow this all had a happy ending. They'd come together in a heated rush and had proceeded to go on with their lives. Only now there was a very large secret between them. One that she knew she had to share.

One that he *deserved* to know.

Yet no matter how she spun it in her mind, she couldn't seem to find the words to tell him the truth.

"But there is something between us, Sera."

Whatever Gavin might question about his feelings and the odd way they'd come in and out of each other's lives— twice now—there was something there.

Wasn't this very conversation proof of that?

Sure, things had had gotten very personal, very fast. That had been true between them from the start. But at the moment, things had also gotten much too serious. So with his dual police *and* dive training in the forefront of his mind, Gavin did what he knew how to do best.

Pivot and attack the situation from a new angle.

"Let's go get some ice cream."

"Now?"

"You ever heard of dessert, Forte?"

"Well, yeah, but—"

He stared pointedly down at his empty plate before looking back up at her. "Do you have ice cream in your freezer?"

"No."

He shook his head and let out a small *tsk* for good measure. "A crime against nature, but we'll address that later. Let's go get some ice cream."

Based on her initial resistance, Gavin figured she'd put up more of a fight, so it was a welcome surprise to find themselves walking into the Sunset Bay pharmacy and heading for their soda counter twenty minutes later.

"Best ice cream sundaes in Brooklyn." Gavin breathed in deeply of the mixed scents of sugar, cream and chocolate as they took two stools at the counter.

Sera slipped onto the stool next to him, and he took her coat as she shrugged out of it, walking it down to the small coatrack at the end of the bar before returning to her.

"Thanks."

"You're welcome."

As he settled himself on his stool, he couldn't help but notice the two of them reflected in the big mirror that stretched along the back of the soda fountain. Although they didn't touch, they looked like they were on a date, the light tension arcing between them evident even in the old mirror with desilvering in small splotches up and down the length of it.

"This place has seen a lot." He said after a quick glance at his menu.

"It was the heart of Sunset Bay while I was growing up. And even more so for the generation before us. Aunt Robin still talks about how Uncle Enzo brought her here when they were dating."

It was interesting. She'd spoken of her aunt and uncle several times throughout the evening, but still nothing about her parents. Were they absent? Dead? Gavin wondered.

He was about to ask, but a skinny, bored teenager came up to them to take their orders.

"What'll you have?" the kid asked Sera.

"Scoop of chocolate with some peanut butter sauce."

"Banana split for me."

The bored teen trotted off, leaving them to their conversation at the mostly empty counter. It was the distinct lack of people that had him drifting straight back to their unfinished dinner conversation.

"So about this something more between us."

She was in the middle of settling her purse on hooks beneath the counter, her attention focused elsewhere, but Gavin didn't miss the wary lines on her face.

Whatever had gripped her in that moment was gone when she gave him her full focus. Her spine was rail-straight as she sat on the backless stool, and her voice held what he assumed was a match for the formidable tones she'd use in the courtroom.

"There isn't something more."

"Sure there is."

"A single night of passion? And while I won't say it's nothing, it shouldn't stand in the way of what each of us wants to accomplish."

"Why are you so insistent on relating the two things at all?"

"Oh, come on, Gavin. Of course those two things are entwined. They're intimately entwined." She leaned closer before seeming to catch herself. "We've seen each other naked."

While he assumed she'd brought up that enticing fact to make a point, he couldn't help but needle her a bit. "We most certainly did."

"Be serious."

"I'm certainly not laughing. In fact, I'm remembering a few things in rather vivid detail."

"You're impossible."

"And you're combining two things together like they somehow cancel each other out. I'd like to know why."

"My work is important to me."

"As mine is to me."

"We slept together. Do you think anyone on that task force is going to take us seriously if we suddenly start up an affair?"

Although there was a thread of irritation starting to simmer in his blood at her continued pushback, he fought to maintain the steady, easy, nearly carefree notes in his voice. If she didn't want to go out with him, he could live with that. But her arguments centered around what others would think or why they couldn't have a shot at something, *not* basic disinterest.

He just couldn't let it go.

"Two single people having a relationship isn't an affair."

"It is when they're paired up on a work project and keeping it a secret."

"So make it public." As he said the words, Gavin realized them for solid truth. "To my earlier point, it's not a crime if the city's employees date each other."

"That won't keep people from talking."

"So let them talk."

Their ice cream arrived, cutting into the argument that was steadily building between them. He wasn't going to get anywhere in this conversation behaving like a petulant child. And he certainly wasn't looking to date someone who didn't want to be with him.

So why was he pushing this?

He'd never put that much stock in the romance dance. You saw someone. You liked them. You spent some time with them. Was it simplistic? Sure. But he'd always had far more important priorities in his life, and no one had ever made him see a reason to change them.

Until Sera.

Something in that time they spent with each other—less than twenty-four hours of his life—had wrecked him. He hated the vulnerability, but more, he hated the idea that what they did for a living needed to dictate their private moments.

Sera had already taken a few small bites of her ice cream and he opted to dig into his banana split, hoping the mix of sugar and heavy cream would cool their conversation off a bit.

"Can we maybe chalk it all up to a complicated situation that we don't have to decide right now?" she finally asked.

"Yeah. We can do that."

And he could. While he wasn't ready to fully back off, Gavin could appreciate that a lot had been thrown at both of them and a bit of time to figure it out would go a long way.

"How's your ice cream?" he asked, their heated conversation fading. He'd brought her here to take her out for a treat and it was actually quite nice to sit and enjoy her company.

"Delicious. I haven't been here in a while. Dessert was a good idea."

"Sugar usually solves most problems. Or at least makes them seem less fraught."

"As someone who solves problems for a living, I'd like to say we're more evolved as a species, but—" She stared down at her ice cream, tapping the side of the small metal dish with her spoon. "It's hard to argue with sugar therapy."

Their dessert seemed to diffuse the tension that had spiked when he'd brought up their relationship status, and they sank back into that easy conversation that had been there between them from the first.

It ebbed and flowed, until they both looked down and realized they hadn't just finished their dessert, but their dishes had long been whisked away by the bored server.

With dessert completed, Gavin collected their coats once more, and then they were weaving their way back out into the early spring night.

"Thanks for the ice cream."

"My pleasure."

Gavin fought the suddenly desperate desire to lay a hand low on her back and shoved his hands into his pockets as they headed back in the direction of her apartment. The lights of the pharmacy spilled back onto the sidewalk and illuminated the deep red tones of her hair.

The rain that had dogged them for days had faded, and in its place was a cool breeze that promised spring, even if winter hadn't quite relinquished its cold grip.

"I still think your lack of ice cream in the home is a

crime against nature, but I'll do my best to reserve further judgment."

"Maybe I just prefer eating ice cream with others."

That breeze kicked up once more as they passed by the alley between the pharmacy and the old shoe store that was its neighbor. The same kid who'd waited on them had obviously been put on closing duty, and he carried two big black bags in his hand to the curb, the distinct scent of the aging garbage filling the air.

"Maybe we'll—" He broke off as a dire look came over her face, the color instantly draining from her cheeks. "Sera?"

But she'd already bolted, heading straight for a city garbage can at the corner. The distinct sounds of misery rose up into the night air as she lost the remnants of her meal, and he made it just in time to hold her shoulders when a second, wracking jolt ripped through her.

"Oh God!" Her choked sob ripped at his heart, but it was the distinct words that followed that robbed him of breath. "I thought I was past this."

Chapter 4

Gavin sat on her couch, his gaze unseeing as he stared at the TV she'd flipped on as a matter of habit when they walked in. She'd wanted to say something deeper, or perhaps even an apology, but had opted instead for pointing at the remote control and letting him know he could put on what he wanted and that she'd be right back.

The strong whiff of garbage as they left the restaurant had hit her, its effect swift and immediate. And although she and Gavin needed to talk, her first order of business was to brush her teeth and give herself a moment to freshen up in the bathroom.

But now the time had come to tell him the truth.

She'd spent the past few months since discovering her pregnancy thinking of scenario after scenario of how she'd tell him about the baby.

Now at the moment of truth her mind was a complete blank.

"The Nets have been playing well this year."

"Hmm?" He glanced up from the basketball game playing out on the screen.

"Um, never mind." She snagged the remote, muting the TV, before taking a seat on the opposite end of the couch. "So I think we need to talk."

His expression suggested an incredulous sort of agreement she imagined along the lines of *you think?* But his words managed a rather different tone.

"How long have you known?"

"About two months."

"All this time…" His voice faded off, his expression oddly blank.

"I wanted to tell you, Gavin. Truly, I did. But I couldn't find you, and then I didn't know how to find you. You'd moved from your apartment, so there was no way of knowing where you'd gone."

"That's an excuse?"

"Well, actually, yes. It's the truth."

"You knew my name."

"Your first name. And that you were a cop. You do realize just how big the NYPD is."

He didn't look convinced. In fact, her argument seemed to ignite something inside of him. "Or maybe you didn't want to find me."

"Excuse me?"

"You walked out in the middle of the afternoon, while I was sleeping. You never had any intention of coming back."

Whatever she'd imagined, no matter how many times she'd played through her mind telling him the news of the baby, this wall of anger wasn't it. "You keep tossing that in my face. What are you really upset about? The fact that I'm pregnant or the fact that your pride is injured because I walked out the door?"

"You're pregnant! I had a right to know."

"I'm not disputing that fact. Our cutesy let's-pretend-we-don't-have-anything-but-this-moment act was heady at the time, but rather inconvenient when I tried to find you after. And you moving only made that worse."

He stood at that, his hands clenched at his sides as he paced back and forth. She wanted to go to him—wanted to comfort him in the same way she'd wanted to be comforted the day she'd discovered the life-altering news—but something kept her rooted to the couch.

His ire? While it was intense, she had zero fear of him.

So what was it? Why was she suddenly itching for a fight? One that would finally—hopefully?—assuage the anger she'd carried for the past three months. "You can stand there and act as self-righteous as you'd like, but it's not like you worked all that hard to come find me, either."

"I had no idea how to find you."

"Neither did I!"

He stilled at that, mid-pace, and stared at her. And in that moment, she saw all the excitement and confusion and raw emotion that she felt herself. "A baby?"

"Yes."

"But we were careful."

"I know. Or I think I know. There might have been that one time. Right around dawn."

His dark gaze clouded with memories, and she knew the moment he took firm hold of that one. "But we—"

"We made a valiant effort, but threw caution to the wind on that one."

And they had. Immense and wonderful, what had been between them had driven both of them nearly mindless. It was wildly out of character for her—she was vigilant about protection—but their conversation earlier in the evening had taken a rather personal turn when both admitted to seeing to their health with regular testing. And she'd believed herself covered with her birth control pills.

Pills she'd forgotten to take with the rush of running around for the holidays and again, after she'd gotten home that day. A lapse that had paid an incredible dividend. One they would now share for the rest of their lives.

"I never wanted to hide this from you, Gavin. Whatever else you might believe, please know that."

"When were you going to tell me? We spent all evening together, and if you hadn't thrown up, I'd still be blithely unaware I was going to be a father."

"Not for long. I was trying to figure out how to tell you and when, but it never crossed my mind not to tell you at all."

He remained where he was but had stopped pacing to stare at her from across the room. That large form she'd so admired, both in and out of clothes, struck her through a new lens as she stared at him.

And in a heartbeat, she *saw* him, their child nestled against his broad chest. She saw him again, hands wrapped firmly around a toddler's as they tried to walk. And even once more, a proud, doting father on one knee adjusting their child's backpack as they headed for the first day of school.

They were bonded by this tiny person who would be here in half a year. A blessing and a gift, one handed to two people who didn't know a thing about each other.

The edge of his lips twitched, a rude awakening in the midst of her thoughts.

"What?"

"Well, come on. You mean you didn't want to share the news in a conference room the size of a cracker box?"

Sera couldn't quite hold back a small smile of her own. "I was actually thinking I'd start our next task force meeting with the entire team. Make the announcement then."

"That certainly gives new meaning to collaborating with your partner."

The humor caught her low and deep in the belly, and she couldn't hold back the peals of laughter that, once started, quickly raged out of control.

Gavin crossed back to the couch, dropping down beside her. His own laughter joined hers, and it was long moments later before they both came up for breath.

But it was that dark brown gaze meeting hers that silenced the lingering humor. "We're actually having a baby?"

"We actually are."

"Garbage scents aside, how are you feeling?"

"I'm fine."

One lone eyebrow shot up. "Try again since I'm finding it hard to believe you. How are you really feeling?"

"I have good days and bad days. It's more the time of the day, to be honest. And I've sort of figured out how to deal with it."

"All by yourself."

"Well, yeah."

"Do your aunt and uncle know?"

It was her turn to shoot him a dark look. "Do you think they'd have been quite so welcoming this evening?"

"Probably not." He waited a few beats before asking, "And your parents?"

"They're not an issue."

He looked about to say something further, but stopped himself. It touched her that he could read her discomfort so easily, even as she felt a strange sort of sadness that she hadn't gotten to share some of that history with him. Some of what had shaped her.

But she stayed quiet and didn't say any of *that*, either.

They might share one explosive night of passion and a child, but there were some boundary lines she still couldn't cross. And there was no way she was ready to talk about *that* aspect of her life.

Which made his next move, so gentle and so innately kind, enough to set her heart to aching.

His hand found hers, his big palm layering over the back of her hand. "Whatever worries either of us will carry for this child, you can remove abandonment from the list." He turned to look at her, his brown eyes searching. "I will be a father for the rest of my life."

He was going to be a father.

The thought flowed in and out of his mind along with his breathing.

Inhale: *I'm going to be...*

Exhale: *...a father.*

Over and over as he and his partners worked the churning waters around Hell Gate.

It was an incongruous thought in an even more incongruous place, yet it was his. *All his*, Gavin thought as his heavily gloved hands moved the silt at the bottom of the East River after a hit on his metal detector. When he only came up with what looked like a key ring, he kept going.

His comms kept up a steady flurry of activity in his ear, both from the team up on the surface. Instructions continued coming down to him and Wyatt, along with separate details for the other pair in the water, Kerrigan Doyle and Jayden Houston.

They took no chances when they dived this area. It was always two teams, and they'd be called up when they still had at least ten minutes of air. It was an extra series of precautions Captain Reed had insisted on after a dive on his watch early in his career had nearly resulted in a Harbor team death.

Although Gavin had been fortunate in his years on the team, he appreciated the extra precautions. While today was fairly smooth going, he was well aware things could change in a minute.

The waters here at Hell Gate were actually a tidal strait, with the confluence of the New York Upper Bay, the Long Island Sound and the Harlem River contributing to the unceasing churn of the water. And the reality of the conditions was that high tide was bad, but low tide only reversed all the flow that had built up pressure in the passage, pushing the water right back in the opposite direction.

They'd deliberately selected this early afternoon window for having the least amount of tidal pressure in the day, but they needed to move. And with the rains of the past several days as well as the water's already roiling currents, the evidence they were attempting to recover could be anywhere.

"Needle in a haystack, friends," one of their leads up above in the police boat advised through the comms. "But you've cleared twelve quadrants so far. Hayes and Trumball, move west, and Doyle and Houston, move south. We'll cover one more swath before you ascend. Submersible's capturing the area north of the bridge."

Their briefing before they'd descended matched Wyatt's description the day before in the conference room. Someone had tossed a gun off the RFK Bridge with its estimated landing closer to the waters beneath Hell Gate Bridge. Although they hated to miss any evidence recovery, the perp was already in custody and two cops were eyewitnesses to the gun being tossed off the bridge, with body cam footage to back it up. It wasn't ideal to leave the evidence at the bottom of the river, but the overarching effort had to be weighed against the benefits.

An odd counterpoint to the clanging reality of his life at the moment. Which was also a clear example of effort versus benefit.

Sera had assured him she would have told him about the baby. But would she?

She'd made several quick assurances now that they'd met again, but if they weren't working the task force, how would she ever have found him?

That thought had haunted him all night and into the morning. What would it be like? To have a child of his walking around without him ever knowing?

He needed to keep his head on straight—they *had* met up again, and he *did* know—but the reality of what might have been haunted him.

"Hayes!" Wyatt's voice was garbled around his mouthpiece, but Gavin got the general gist, made even more specific when Wyatt grabbed his calf. They had a variety of physical signals they were all trained on, but this one was pretty straightforward.

He stopped his forward movement, allowing Wyatt to move up beside him. The water was murky, but their headlamps as well as the bright sunshine above gave him a decent view of his dive partner's face.

Gavin pointed toward the floor of the river, turning his hands up in an empty motion.

But it was Wyatt's face, visible through the clear veneer of his mask, that had Gavin doing a double take. The man held up a gun, the shape more than clear in the murky water, before waving him on.

And although his voice was garbled when he spoke, Wyatt's instructions were clear.

"Wait until you see what I found."

What they found was a cache of weapons that they'd be hauling up for hours, Gavin thought as he stared at what they had laid out on the floor of the police boat.

No weapon was designed to shoot flowers and sunshine, he admitted to himself, but these were some of the worst. Retrofitted guns designed to do maximum damage, all with serial numbers removed.

They'd called in a second dive team, who was working the scene now while he, Wyatt, Kerrigan and Jayden took a break.

"What a mess." Wyatt shook his head as he got to his feet. He'd called in for reinforcements, and even now Gavin saw Detective Arlo Prescott, a fellow officer and one of the most decorated detectives at the 86th, stepping onto the police boat after being ferried over.

Arlo and Kerrigan were dating, and Gavin saw them briefly speak, his hand tenderly rubbing her shoulder, before Arlo continued on to the cache spread out on the deck. The man let out a low whistle before crouching down in the same pose Wyatt had just come up out of. "This gives new meaning to evidence recovery."

"You're not kidding." Wyatt pointed toward the three sawed-off shotguns at the edge of the area. "Got a hit on the metal detector, but as soon as I saw the butt of that first one, I realized what we had. And not one damn serial number among them."

Arlo glanced up, frowning. "Kerrigan's talked often enough about hating to dive Hell Gate, but you all are still down there pretty regularly. How long do you think these have been there, unnoticed?"

"Forensics will do some testing," Gavin put in. "But based on some of the decomp on the metal and the state of a few of the barrels we've looked at, I'd say well over six months. Maybe a bit more since much of that would have been winter."

"You think we'll get any prints?"

"We've been careful bringing it all up." Gavin shrugged. "But that's hard to say."

They had been careful, well aware with this much evidence it would be more than possible they'd get a hit on some careless act like fingerprints or a partial serial number.

And still…

Something gnawed at him.

"Something this big?" Gavin finally spoke. "Whoever did it would have to realize they were going to attract attention once everything was found."

Arlo glanced over from staring at the cache of weapons, a faint smile on his lips. "You're assuming this was done by a party of masterminds. Panicked people do stupid things. It's why we get our fair share of cases that wrap up with minimal fuss."

"Maybe—" Gavin let his thought die off. Something about this troubled him, beyond the broader issue of such a large criminal act, but he hadn't quite worked it through in his mind. But there was something.

"Tell me what has you bothered, Gav," Wyatt pressed. "Is it the way we're handling the evidence?"

Despite the display currently on the floor of the police boat, there was a team en route shortly behind Arlo to quickly manage both the chain of evidence as well as the more sensitive aspects of handling the weapons. The Harbor team was well trained in basic recovery to ensure as clean a sample as possible, but they always breathed a bit easier once it had moved on to the folks actually responsible for evidence handling.

"No, not that. We've done this by the book. It's just the volume of it. The location. Whoever did this knew what they were doing." He shot a look at Arlo and offered a grim smile of his own. "These weren't run-of-the-mill criminals or a group of lackeys low on the food chain. Destroying evidence like this? And up at Hell Gate? It feels to me like whoever is responsible has knowledge of our work."

Arlo and Wyatt both stared at him, their gazes focused as they gave consideration to his assessment.

"Knowledge how?" Wyatt asked.

"The tides, for one. Hell Gate doesn't just have a scary name. That channel's always been difficult, and we have protocols specifically for diving there."

Wyatt nodded, his mouth grim. "I can still see you circling. Keep going."

And that was when he hit on it.

"It's the volume, Wyatt. You need time to dump that much, but you also have to know this area's a great place to hide. The tides work in a criminal's favor on that front."

"Tell me more about that," Arlo said. "You know I'm a big fan of what you do, but that's the stuff I'm fuzzy on."

Wyatt brought Arlo toward one of the large maps they

had up in the boathouse, one specifically mapping out the East River. But as one more obvious sign of his leadership, he gestured Gavin toward the wall. "Please, Hayes. Go ahead."

"The tidal patterns are wicked here." He pointed out the various points, the overall geography and the way multiple bodies of water—all with their own tidal push and pull—came together.

It was a credit to Arlo how quickly he picked it all up. "So what you're saying is high tide isn't your friend, but low tide's not much better."

"Exactly." Gavin nodded. "What comes in hard and fast goes right back out the same way. Which means if Wyatt hadn't accidentally discovered that gun there's every chance this dump site would continue to go unnoticed. Over time, especially as things piled up, they'd inevitably get moved with the currents."

"Speaking of which." Wyatt stepped in. "We need to get the team up. Low tide's going to start causing problems next. We'll prep and go back down later."

Wyatt headed out to the dive master manning the comms out on the deck, and Arlo turned away from the map, his gaze veering right back to the cache of weapons already laid out. "We don't have any recent pulses on gun trade activity. With what you found down there, you think there are about fifty weapons?"

Gavin nodded. "Initial estimate, but I think we're going to net out in that range."

"It's a lot in one place, but it's still not huge. Citywide, we take down that amount in an average weekend."

Gavin knew Arlo was right, and in the scheme of overall crime, fifty guns was the tip of the iceberg. And yet...

Was this something for the task force?

The thought popped in with little fanfare, but as Gavin considered it, he realized it could be an interesting approach to the project he and Sera were working on. A real-life case they could present and which then could use the extended brainpower of multiple teams.

He vowed to think on it later as a shout came up from the edge of the police boat. The second dive team had surfaced, more evidence in hand. Arlo and Gavin moved over to help, carefully securing what came up following each of the recovery steps they were all trained in.

Wyatt's focus on planning for a second dive altered Gavin's responsibilities for the rest of his shift. He put together a plan for the next day's dive teams, as well as setting up a pair of uniforms on both ends of the bridge to watch from above and a police boat to keep watch over the cache location still under the water.

It was good work. Solid police work. But as daylight slowly faded, the lights of the bridge coming up over them, he kept circling back around to using the task force and Sera.

Always Sera.

Which was how he found himself knocking on her door after his shift ended, dinner in hand.

Sera glanced down once more at her laptop before standing to head to the front door and whoever stood on the other side. Aunt Robin had mentioned stopping by one evening this week with some legal paperwork on one of their rentals, and Sera figured it would be a nice break from what she'd dubbed the legal brief from hell.

Although her workload had been significantly reduced

so she could participate in the task force, she still had the cases David had requested she retain. And for some reason, the brief on the Nicholson murder case she was handling was giving her headaches.

The bigger problem, to her mind, was why.

She usually enjoyed this part of her job, organizing her thoughts on a case and then writing the encapsulation of all she'd reviewed. It not only helped her consolidate her thoughts, but inevitably in the process, she gained more clarity and refined the approach she was going to use to argue the case.

"If clarity's what you're after, maybe you need to write a legal brief on Gavin," she muttered to herself as she crossed toward the door.

Which made the fact that he stood on the opposite side an unexpected shot beneath the armor she'd vowed to put into place. "You're not Aunt Robin."

"Not last time I checked." He held up a bag that emitted the most delicious aromas. "But I do come bearing dinner."

She recognized the logo on the side of the bag. "You brought shawarma."

"It struck me as I was walking home from work that I wanted this for dinner, and then I thought, maybe Sera would like it, too."

"I love it."

"Then I chose right." He leaned forward as if checking out the inside of her apartment. "Is it okay if I come in?"

"Oh! Yes!" She quickly gestured him in, her surprise at seeing him obviously killing any semblance of manners. "I was just doing some work."

"You usually work through dinner?" The question was casual, but she caught the subtle notes of censure. Before she could call him on it, he'd already turned from where he'd set the bag down on the counter. "I'm sorry. I was thinking about you *and* the baby on that one."

"Since the baby is the one who has put me off food for the past few months, I'd say you're putting blame in the wrong place." Since he looked genuinely chagrined, she opted to cut him some slack. "But since we're both hungry this evening, I'd also say your timing is perfect. And," she added, "it's further proof I'm hungry since I'm grumping at you even as you come bearing one of my top three favorite foods."

With that particular land mine disarmed, she crossed to the cabinets to get plates. "Help yourself to anything you'd like in the fridge. I've got some beer leftover from a party last year and a few bottles of wine in addition to diet soda."

"You sure about the beer?"

"Please, help yourself."

"It won't bother you if I drink and you can't?"

The deep, genuine sincerity in his gaze caught her up as she stared at him across the small expanse of the kitchen. "No, I don't mind at all. But thank you for asking."

It was a small kindness, but a welcome one. And it was only as she sat, nestled in the small drop-leaf table for the second night in a row, that Sera saw the sheer exhaustion that rode his features.

"Is everything okay?"

"Sure. Why?"

"It looks like you might have had a tough day." She stopped, realizing going any further would add a layer of intimacy she wasn't sure they'd progressed to. "You just look a bit tired."

When he didn't immediately say anything, the conversation the day before in the precinct conference room came winging back to her.

"Today was Hell Gate. How was it?"

"Tough, as usual. That stretch always is."

She'd read up on it last night after he'd left, curious what something so darkly named might be like as an actual dive site. The confluence of waterways and the sheer history of the location had sparked her worries, and she'd quickly closed her laptop for fear of moving down a path she wasn't entitled to.

He had a job, and it wasn't her place to question his choices. Nor did she have a right to those questions—to *any* questions, really—simply because she was carrying his child. Even if the reality of what he did for a living had embedded a level of worry in her chest she'd never expected to feel.

Which was just one more layer of weirdness in all that was happening to her.

No, she corrected herself, to *them*. And to the family they'd inadvertently created.

Gavin smiled as he unwrapped his meal. "Those look like very heavy thoughts in the face of this delicious pita wrapper full of seasoned meat."

"I—" It had happened so many times in the past thirty-six hours that she should be used to it by now, but as she set down her dinner, Sera had the odd sensation of not knowing what to say. Or more, feeling she had to say something yet having no idea how to navigate the discussion.

She hadn't felt this out of her depth since she was a teenager, trying to move on after her mother's death and feeling like the person she used to be was gone. It had been true then, and Sera suspected it was true now.

Why did it feel as unsettling at thirty-two as it had almost two decades ago?

"Why don't you start wherever you want to start?" His suggestion was gentle yet seemed like the exact right choice.

"I worried about you today. Quite unexpectedly, actually. What you do for a living, it's…dangerous."

"It is."

"And then you showed up, and you look really tired, and you sort of pissed me off with the eating thing, which…" she waved a hand "…I'm over. Truly I am. But I don't know what to *do* with you."

"What to do with me?" He grinned, quite at odds with the serious expression that had ridden his face through her outburst. "I'm not a pile of laundry."

"I—" She stared back, not sure if he was laughing at her or just making a joke.

She and Gavin didn't actually *know* one another's quirks or moods or what set them off. Because that came in time. After you got to know someone. Day by day.

Not after a night of fevered passion that resulted in a degree of involvement with each other that was going to last, oh, about forever.

"I stand by the statement," she finally said, sounding rather lame even to herself.

"Then I guess it's my turn to stand by something, too."

"What's that?"

Before she knew what he was about, he'd actually stood up and moved beside the table, extending a hand.

"What are you doing?"

"Isn't it obvious? I'm standing." He reached for her hand, tugging lightly. "Now it's your turn, too."

"Okay."

It was the last thing to escape her lips and, she'd admit later, the last coherent thought she had for quite some time.

The moment she stood, steady on her feet, Gavin had an arm around her waist, pulling her close. And in less than a heartbeat later, his lips captured hers in a kiss so intense, she could only wrap her arms around his neck and hang on.

Chapter 5

It might not have been one of his most inspired moves, Gavin thought as the kiss spun out, but it was hands down the best choice he'd made all day.

All month, if he were honest.

He'd wanted Sera back in his arms, and all the strange tension swirling around them since he'd arrived at her place seemed in need of taming. So he'd gambled, figuring kissing her could go one of two ways.

And he was damn glad it was this way, with her arms around his neck and her mouth open beneath his like a warm welcome home.

Because whatever else she was, Gavin thought as a hand drifted down over her spine while the other one remained firmly wrapped around her shoulders, Sera Forte felt like home.

She had from the moment they'd met.

A small sigh rose up in her throat as their tongues met, a joyful sort of remembrance that let him know whatever fantasies he'd had these past three months, nothing could compare to the real thing.

Nothing in his whole life had ever felt like Sera in his arms.

Memories of their time together blended with the reality of holding her again and Gavin recognized the truth. Reality was so much better.

Another small sigh lingered between them as he shifted the angle of the kiss, and he couldn't help but smile at her full response. Whatever else was between them, they had this.

Even if he'd nearly bungled it beyond recognition.

He was still frustrated with himself for his behavior on their first day of the task force. Yes, he'd been shocked to see her, but he'd been even more shocked at that pure rush of emotion during their reunion.

And with all those feelings he had no business swimming in came the endless questions that had haunted him since the new year.

Why did she leave? What could he have done differently? And perhaps the scariest of all—why had it mattered so much? It was that persistent confusion—and the sheer power of whatever it was between them—that had him pulling back.

I don't know what to do with you.

Her words still lingered in his mind, even as he had a few ideas of exactly what they could do together. But if he were honest with himself, Gavin thought, there was also way too much unspoken between them to jump back into bed.

But oh, the temptation…

Even as he thought it, Gavin admitted temptation was too simple a word. These feelings for her? They haunted him. Made him want a future with someone who, by all accounts, hadn't wanted one with him.

His behavior was ridiculous.

All of it.

His moony attitude. His inability to shake these feelings. Even his mental gyrations that insisted they had a connection that went deeper than a one-night stand. A feeling he'd had long before he'd known they'd created a life.

"Gavin?" Her voice was soft, a bemused expression tilting her still-wet lips.

"I interrupted our dinner. We should probably get back to it."

Bemusement shifted to subtle confusion, and Gavin recognized, once again, his behavior was so far out of the norm for him it was almost laughable.

He simply wasn't a person set with wide-sweeping emotions. He wasn't made for that; his early life as a "Park Avenue Hayes" ensured that he knew decorum and had a certain measure to his emotions at all times.

A range of emotions flitted across her face, some he could decipher and others that remained a mystery, before she finally spoke. "Why are you pulling away?"

"Is it that obvious?"

"No more obvious than my own hesitation. So why don't you grab a fresh beer, and we have the talk we really need to have?"

"About the baby?"

"No." She shook her head. "About us, Gavin. We need to talk about us."

Sera had always considered her willingness to tackle conflict—especially when rooted in the vastness of what remained unspoken—as one of her greatest assets in the practice of law. She'd understood from a very early age that the things people said or didn't say often hid something far deeper going on inside.

A point that became patently obvious when those words didn't match behavior.

She used that skill—honed it, really—to a sharp point in her legal work. What were the circumstances that led up to a crime? What was the perpetrator's motives? And what made them act in that moment?

There were times, of course, when people simply acted poorly. But more often than not, asking the questions that probed deeper gave far more insight into a case than simply assuming the worst of someone. It was the lodestone she hung onto, even on some of her worst cases. Finding that humanity in others. *Believing* it existed.

It was essential to how she lived. She needed it like she needed air.

To make sense of her past.

To believe she was making a difference.

To move beyond her parents' choices.

And with that knowledge, Sera recognized something else. She hadn't been at her best these past few days, and she knew herself to be a decent person. Which only made it fair to question what was driving Gavin.

From their tense moments on the first day of the task force to his sudden reappearance two nights in a row, they needed to get underneath it all. Because however much they didn't know about each other, she *knew* he was a good man.

She took her seat and waited until he sat back down before launching in. "I know we haven't been an 'us' for all that long or with any level of permanence, but there's a lot we haven't talked about."

"Is there something specific you'd like to know?"

As questions went, Sera had to admit, it was a good one.

Because the reality was, there was a rather large chasm between claiming she wanted to *talk about us* and then knowing exactly what to say on the matter.

"Are you a native New Yorker? Why police work and the dive work specifically? Why Brooklyn?" She lifted her hands and knew the smile on her face had to be distinctly rueful. "Who are you, Gavin Hayes?"

"An expectant father."

It was sweet that he started there, and Sera felt a small clutch beneath her heart. Especially because the sheer look of awe that filled his face as he spoke the words touched something she'd never thought possible.

"And as you said, I'm a cop." When she only nodded, saying nothing, he kept on. "I didn't grow up wanting to be a cop. It wasn't in my life plan, as it were. But—" He shrugged, and while the action was casual, Sera sensed a pain there she'd never have expected.

Something tugged on her to probe further, but she'd finally gotten him talking, and although she couldn't explain it, every instinct she had told her if she pushed too hard on that front, he'd shut down entirely.

So she tamped down on her own curiosity, instead following whatever he was willing to share. "But what?"

"But it's who I was meant to be."

"And the diving?"

The flash of a quick grin erased whatever lingering melancholy she saw in his face. "That's the fun part of being a cop."

"Risking your life and diving in the shockingly disgusting waters that surround our wonderful city is fun?"

"Why does everyone focus on that part?" Gavin reached for his sandwich, taking a large bite, the direction of their conversation apparently having zero impact on his willingness to finish his dinner.

"The dirty part?"

"Yeah." He waited until he was done chewing his bite. "It's getting better."

"Than what? A vat of toxic waste?" She picked at a small corner of her pita, unable to hide a smile of her own. "Or is that an insult to toxic waste?"

"It's not quite that bad. And yes, as the Harbor team we're encouraged to avoid opening our mouths or allowing any water to get past our lips. I also have a few extra shots each year to ensure my safety and physical health."

Sera shuddered at that. "And that's just the water risks. What about the other risks?" Her eyes widened as a new risk popped into her mind. "What about animals? Sharks? Eels?"

"No sharks. Eels yes. And feral goldfish, to name another."

"No way! Goldfish can be feral?"

"Absolutely. I've seen some that are as large as four pounds. Where do you think all those innocent little fish won at street fairs go?"

"I assumed the trip down the toilet and on into the sewer system was too much for them."

Gavin set down his napkin and leaned back in his chair. "Perhaps all aren't up to the trip, but a lot of people think taking their fair winnings and dropping them in a body of water themselves is a good idea. News flash. It isn't."

"I'm not sure I can keep eating."

"Which is another important fun fact. Women under fifty are encouraged to avoid any and all fish pulled out of local city waters."

Although she knew it was a reference to child-bearing age, Sera couldn't resist teasing him. "What about women over fifty?"

"They should plan their menu at their own risk."

It was a silly, innocuous conversation, and Sera was surprised by how good it felt. Especially because when she'd started down this path, the need to question him—to *know* him—had felt weighted somehow.

"See," she said, unable to hold back the smile even as the creepy concept of a four-pound goldfish would likely haunt her for days. "That wasn't so hard. A few fun facts about Gavin."

"Which means it's my turn. Tax, title, license." He made a come-hither motion with his hand. "Come on."

She knew this moment would come. Turnabout, after all, was more than fair.

Yet now, faced with the chance to tell him something that mattered, she felt the mental noose tightening around her neck.

What should she actually tell him?

That she was a workaholic with an unquenchable need to prove herself? Or maybe that she was a semi-loner adult whose guarded attitude had resulted in minimal friendships?

Or perhaps she should just go for it and watch him walk out the door. After all, who didn't wonder about a person who'd been abandoned by their parents?

Oddly, she felt the need to tell him all those things and so much more.

It was a first for her and no matter how much she believed he'd listen, a lifetime of *not* sharing those aspects of her life held her back.

"I'm a lawyer, which you know."

"I do."

"But you may not know why I chose public defender."

"I assumed it was your unerring need for fairness and justice."

"Not too far off the mark."

"Then what is it?"

"It's people, Gavin. I have a need to believe in people. In their innate goodness. Their ability to be fair when really pressed to the wall. And that even if they make a bad decision, they don't have to be defined by it."

"And what about you, Sera?"

"What about me?"

"Do you give yourself the same credit?"

The conversation had turned far deeper, far more quickly than he'd have anticipated.

And yet…

Something about the look in her gaze and the way she'd leaned forward slightly in her chair and the earnestness in her voice. Those emotions all spoke of something even more than passion.

They spoke of desperation.

And maybe, Gavin considered, he'd been a bit too focused on himself to think about what really happened on New Year's Day. He'd let his pride keep him from thinking that she'd left for any reason other than she had no interest in seeing him again. How humbling, then, to realize he'd not only missed the mark, but had lost three months out of sheer, stubborn idiocy.

As if realizing she'd stalled out their conversation, Sera finally spoke. "I don't know what you mean."

"This need to believe in other people. Do you give yourself the same credit?"

"Well, of course."

"Then why did you leave on New Year's? The real reason, not the potential for it to get awkward."

He wasn't sure why he was pressing it, but somehow, Gavin knew that he needed the truth. He needed to *know*. And he needed to hear her reasons, instead of living with the ones he'd made up in his mind. Perhaps he wouldn't like them, but at least they'd be the truth instead of something he'd managed to manufacture out of his own battered pride or bruised ego.

"It was a one-night stand." Although she didn't put nearly as much heat behind that argument as the day before, Gavin still sensed that reason was a lifeline she was hanging on to by the edges of her fingernails.

"It was."

"Most people prefer those have no strings attached."

"I'm not talking about most people. I'm talking about us. About our night together. About the connection we had that put us together in the first place."

Because whatever else he wanted to think or believe, he couldn't shake that sense of connection.

Of belonging.

It wasn't a sensation he was familiar with beyond his work with the Harbor team, and it had stuck with him for all these long months. Upended him, really, because for the first time in his life he'd felt attraction and desire in lockstep with the innate sense that he *fit* with another person.

And he'd reveled in that sensation of belonging in those hours with Sera. Of being understood.

Of fitting.

Maybe it was why her attempts at being casual—dismissive even—had him finding an odd sort of humor in their situation.

Sera blew out a breath that fluttered the hair that framed her face. "You do realize there are about a million articles in women's magazines saying not to have feelings for your one-night stand. And about ten times that of cautionary tales told on social media sites, talking about what a bad idea it is to bring emotion into casual sex."

"And there we have it."

When she only looked at him, he realized that she'd inadvertently given him the opening he needed.

"You're assuming what was between us was casual. Or scratching an itch."

"Scratching an itch?" A small bark of laughter escaped her. "How eloquent."

"Giving in to desire, then?"

"What does it matter?"

"It all matters, Sera. I was attracted to you, yes. And there was a hell of a lot of desire." He reached out and laid a hand over hers, willing her to understand what was so damned hard to put into words. "But nothing between us was casual. Nothing at all."

She sat there, her gaze focused on their hands for several long moments. Whatever progress he'd believed they had made seemed to fade, wisping away like smoke.

Until she turned her hand beneath his, their fingertips meeting the other's palm.

"It wasn't casual." She stared up at him then, those irises as blue as a spring day meeting his. "But we don't know each other. A single day, even a non-casual one, doesn't negate the fact that we don't know each other."

"So we get to know each other. Day by day."

"Fate seems to think that's a good idea. Between the baby and the task force, we've got a lot of together time in front of us."

"Then let's take it."

She nodded and didn't remove her hand from where it linked to his.

Gavin gave himself a few more moments to revel in the simplicity of that connection before his day came rushing back to him. "Lest you think I'm just the neighborhood stud you can ogle, I did come here with information we might be able to use for our task force project."

"The neighborhood stud?" She snatched her hand back, the slight shake of her head proof she already knew him well enough to get the joke. "Smooth, Hayes."

"I am that, but tell me you're not intrigued all the same."

The raw intimacy that had arced between them since the kiss began to fade as they both shifted toward work. Whether by design or simply to find some ease after several tense moments, he wasn't sure, but the shift was welcome.

"Oh, I'm intrigued. So tell me more about how we're going to create the best plan of all the task force teams." She picked up her shawarma and took another bite, her renewed interest in dinner a good sign they were back on level ground.

"My team and I had a big day up at Hell Gate."

"You find a school of feral goldfish?"

"Not letting that one go, I see. But what we found was way better."

With the economy he'd learned in briefing his captain on case progress, he quickly caught her up to speed on the cache of weapons they'd discovered and the work underway to bring everything up to the surface.

And with her legal mind and understanding of local crime, Sera caught on quick. "Someone had to know that was the perfect place to make an illegal drop like that. Difficult waters. Active tides."

"Without question. Add on that we haven't found a serial number on anything we've brought up, and it looks like this was deliberate."

"There are potential trafficking elements here. The Feds are going to want in."

"Which is why this is the perfect subject for our task force project. It's real work, and we can use it to map out a plan of action in real time."

"I like it for the project, but, Gavin, what about the actual implications? Something that size? And that deliberate disposal? *Especially* when it wasn't the reason you were diving that area to begin with."

He'd turned the case over in his mind, but it wasn't until she doubled down on the real-world implications that Gavin realized all he'd missed. He'd been so focused on making a success of the task force that he hadn't fully appreciated the advancement this case would provide all on its own.

"It's a lucky hit, no doubt."

"It's more than luck, Gavin." Those notes of justice—the ones she was so determined to find—lit up her gaze. "Whoever put that stash of weapons there didn't think they were going to get caught."

The day's news out of the 86th was late in arriving but pertinent all the same, the Organizer thought as he considered the details.

The damned Harbor team had struck again.

The ongoing drop at Hell Gate had been an inspired approach to their problems around weapons disposal. And they'd been getting away with it for some time now.

Until the water cowboys over at the 86th nosed around.

And now that they knew, it was time to not only find a new drop but deal with the fallout of this one. He glanced at the other items spread over his desk. The ones he kept secreted away on his person, pulling them out only in his private moments.

The burner phone he changed out religiously each week.

The single sheet of paper on which he kept a list of rotating passwords, also changed out every seven days.

And the phone number he planned never to use.

Although he'd committed that number to memory, he knew well enough that should he need to use it, he'd have no time to worry if he could recall those digits in their precise order.

So yes, he held on to the number, the paper it was written on faded and thin from where it had worn, rubbing against the inside breast pocket of his suit jackets.

Even as he took great pride that he'd never had need of it.

Pushing aside thoughts of his *partner*, the Organizer tapped a finger on the burner phone, considering all the angles.

None of the weapons had serial numbers. It was a requirement of the work he'd insisted on from the first, along with a distributed work pattern so that no one person had access to all the information of the operation, and things had been progressing smoothly.

He considered himself the finest puppet master, after all.

And, as such, he understood his other options. Knew where he could push or pull, shift and maneuver the situation to his bidding.

This was a bump in the road.

Those guns were untraceable, after all.

And he'd simply find a new way to dispose of his garbage.

Chapter 6

Gavin stood at parade rest as Captain Dwayne Reed considered all he, Wyatt and Arlo had just shared about their recovery dive up at Hell Gate.

Captain Reed had first listened to their overview, and now his deep brown gaze was engrossed on the report Gavin had come in early to write up.

The man's attention was laser-focused on the work. It was a style, Gavin knew, that showed both a measure of respect to his team as well as a razor-sharp intellect that was already processing implications with each word he digested.

He listened.

He considered.

And then the man never failed to seamlessly nail the most pertinent questions in a matter of minutes.

Kerrigan and Jayden had already gone out again this morning to direct a second team who was fresh for the work while Gavin took point on the briefing. He'd already been scheduled off the Harbor team today because of his task force work, so Wyatt had given him the opportunity to debrief their captain.

That was Wyatt's style, too. He was more than comfortable sharing the work of their team, allowing everyone to shine. He might be their de facto dive head, but he ensured the leadership at the 86th always knew harbor work was a full team effort.

"This is good work, Gavin." Captain Reed looked up from the report, deep lines grooved in his deep brown skin, framing his mouth, forehead and beneath his compassionate gaze. Although he wore the mantle of responsibility incredibly well, the pressure of the work was never-ending. "And this cache is a big deal. Based on what you've got here, you're confident this would have gone undetected for some time?"

"Yes, sir. The dive was a recovery mission, and if the waters hadn't been so churned up from the storms earlier this week, we'd likely not have moved into the quadrant where the weapons were discovered."

Gavin kept his comments brief and saw a solid gleam of approval shining from Wyatt's eyes.

"Would someone have a way of knowing what quadrants you regularly dive?" the captain asked.

The question cut straight to the heart of the matter and a theory Gavin had been playing around with on his own. "We don't publicize our dives or the patterns we follow, and the quadrant management is as much how we map out the area ahead of time that we're going to dive rather than being an actual location."

"So you'd have missed these for an indeterminate period of time?" Captain Reed persisted.

"Yes. The rocky area beneath the surface where we found the weapons isn't directly aligned or easily reached simply by tossing something off the Hell Gate Bridge. Or the RFK Bridge to its south. To position the guns in the place we uncovered, you'd need to do it deliberately and down near the water to make a drop."

"Nor is that an area we regularly check for incendiary devices," Wyatt added.

It was a sad reality that some of their team's work was aligned around regular bomb checks under bridges and city access points. Wyatt's added comment only reinforced the situation—that these guns were also in a place where they'd not be discovered on those regular dives.

Captain Reed stood and came around his desk, taking a spot perched against it. "I'd like you to work this, Gavin. I know it's a lot, and I don't want to take away from your task force work, but I'm hoping the additional days off the water will give you the time to lead this investigation."

That same shot of excitement that had filled Gavin when he'd been chosen for the task force lit him up, a deep sense of pride welling in his chest. Captain Reed was exceedingly fair in his distribution of work, and Gavin had never felt overlooked, but the task force and now this opportunity demonstrated he was getting the chance to show he was increasingly ready for the rank of detective.

"I'll give it everything I've got."

Captain Reed smiled, his first of the morning. "I believe it."

"The task force might be a good conduit for this one," Arlo offered up. "A way to talk with other teams and discuss how to approach something like this."

At the man's words, thoughts of Sera filled Gavin's mind, and the anticipation of seeing her once he wrapped up this meeting grew. Their conversation the night before had been a revelation. Part getting-to-know-you and part professional brainstorming session, it amazed him to see how easy it was with her to shift seamlessly between any number of topics.

Even that kiss—hot and needy in her kitchen—hadn't stopped their ability to talk to each other. To listen to one another's opinions. And to willingly share thoughts with each other.

He wasn't used to that. He was raised in an environment of *children should be seen, not heard*, and after he was past the point that such a rigid structure would matter, life took a dark turn that left him far more willing to keep his own counsel than share parts of himself with others.

And wasn't that the miracle of Sera?

They didn't know each other, and there was a long road toward whatever the future held for them, but he had this clear sense that they *would* figure it out.

It was Wyatt who spoke first, clearly finding humor in Arlo's words. "This suggestion from the man who famously loves to close his cases with as little help as possible."

"I take help. I just don't need it," Arlo shot back at Wyatt, their long-standing friendship more than evident in the banter.

"I think I want to watch you say that in front of Kerrigan."

It was Captain Reed who finally broke up the byplay. "While Detective Prescott's lone-wolf status has taken a hit these past few months, I think his point's a good one. Use this time, Gavin. Talk to others and see what they think. Working through a case with someone else is never a bad idea, and getting a different perspective can open a new line of thinking."

"I will, sir. And I'll have an updated report on your desk

tomorrow after seeing what the team brings up today. I'll head over to the site later this afternoon."

Their captain nodded before circling around back to his chair, signaling the close of their meeting. They all thanked him for his time before Captain Reed called out to Gavin, "A few more moments, Hayes?"

"Of course, sir."

Arlo and Wyatt kept on going, their obvious trust of their captain ensuring they didn't even look back. A sign of respect to Captain Reed and, Gavin realized, one to him, as well. He had this case, and he'd do it well. It felt good to have colleagues who believed that, too.

Captain Reed tapped on the printout of Gavin's briefing. "This is good work."

"Thank you."

"You understood the implications on this one immediately, and you've suggested some strong lines to tug quickly to see what's going on."

He nodded, curious to see where the man was going.

"Arlo's task force suggestion is a good one, as well. Use your partner there. Get their feedback."

"I will, sir. I—" He stopped, careful with his words. "I admit, I'm a bit surprised. Are you open to other jurisdictions coming in on this one?"

"*Resigned* is maybe a better word."

"Resigned how?"

Those lines that had been so obvious earlier only cut deeper in his captain's face. "These guns are concerning. They're going to draw attention. A find like this is going to get the FBI involved, and I get why. This smacks of a criminal ring with potential interstate traffic."

"Of course."

Although he avoided sharing any disappointment, Gavin knew himself and knew how much he wanted to handle this on his own. *Without* federal interference.

"If you can demonstrate from the start that you're open to support and collaboration, it'll grease the wheels early. Show you can run an op and work well with others."

"Yes, sir."

Captain Reed's smile, normally soft and gentle in the way he spoke to his team and dispensed his leadership, turned positively wolfish. "And when you do all that great work and communicate well with others, I'll have a very clear pathway to step in and ensure that you can remain lead on the case. This is your show, Officer Hayes. You have my full endorsement on that."

Sera showed her credentials at the front desk and put her work bag and purse through the X-ray machines at the entrance to the 86th. The spring day was bright and crisp, and she'd gotten away with only her raincoat as she'd headed out that morning.

The air had a decided nip in it as she hoofed it from the subway to the precinct, but she simply couldn't wear her thick winter coat one more day if she could help it.

The bracing fresh air had an added benefit, helping the morning queasiness she hadn't fully shaken yet. Her sour stomach was slowly improving day by day, but bright sunshine and a cool breeze certainly helped.

All of which served to put her in a very good mood when she walked into that small conference room Gavin had reserved for them again.

He wasn't in the room, but had obviously beaten her to work, because his notebook and files were at the end of the conference room table, along with a scrawled note that he'd be right back addressed to her.

Sera took in the bold scrawl and nearly picked up the note to trace her fingers over the letters before she caught herself.

Tracing his handwriting? Seriously?

For someone who was doing her level best to keep her heart in check, she certainly had her moon-eyed moments. Especially after the past two evenings in his company.

Last night had been…special.

Even if at times she'd felt the intimacy clawing at her, knocking on the doors of her past.

It was a silly thought, Sera admitted, but it was a fit for how she felt. And last night's discussion—and her deep need to know more about Gavin—had left her more than aware that if she wanted answers from him, she'd need to be prepared to share some of her own.

Wasn't that the whole reason she'd avoided building deeper relationships with others, sexual or otherwise? Her friendships were surface level. Even Uncle Enzo and Aunt Robin, who knew her past, were kept at an arm's length most of the time.

They tried to get in, and Sera probably gave Aunt Robin the most leeway when it came to deeper discussions about life, especially her own, but that was the extent of it.

She'd always told herself it was a matter of privacy, but was it?

Or was it initially an armored response to life that had somehow become a prison?

"Sera!"

She glanced up to see Wyatt Trumball framed in the doorway. "Hey, Wyatt."

"I had to run up here to check in on another team and realized you were here waiting for Gavin. We just had a briefing meeting with the captain, and he needed to stay a few extra minutes to wrap up."

"Of course. I've got plenty to do while I wait."

He looked about to leave before seemingly thinking better of it. "Gavin mentioned that he told you about our discovery yesterday and that he'd like to put it up as an item for consideration on the task force you're both working."

"It seems almost purpose-built for what we're doing. How to share jurisdictions and more seamlessly communicate and hand projects back and forth."

"I was more intrigued that you pushed him to focus on working the case."

"Intrigued?"

"I get this task force is important. Everyone selected for it was handpicked by their leadership, and it's a sign you're being considered for more. To encourage Gavin to work the case before prioritizing the task force, that's a credit to you, Sera."

"Thank you. I—" She wasn't entirely sure what to say in the face of such obvious praise, so ended up simply sharing what she truly felt. "I appreciate the opportunity to grow my career and my work. But the reason we're even on a task force? It matters because we're keeping the city safe. No amount of ambition can stand in the way of that."

"Not everyone can say that. I hope you know it only reinforces why you were selected for the task force in the first place. I will make sure Captain Reed communicates the same to your DA."

"Thanks, Wyatt. I appreciate that."

Visit at an end, the man headed off almost as quickly as

he'd arrived. Even so, Wyatt's support of her lingered in her mind long after he'd left.

That ready sense of encouragement was special. And while she'd never have said David Esposito didn't offer similar encouragement to his team of ADA's, she could also honestly say there was a distinct sense of competition in her team. One that came from a pace and tone David set with all of them as their district attorney.

"What's the frown for?"

She looked up from her laptop to see Gavin standing behind his seat at the table.

"Frown?"

"Yeah, you looked like a cross between angry and sad with distinct notes of annoyed." He laid a hand over his heart. "What did I do?"

She had the urge to toss her pen at him but held back. "Every thought in my head doesn't include you."

"Pity." Gavin pulled his phone and a thick leather folder that held his badge from his pockets before taking his seat. "Why'd you think I was angry?"

"I don't know, but you just looked really upset there when I walked in."

"Wyatt stopped in to tell me you were delayed by your briefing. And he said something quite nice." Without knowing why, Wyatt's words fell from her lips, and she couldn't deny how much it had meant to her that he'd acknowledged her in that way.

"And that put an angry look on your face?"

"That's just it. I realized that there's a lot of competition in my own team. I guess I always saw it as a good thing, but maybe it sort of pisses me off, now that I think about it."

"Teams are all about personalities. I see that with the

Harbor team, which is a good blend of personalities. But further back, when I went through training with my academy team. We were—" he shrugged "—let's just say I've heard more than one person mention my class had a lot of high-maintenance personalities."

High-maintenance personalities.

Wasn't that the very definition of a lawyer? Yet even with the realities of living a cerebral life, constantly strategizing and building counterarguments, Sera sensed there was something more beneath the surface.

"Well, I guess I never realized our collective personality in the DA's office is a bit like a rabid wolf pack." With an odd sort of sinking in her stomach, she added, "Or how much I seemingly enjoyed running with the pack."

"I wouldn't be too hard on yourself. A little healthy competition isn't always a bad thing."

"Maybe so."

And there it was. Once again, Gavin had a way of seeing straight through to the root of her questions, nailing whatever it was she was gnawing over in her mind.

"You know, that might be an interesting angle to apply to the task force work," she said.

"Competition?"

"Oh, we've got plenty of that. But I mean more the dynamics of interdepartmental groups through the lens of team personalities."

Although they'd maintained a solid veneer of professionalism in public, Sera didn't miss the distinct heating of Gavin's dark gaze as he stared at her across the table. "Inter-departmental dynamics, you say?"

"Not *those* sorts of dynamics." Heat flooded her veins in response to his innuendo, the magnetic draw of this man something she was helpless to fully deny. A fact that felt more than clear when her voice quavered at the edges all while the space of the table felt like it was shrinking somehow, so that nothing existed in the room except her and Gavin.

It was a heady sensation, one she'd never had to juggle in a professional setting before. Heck, she admitted to herself, not really in *any* setting.

"Why, Sera Forte, whatever do you mean?" His gaze had grown even more heated, and she could swear she felt that gaze on her body like a caress.

She felt the heat, but underneath it, she also felt the subtle play of humor. And wasn't that something? Although she wouldn't have called past relationships staid, now that she'd met Gavin, she had to admit there was a deeper dimension there. One she'd never have expected.

There was fun.

Which made her next comment as easy as breathing.

"You know exactly what I mean, Gavin Hayes. The naked kind."

The naked kind.

The implications of *that* hit him with a tsunami of sexual longing that, if he wasn't sitting, likely would have had his knees buckling.

Gavin knew this way lay madness, but he was helpless to turn away from the simmering physical need that wasn't far from the surface where Sera was concerned.

It had been that way from the first.

Those initial moments in the bar, when she'd come up and asked to share his high-top table with her friends on New Year's. He'd quickly obliged, and his own group had opened the space in the crowded bar to welcome the new-comers. Their group had fallen into conversation, one of his friends recognizing one of Sera's friends as a mutual acquaintance, and talk had come easily from there.

The two of them had found a rapport instantly, one that was as much steeped in attraction as it was in the sheer enjoyment of each other. They'd only briefly talked of their jobs, instead focusing on everything from favorite museums in the city to deep discussion on their latest binge watch on a streaming service. Whatever the topic, they'd flowed in and out of it with ease.

It had also been the first time in a long time that his social conversations didn't hinge on work or on his family. He loved his job, but a group of cops tended to talk almost obsessively about work.

And time spent with his family was…fraught.

Yet with Sera, he'd experienced neither.

And because of it, for the first time he could ever remember, he'd felt like Gavin Hayes.

Not Gavin Hayes the cop.

Or Gavin Hayes the survivor.

It was *that* reality about himself that had him stepping back from the sexy talk.

Time to get back on track.

Putting on a faux, world-weary voice—and adding a wink for good measure—he said, "Much as I'd like to interrogate that line of thinking, Ms. Forte, I'm afraid we have work to do."

"So we do."

They caught each other up on the work they'd done independently against their project. While they would come together to create the final project, they'd also decided it would be helpful to map out how each of their team's interacted with each other, pinpointing all the places where a case could be handed off from one owner to another.

"That right there." Sera pointed to one of the handoff steps Gavin mapped on the room's whiteboard as they'd talked through the various angles each had sketched out. "The chain of evidence. There's risk there."

"Risk how?"

"Your team captures it and goes through several areas of documentation within the police department. All those details are handed off to the DA's office, and we have matched handling rules on our side. But how clear is the handoff itself?"

"There's standard operating procedure. To your point, it's all noted and documented."

"But is it a gap? We're focused on city-based jurisdictions, but what about when the Feds are involved? Or what if something has to be further reviewed between two jurisdictions?"

Gavin considered what she was saying. Although evidence was taken very seriously, people were human. And those moments where evidence shifted between parties were the places where there was the most risk for a mistake.

"We could use the new case I'm working on. The captain endorsed us considering it for the task force, and I'd honestly welcome a set of eyes that aren't, first and foremost, cop."

"The weapons find?" She stepped back from the whiteboard and took the seat beside him. "It makes sense to use that. Walk me through it."

Since he'd already given her the key elements over dinner the day before, he focused instead on the evidence recovery and handoffs specifically.

"So your team brings it up, with the rules you follow when making a retrieval."

"We do. There's nearly always another handler on the police boat as well, who will take point on keeping track of everything and do a quick log as we're bringing it up."

He remembered that time well. Those early days of his training when he so desperately wanted to be under the water, but he had to pay his dues by learning the ropes and every single aspect of the Harbor team's work.

"Do you bring the evidence in or does a team come to you?"

"It depends on what we've retrieved. We went out yesterday to recover a single weapon. If that was all we'd found, we'd bring it in and hand off to the team that does intake on evidence."

"But in this case?"

"Because it's so large and the recovery area needs photographing, too? A team comes to us."

He watched, fascinated, as she considered what he'd shared. He could almost see her processing the information, working through the angles. But it was her next question that made him realize Sera wasn't one to sit and wonder.

Instead, she was a woman of action.

"Can we go out with the evidence team? See how they're handling what your team's brought up?"

He glanced at his watch, but already knew they'd be in time. Kerrigan and Jayden had gone on shift about an hour before, and they'd likely be there until early afternoon.

"You sure the water won't upset your stomach?"

"I'm sure." She glanced down where she laid a hand over

her ever-so-slightly rounded belly. "I think I could ride roller coasters and be okay. It's the smell of food that seems to set me off." She glanced up. "Or should I say, sets us off?"

What had started out as a simple question quickly turned profound as he realized it was his child beneath her palm. His child they were speaking of.

His child in the small space between them.

"The good news is there's nothing in the way of food on the boats. I can't promise you there aren't any smells. It is the East River."

"I'm willing to risk it. I really want to see the whole operation."

Gavin allowed his gaze to linger another few beats on her stomach before turning to look at their work on the whiteboard. He reached for his phone to take some pictures, capturing their discussion, before erasing all they'd mapped out.

When he turned back, she'd already gathered her things, an eager look on her face.

"Let's get out of here, Hayes, and go kick some task force ass."

Chapter 7

Although she knew the Harbor team who worked out of Brooklyn were based out of the 86th Precinct, Sera had never realized how extensive the dock area was or appreciated their impressive setup.

She should have, she admitted to herself as Gavin led her out to the dock situated about five hundred yards from the precinct building. They'd stowed her personal items in his locker, and she felt a bit empty-handed, out on a workday with just her purse, a small notebook stowed inside.

But wow.

She *really* should have imagined this setup, she thought as she took in the array of boats and equipment, immaculately kept and all neatly ordered around the open-air structure. The Harbor team was a small unit compared to the overall size of the NYPD, but it was still a large operation, tasked with covering hundreds of miles of shoreline and waterway. Their equipment was testament to that.

"So this is where the magic happens." She turned to Gavin, surprised to find him watching her closely.

"It all starts here."

"It's quite a set up. And a much bigger operation than I'd have ever imagined."

"We have an incredible number of tools at our disposal. It's a privilege to work on a team outfitted like this."

While she'd never argue that point—and was beyond grateful there was an infrastructure in place to keep him as safe as possible—she also recognized the NYPD was exceptionally well funded for their work.

"I wonder if you realize how obvious it is on your face when your mind starts working."

His statement was voiced in low tones, with an intimacy that went straight to her very core, as she stared up at Gavin.

"I'm sorry."

"Don't be. It's fascinating." He reached out, tracing a soft line over one of her eyebrows before smoothing a fly-away piece of hair that caught in the breeze. "The way your forehead scrunches up a bit when you're considering something."

"Oh, lovely." She meant it as a bit of a joke, but her voice came out sort of like a croak and her skin was all warm and tingly where he'd touched it.

"It is lovely. And incredibly cute."

"Thank you."

Thank you? *Really, Sera? That's the best you can do when a sexy man's touching you at 10:00 a.m.?*

She wanted to play this cool. Wanted to be one of those women who came off like they ate men like this for break-fast and found a new one by dinner. Women for whom flir-tation came quick and easy.

Women who didn't carry the scars of abandonment into adulthood.

But she wasn't.

Which was why she stepped back, instead focusing on

the questions that had rolled through her mind as they'd come onto the harbor docks.

"Well, um. I *was* thinking, actually…"

Gavin seemed to sense her reluctance and stepped back himself. "Go on."

"What about other jurisdictions? There are endless miles of waterway in and around the country. How do other places do the same sort of work? This is an impressive outfit you've got here, and I can't imagine it's nearly this sophisticated in other places."

"Most large cities have the same. Los Angeles and San Francisco are well outfitted. Miami and DC, too." He stopped and looked around at all that lay before them, from boats to equipment to an even larger ship docked outside the shed-like overhang that protected this area of the marina. There was a crane built into the boat and an oversize deck wide enough to hold several vehicles.

"But yes, we're incredibly fortunate to have all this. And there are a heck of a lot of water-based locations that simply get by with what they have. Several have volunteer services, too. Better-than-amateur divers who choose to train for rescue certifications and offer their skills."

"I saw something about that recently," she realized. "That big news story out of Bucks County last summer, down between New Jersey and Pennsylvania. There was a whole team of volunteers who saved several people from the rushing waters of the Delaware River."

"That's exactly it. There are many municipalities who benefit from that sort of support."

"Which circles us back to the start of this. How is evidence managed in those places?"

"It's part of training."

"Sure, but I have to imagine your training and the professional expectations of you are considerably higher."

"They are. But those groups are also more search-and-rescue-based than evidence recovery. Much as we'd like to believe every criminal is caught, a lot of people get away with a lot of bad things. And capturing the evidence correctly makes it easier for you and your colleagues to do their jobs."

As if to punctuate his point, a loud shout of laughter echoed off the cavernous space as a team came walking down to the dock. Several had large bags swung over their shoulders, and despite the obvious camaraderie, there was a seriousness in their demeanor as they all headed for the boat she and Gavin stood in front of.

"We picked a good time," he said. "That's the forensics and evidence crew. We'll go out with them if you're still up for it."

"Absolutely."

After brief introductions and an explanation of what they were doing, she and Gavin boarded a large boat with the NYPD's logo printed on the side. After safety checks and a quick run-through for her on where to find life vests and where the radio system was housed, they were on their way.

Gavin moved into a discussion with the leader of the forensics team, getting an update on the day before. Sera used the time to head for the back of the boat. The slip they'd left and the overhang that protected the docks grew smaller as they pulled out of Sunset Bay and began the journey toward New York Harbor and the entrance to the East River.

The city rose majestically in the distance, the iconic New York skyline unmistakable beneath a gorgeous blue sky. That decided nip in the air she'd ignored on her morning walk was positively frigid in the breeze kicking up off the water, and she crossed her arms, unwilling to go back inside the boathouse and miss the views.

Which made the jacket that came around her shoulders, already warmed by Gavin's body heat, a welcome treat. Especially when she could inhale the soft scent of him enveloping her. It wasn't anything she could put a name to, but she was attracted enough—and pregnant enough—to know there was a sizable hit of pheromones making her own hormones work overtime.

Who knew her increased scent receptors that had made it so difficult to keep food down would augment the scent of him in such a wonderful way?

"It's cold out here."

"It's too pretty a day with too gorgeous a view to sit inside."

He pointed out a few last things around the Brooklyn shoreline before they made the turn for the East River. "It won't be too much farther, and you can see the team in action."

She glanced around once more, her gaze seeming to look everywhere all at once. The Manhattan skyscrapers to the west, the Brooklyn and Manhattan bridges rising above them as they passed beneath and the East River stretching before them as they navigated north.

"We're almost there."

"I can't believe you do this all the time." She turned to him, and once more was caught up in that warm gaze.

No, warm *hungry* gaze, she corrected herself.

Each encounter they'd had since the start of the task

force only grew more intense than the last. Only made what they'd shared at New Year's feel that much more tangible.

As if a baby hadn't already done that.

Even so, she'd managed to separate her pregnancy from her feelings for Gavin in her mind. She loved this baby already and had from the very first moment she'd discovered she was pregnant. But the father...

What she felt for Gavin was complex and confusing and...well, wonderful. She kept trying to ignore that fact, yet circled back around to it, over and over again. She enjoyed his company.

So as they stood there, side by side on the back of a boat navigating the East River, Sera let down her guard and leaned into him.

And didn't try to move away when his arm came around her shoulders, pulling her close.

The stealth surveillance cameras caught the work up near Hell Gate in exquisite clarity. Proof that you could get what you paid dearly for, the Organizer thought as he watched video so clear he could make out the puffs of breath from the divers coming up out of the water in the cool morning air.

The cameras had been a risk: discovery always a possibility, but a worthwhile one. He hadn't regretted their installation for a minute.

But it was this moment that had paid off.

He'd had a clear view of the work pulling up the weapons he'd so carefully hidden. And he'd watched the crew managing the find, already thinking how he could take care of each and every one of them.

They were liabilities.

Even as the fantasy played out, one thought more grue-some than the next, he knew it was just that. A fantasy. No matter how angry, you simply didn't take out roughly a dozen NYPD officers without anyone noticing.

But someone would have to pay.

He wasn't sure who or how, but there would be some ret-ribution demanded for this. A needful sort of accounting.

Although he kept himself separate from the operation as a whole, his inner circle still gave him a wide berth. They all realized his carefully leashed temper could turn on them, and everyone was keeping their distance, hard at work looking for a new location.

Nothing would be quite as perfect, but there would be other places. Other forgotten spots that could take the place of this one.

He just needed to do damage control in the meantime.

The activity had been robust around the dump site, and he'd cataloged what was coming up out of the water and the speed of the operation. At the rate they were going, they'd likely have every last weapon by the end of the day.

Which meant he needed to put his plans with the evi-dence team into motion.

He'd nearly shut down the feed of the dump site and the waters beyond—he would watch more later—when movement at the edge of the screen caught his attention. No sooner did he lean in closer to the monitor when one of the evidence boats moved into view before nearly heading out of the top of the camera's frame.

But it was the figures on the back of the boat that caught his attention.

Two people, huddled together.

He paused the video, recognition instantly flashing as

he looked at the slender figure wrapped in an oversize coat, leaning into the man beside her. Zooming in on the couple, he watched Sera Forte fill his screen, the man beside her looking far more like a companion than a colleague. What the hell was a Brooklyn assistant district attorney doing on the back of the evidence boat?

And why did he have the sinking feeling that the task force he'd used to get her out of the way for a while had just reared up to bite him in the ass?

Unlike his earlier fantasy of just doing away with his enemies, this particular betrayal needed addressing. He'd think on it, but he would find the right moment. In the meantime, it might be worth tossing a diversion everyone's way.

He hated acting on impulse—it rarely paid off—but his gut told him this required swift action.

And with all those people out on the water, he was pretty sure he knew what would shake them up once they all came home.

The discovery site was a hive of activity, and Gavin took it all in after helping Sera back into the large cabin set atop the recovery boat. A big part of him itched to be in the water with Kerrigan and Jayden and the rest of the team, diving down to pick up the weapons, even as a bigger part of him knew that the opportunities he was being given above-ground mattered.

Captain Reed's faith in him mattered.

And if that meant he would spend less time in the water over the next few weeks, he had to accept that.

The evidence crew that had joined his Harbor team that morning was pulling out, heading back into the precinct to continue cataloging the weapons. In its place, the boat he and Sera had ridden over on pulled up alongside the NYPD boat that was the epicenter of the Harbor team's work.

"This is quite an operation." Sera looked around, her continued questions and awe at the work evident in her voice.

"We're usually not this heavy with personnel and boats concentrated in one place. Normally, our work's spread out around the city each day, but this is priority one right now."

"Yo, Gav!"

He turned to see Kerrigan Doyle waving at him from the water. She was in full gear, and all that was visible was a bright, vivid smile beneath her heavy face mask.

"You've got the whole damn department doing your bidding, Doyle! Crews are coming and going for you."

If possible, that grin grew even wider before she gestured that she'd come up on the boat.

Gavin turned to find Sera taking it all in, her hands on her hips.

"You surprised a woman's competently doing that job, Hayes?" She'd teasingly called him Hayes before, but this time Gavin didn't miss the distinct notes of challenge in her voice.

"Never."

"Good. I don't want to be wrong about you, you know."

As he moved around to the ladder side of the boat, he had the distinct realization he didn't want Sera to be wrong about him, either. A stark reminder that for all they didn't know about each other, he couldn't stop the increasing hope that they had a way forward. One that wasn't just co-parenting, but something more.

"Kerrigan's one of the best divers on the team," Gavin

said with absolute sincerity. "And she's an incredible cop. She and another detective in the department were responsible for bringing down that up-and-coming crime ring last fall."

"Incredible work that we're still processing in the DA's office. Wendy Parker managed to do a heck of a lot of damage in her quest to rise to the top of the New York crime syndicate pecking order."

"She was a determined woman. And she left a wake of destruction, a term I'm using quite literally."

They'd dived the wreck of a boat in the harbor in the midst of a nor'easter the prior October, a drug trafficking incident gone very bad. The sunken boat and the violent murders of two of the drug runners on it had opened up the case, and Kerrigan had worked it with Arlo Prescott.

"It was great work. And I shudder to think what Wendy would have done if Kerrigan and Arlo hadn't figured out she was the source of it all."

Kerrigan crossed over to them after shedding her mask and tanks. "Are you talking about my former high school classmate?"

"You went to school with Wendy Parker?" Sera asked.

Kerrigan nodded as she worked the tight confines of her wet suit down to her waist. "Sure did. And while I'd never have said we were close or even all that friendly, I can honestly say I never took her for a crime lord wannabe." Kerrigan screwed up her mouth. "Or is that a crime lady? What's the equivalent of a crime lord?"

"I'm not sure it matters." Sera laughed, extending her hand. "Sera Forte. I'm from the DA's office and am working with Gavin on an interjurisdictional task force. I'd love to find out more about what you do."

"He hasn't talked your ears off about it yet?" Although Kerrigan was friendly and warm, Gavin didn't miss the way her gaze cataloged the fact that Sera wore his jacket.

Or the fact that she was on the boat at all.

"I figured this would be a good chance for Sera to get firsthand knowledge of how we manage evidence," he quickly jumped in. "It's an angle we're playing for our task force project. Especially those instances where evidence is handed from one group to another."

Whatever speculation she might have carried vanished as Kerrigan pointed toward the front of the boat. "Let me show you how we've been doing this. I think it'll give you a sense for our steps, even though these are all still NYPD protocols, not handoffs outside the department."

Kerrigan stopped, her gaze drifting toward the water, Hell Gate Bridge rising in the distance. "You know, this is a really good case to use. It's not busywork or theoretical, but something that can help make our work better, and it's good you're here to see it in person."

"Thank you," Sera said. "That's one of the things that's been impressive about the task force so far. It's set up to be more than just theory. We're working on outcomes that can have practical application."

"I think you'd take away a lot from the Parker case, too. The volume of evidence, and bringing that boat up off the harbor floor, is a textbook case of evidence management."

"I'd love to talk to you about it."

Kerrigan and Sera exchanged a few more questions before the action commenced on their boat. Jayden and another diver, Marco Hennessy, were on point to bring up additional guns.

Gavin considered the initial find and his and Wyatt's

estimates of how much was on the riverbed floor as he gave Jayden a hand up. "How much is left down there?"

"This should make thirty-five and thirty-six," Kerrigan said from where she took the evidence package from Marco, her facts on the dive well in hand. "I figure there are about fifteen more to bring up."

"And you're doing it one by one?"

"One by one?" Jayden asked as he slipped off his tank. "If she had her druthers, we'd bring up each piece in pairs."

"I'm not quite that bad." Kerrigan playfully stuck her tongue out at Jayden, the member of the team she was closest to, before updating Gavin on the past twelve hours. "We considered bringing down a container and trying to retrieve multiple pieces that way, but after talking through it, we really want to keep as much integrity as we can with each piece. So we're bagging everything down there, bringing it up one gun to one diver."

"It's tedious work."

That grin flashed once more, Kerrigan Doyle's excitement and enthusiasm for her work stamped in that wide smile.

"Oh yeah, but it'll all be worth it when we catch the bastards with airtight evidence."

Airtight evidence.

She'd overheard Kerrigan use that term earlier, and as Sera looked over the expanse of guns laid out on the floor of the evidence boat, she recognized that was clearly the goal.

Late morning had drifted well past lunch and on into the afternoon as the work went on and on around her: photographs; audio memos recorded by each diver on how they found the piece under the water; and the tapping of keys on several laptops as each evidence recovery agent managed their portion of the haul.

After making her initial observations, she'd asked where she could help and had been quickly put to work with a laptop of her own, cataloging what was on the ground and adding her impressions. After laboring over each piece and thinking about how to describe it, she added in the same impressions she would use when building a case.

And now, reading through her notes, Sera felt a distinct shot of pride at what she'd added to the process. She might not know how to scientifically and accurately assess decomposition timelines, but she knew exactly how to use decomp stats to make a case around intent, possible motive and probable guilt.

"You want some lunch?"

Sera glanced up from her screen to find Gavin standing before her, a paper plate full of a sandwich and potato chips. "What time is it?"

"Almost two thirty. I know I said there's no food on the boat, but when they traded out the last team, they brought in sandwiches, too."

"Then I'd love some lunch." Her eyes widened just as her stomach let out a low gurgling sound. "I'm not sure how, but for the first time in two months this work has made me forget about eating. It's a novel experience, let me tell you."

She gently closed the laptop lid and put it on the bench beside her, gesturing Gavin into the seat next to her. He'd built a plate for himself, and they sat in the bright sunshine with their meal, eating in companionable silence.

"You've made quite an impression on everyone," Gavin said as he picked up a chip.

"All I can say is likewise. I never doubted the work your team did was impressive, but this is something beyond my wildest imaginings. It's grueling, yet everyone seems to have an endless drive for the work."

"We're a bit of an odd lot."

"You're a family."

She saw the moment her words registered, something between a direct hit and a shot clean through the heart.

It made no sense—and she had no idea how she *knew*—but in that moment, Sera recognized the truth beneath Gavin's demeanor and those sometimes-sharp spikes she'd seen in his personality. Those moments where he fumbled to articulate what he wanted or needed. She'd sensed it from the first, but hadn't had words for it. Only now she knew.

The concept of family didn't come easily to him.

And with that understanding came one of her own. It had never come easily to her, either. Yet here they were, making a family of their own.

"We certainly have each other's backs."

Which, she almost added, was one of the definitions of family, but held herself back. There was no need to press her point, and she could circle back to it later. When he'd had time to process it, and so had she.

His team did have his back, and he had theirs. The ease between all of them—and the reality of how dependent they were on one another for each drop beneath the water— had forged serious bonds. Ones that went well beyond the professional.

Most cops had it, she admitted. She'd seen it in her work from the earliest days of her career: so much of what they did in the DA's office linked to the work of the NYPD. That sense that their professions weren't just what they got up each day and did, but were a calling that each went into, knowing full well the risks.

Being a lawyer wasn't risk free, and her office certainly got its share of threats, but they weren't out on the front-lines, either. Nor were she and her colleagues putting their lives on the line when writing a brief or arguing a case.

But what Gavin did? Not only did he face the standard risks a cop did, but he then did this incredibly difficult, physical job that carried additional danger.

Their gear alone fascinated her. Each diver that came up was outfitted in suits and air tanks and an additional, smaller tank Gavin had called a bailout bottle. And then there was all the additional equipment, from cutting tools to communications equipment to camera and video equipment when needed. All while putting the body through the physical rigors of a dive.

If that didn't make a family by choice, Sera didn't know what would.

"You do have each other's backs," she finally said in agreement. "It's impressive. But I wonder if you know how special it is."

"I work with a great group of really dedicated people."

That subtle resistance from him—the one that didn't want to fully acknowledge what she was saying—had her reaching for her sandwich. She'd been pressed in the past by well-meaning comments she wasn't ready to hear and could recognize carefully built armor shifting into place.

What was the real surprise was how her own carefully constructed armor had begun to chafe, rubbing at convictions she'd held so long she'd nearly forgotten the armor was even there in the first place. Because if she wanted to poke at Gavin, she'd have to accept the requirement to open up, too.

And, oddly, it didn't fill her with the same sense of panic it might have in the past.

There was no way she could have a child with someone who had no idea who she was or what she'd lived with. It was uncomfortable and took the concept of intimacy to a place well beyond friendship or deep conversation or even sex.

But he deserved to know.

And, if she were fair to herself and even more fair to their child, she deserved to tell him. About those experiences that had shaped her from the earliest age. The memories she fought to keep buried and hidden away from others. The ones that, on the rare occasions she took them out and examined them, left her feeling wanting and less than, even though she knew she shouldn't feel that way at all.

Which meant she needed to figure out how to tell him. And as they sat there, each of them taking a few minutes of respite with each other, she had the first inkling that it might be okay.

She could *do* this.

Because, in an odd and deeply strange parallel, it was a lot like those weapons laid out at the front of the boat.

What Gavin chose to do with the evidence was going to be up to him.

Chapter 8

Something had changed.

Hell, Gavin thought ruefully, a lot had changed.

But specifically today, something had decidedly and determinedly shifted course between him and Sera. Something that went well beyond what happened at New Year's or their work on the task force or even the baby.

It was the *something* between them.

He could see her now, talking to Kerrigan at the front of the boat, both of them perched over the evidence and talking about the various aspects of the weapons recovery. He'd joined them at first, but after the continued distraction of all that consumed his thoughts, he'd made an excuse to go talk to the evidence lead, leaving them to their discussion.

You're a family.

Her comment was made so simply—so casually, even—and it had haunted him.

For a man who considered himself fitted with rather loose familial bonds, it was jarring to realize that he had formed them anyway. He just hadn't realized it.

"Hey, Gav." The greeting was punctuated with a mild pat on the back as Jayden Houston came up beside him, his demeanor casual as he took up the spot beside him at the back railing of the boat.

Gavin wasn't fooled for a minute. Jayden was a stellar member of the Harbor team, his physical conditioning and dive skills making him excellent in the field. But it was his innate kindness and understanding of the crew he worked with that truly made him a standout.

His body language might be saying cool-as-a-cucumber, but Gavin was well aware the man missed nothing. He was also inscrutable about it.

The fact that he'd come up to Gavin in a relatively deserted area of the boat meant he likely had something on his mind. But since Jayden didn't give anything away until he wanted to, Gavin figured he'd lead the conversation and see where it went. "That was some damn fine work today. The recovery was really smooth."

"Thanks. All the credit to you and Wyatt for the first on scene. You both knew what you had."

Gavin let out a long, low sigh. "And what we have is a lot."

"A whole freaking lot. Any theories yet on who's doing it?"

"Not a one. I briefed the captain this morning. He's put me on point on the investigation since I'm already splitting some time above the water for the task force."

"That's fantastic!" Jayden's dark eyes lit up, even though exhaustion rode his features after two straight days of diving. "And don't fool yourself that this is just about being on land with the task force. Good things are happening for you, Gav, and no one deserves it more."

It was just like Jayden—a man who had confidence in himself and support for his colleagues in equal measure.

And once more, Sera's telling comment pushed through

Gavin's thoughts, refusing to be silenced no matter how hard he'd tried to push it away.

You're a family.

"The task force is turning out to be quite an experience so far."

Jayden tilted his head in the direction of the boat. "If Sera's any indication of the caliber of people chosen for it, you're in really good company. Man, she's great. Sharp. Smart. And super interested in the work."

"She's amazing." He waited barely a breath before pressing on. "She's also Miss New Year's Eve."

Jayden turned from where his gaze had drifted to the Brooklyn Bridge overhead and simply stared at him. "She's what?"

"The woman. The one I told you and Kerrigan about. From New Year's Eve."

Gavin wasn't sure why he was sharing this or why he'd chosen this moment to do it. Maybe because Jayden would have pulled it out of him anyway. Or maybe it was because his head had been so far in the clouds the past week, he just needed to get it off his chest.

But here they were, heading out into the open waters of the harbor, and he was spilling every bit of his life's current events to one of his dive partners.

"I thought you didn't know how to find her."

"I didn't. And then I walked into the task force meeting Monday morning, and she was standing at the sideboard they had set up with breakfast pastries and coffee, talking to some guy she went to law school with."

Jayden shook his head. "Seriously small world, dude."

"Minuscule sometimes."

"And mind-numbingly vast when you're looking for someone."

Even now, Gavin had no understanding of why he'd shared the whole story of his mystery woman with Jayden and Kerrigan. He had vowed to not only keep it to himself, but he'd believed he was getting past the subtle ache that he'd carried those first few weeks of the year each time he thought of her.

Instead, he'd found himself spilling his tale of woe over a few beers after a tough shift in late January.

Like a sap, Gavin thought, still unsure why he was continuing to share now. Especially because he'd tried to play it off after they'd left the bar, outside in the cold hoofing it to the subway, but both had seen through it. And neither of them had been fooled by his attempts at smoothing over his confession.

They'd been equally fair in avoiding asking him the more obvious questions of why he hadn't shored up his problem to begin with and gotten his mystery woman's full name and phone number.

"Well, now that I've met her," Jayden continued, "I can see why you weren't ready to let her go. She's great, Gav."

"She's pregnant."

Although he mentally braced for something between shock and overt sympathy, the sudden whoop of laughter and grab for a tight, backslapping hug was its antithesis. "Gavin, that's amazing. Congratulations, man."

He leaned into the embrace, surprised to realize how good it felt to tell someone. And how much better it felt to hear such elation from another person at his news.

News he hadn't shared with anyone else yet.

And as Gavin pulled back, he couldn't hide the smile.

"It's really good. And it's all pretty new, but it is most definitely good."

"I'm happy for you. My mother has always said it, and it's one of the truest things in the world. Babies are wonderful news."

"Since Mama Houston's never wrong about anything, I'll take that as the best validation when those moments of sheer panic rear up and grab me by the throat."

"She's going to be over the moon with this. You and Sera had better expect an invite for Sunday dinner soon."

Gavin's apprehension must have shown through because Jayden added, "My mother doesn't care about what's going on between the two of you, though she'll find a way to give you a talking-to regardless. When she brings you out to her small cookery on the back porch and waves everyone else away is usually when it happens."

Gavin could already picture the small prep area off the kitchen in the Houstons' Sunset Bay row home and braced for whatever was coming. Not only because it came from a place of love, but because he deserved it. "Forewarned is forearmed."

"Did I ever tell you the set down I got over Darius?"

"I don't think so."

Jayden smiled, warming up to his story. "We'd been dating for a few months when it went down. My family knew I was gay, but I preferred to keep my relationships away from them."

Gavin realized he hadn't heard the story before, but also realized it seemed disconnected from what he knew of Jayden's welcoming and effusive family. "Because they weren't okay with your relationship?"

"Nah, it was all me. Because I wasn't comfortable." Sadness seemed to increase the exhaustion beneath his dark brown eyes. "I almost lost Darius because of it, too. But well, with her bat ears, Mama heard through the neighborhood grapevine I was getting serious, and this wasn't something casual.

"She dragged my ass out there to her cookery the first opportunity she got and waved a wooden spoon at me. Told me she and my big beautiful Black family loved me and whoever I loved, and if I was going to hide something special from the rest of them, I didn't deserve to have it. And that I was insulting all of them, too, while I was at it."

"That sweet woman who welcomes me with kisses and hugs and sends me home with leftovers for a week?"

"Don't let it fool you. If you're acting like an ass, she'll make sure you know."

"Darius is a good man. It would have been a shame to let him get away."

"I think about it every day, man." Jayden turned to look back toward the boat. Sera was just visible through the windows where she and Kerrigan were still talking. "Every. Damn. Day."

Gavin's gaze followed Jayden's before turning back to his friend. "Is the back of this boat the equivalent of your mother's cookery?"

Jayden grinned at that, the flash of white teeth and laughter breaking through that lingering exhaustion. "She'd love the comparison, but no one dispenses the wisdom and sass in equal measure like my mother." Jayden slapped him on the back once more as they turned to look out over the water. "And besides, I don't have a wooden spoon."

Gavin laughed at the image as they made the last turn into the waterway that led to the 86th's docks.

The words that had haunted him this afternoon settled a bit, along with the lingering excitement Jayden had shared over the baby.

You're a family.

It was a compliment in every way.

And as he and his brother-in-arms headed for the ropes to help secure the boat to the docks, Gavin figured that was something well worth leaning into.

"Club soda for you," Kerrigan said as she deposited drinks on the high-top table at Case Closed.

The bar was old, dating back a good two decades, started by a retired detective. One who knew cops liked a place to call their own. Although anyone was welcome, tables were reserved for parties of cops, and in kind, the 86th generously rewarded the owner with their business.

"News travels fast," Sera said, surprised she didn't feel more anxiety about the fact that Kerrigan knew she was pregnant.

"Good news certainly does." Kerrigan clinked the top of her beer bottle to Sera's glass. "So. You and my pal Gavin."

"So."

She'd originally thought to hide the news of her pregnancy, but Kerrigan had surprised her by leaning in and whispering that she figured it out as they all walked into Case Closed. Sera had been too shocked to deny it and too happy to have been invited out to complain.

Which now left her with the very real question of just how obvious she was. As a pregnant woman, yes, but also as a pregnant woman who couldn't stop looking at Gavin in a way people noticed.

"He's a good man," Kerrigan continued, ignoring the

lack of a response. "His outer shell is way too tough but not in the grizzly bear sort of way."

Although he'd been prickly when they'd first gotten re-acquainted, it was interesting to hear Kerrigan's perspective. More than interesting, Sera admitted to herself. She was hungry for the information.

"He's definitely not grumpy or unpleasant."

"That's how you miss it!" Kerrigan snapped her fingers. "You think he's all salt-of-the-earth, Mister Easygoing, and then you hit a point where you open your eyes and realize just how crafty he really is."

"How so?"

"That man's fathoms deep, and he never lets anyone deeper than a foot."

It wasn't quite how she'd have characterized him, yet as she turned over Kerrigan's comments, Sera had to admit they fit. Hadn't she sensed his reluctance to discuss his family? And even with their conversations the past two evenings, there was a definite sense she'd been held at arm's length. It wasn't cold or even distant, it was just…well…to adopt Kerrigan's term, it was well crafted. As if he'd figured out how to orchestrate the world around him to stay just outside an invisible fence.

Like someone else you know, Forte?

Maybe that was their real connection—that ability to fit in without giving much away. Giving people a foot, as Kerrigan put it, where most gave a fathom.

It was also humbling to realize how much deeper she wanted to go.

"I didn't mean to upset you, by the way, mentioning your pregnancy. I come from a big family, and I can smell baby hormones at fifty paces. I'm not a gossip, and I promise to keep it to myself."

"No, it's fine. Really. I mean, well, I haven't told work yet, but I'm three months along, so it's only a matter of weeks before I can't hide it any longer."

"No, I get it. There's already an assumption we're delicate. Add on the worry that it'll affect how you're seen at your job, and I don't blame you for holding on to the information."

"The baby is Gavin's."

"I figured as much."

"Was it because I was wearing his coat?"

"Not a bit. Like I said, he's a good guy. If anyone was cold, he'd have given them his coat." The young woman with the sharp gaze took a sip of her beer. "It's the way he looks at you."

"Oh...oh. Well." Sera caught herself before curiosity got the better of her. "How does he look at me?"

"Like you're precious."

She'd never felt precious before. Competent, yes. Effective, that, too. But precious?

It humbled her to know that someone saw that sort of attention for her in another person. Like she mattered.

"Well, if it isn't the princess of Hell Gate." A large man with tawny blond hair and vivid blue eyes made the pronouncement just before pulling Kerrigan into his arms for a big smacking kiss.

The sassy friend Sera had made that afternoon turned into a pile of mush, staring up at the big man once the kiss ended.

He recognized they had an audience, and he naturally shifted gears, extending a hand. "I'm Arlo Prescott."

Sera introduced herself, with Kerrigan quickly adding in color commentary about their day and the fact that Sera was part of the same task force as Gavin.

Arlo was kind and attentive throughout, but as the conversation shifted around the table, Sera didn't miss how his voice lowered, all hints of earlier humor vanishing as his attention narrowed in once more on Kerrigan.

"Heard it was a hard day. How are you?"

"I'm good."

Sera looked away to give them their privacy, quickly introducing herself to the other newcomer to the table. A gorgeous Black man, still dressed head-to-toe like he was ready to take on Wall Street—or had just finished conquering it—extended a hand. "I'm Darius St. Germaine." He pressed a quick kiss to Jayden's head. "This one's husband."

"Sera Forte."

"How'd you fall in with this motley crew?"

"Luck?"

"Well, who can argue with that?" Darius took a seat next to her with his glass of whiskey over ice, that smile still in place. "Are you part of the Harbor team?"

"No, I'm an ADA with the Brooklyn DA's office. I'm working on an interdepartmental task force with Gavin, and he was kind enough to take me out on the recovery today. It's tied to the approach we're taking on the task force."

Darius nodded. "What they do is intense."

"And they're amazing in how they orchestrate it all. I was able to see a lot of the evidence recovery today. They're athletes and serious jugglers with all that equipment in addition to being cops."

"I tell Jay that all the time. I swear he's part fish." Darius shot his husband a wink across the table where Jayden had glanced over at their conversation.

It was a warm moment. Intimate, even, yet not out of place. Just like when Arlo had come up to wrap Kerrigan in a tight hug.

It made her...*want*.

There really was no other word for it. That easy intimacy at the end of a long day that wasn't overtly sexual but rather was a sort of caring awareness of each other. And the absolute delight of being together.

Since she wasn't there with Gavin in the same capacity, she willed the emotion away and turned back to her new friend, the very interesting Mr. St. Germaine.

"And what is it you do?" She tapped a finger lightly over the cufflink that winked off the edge of his shirt, visible now that he'd settled his suit jacket on the back of his bar chair. "Not diving, I presume?"

Darius let out a hard bark of laughter. "God, no. I don't even like putting my head under the water."

The two of them fell into easy conversation after that, and it was only twenty minutes later, as a second round of drinks made its way to the table, that Sera realized she'd made a fast friend.

Gavin had kept his distance throughout, obviously unwilling to overtly pair the two of them up in front of his friends. They both went out of their way to talk about their partnership on the task force and that seemed to allay any discussion of their relationship.

Or lack of one.

Realistically, she should have been grateful for that. She and Gavin didn't know each other well, and they'd both gone through a lot this week while getting reacquainted. So why was she increasingly irritated that it felt like they were the only two at the table not a couple?

They *weren't* a couple. They were two people who'd had sex and were now having a baby.

Yet because of their circumstances, all that *want* that seemed to be swirling in her gut suddenly had no place to land.

Similar to Kerrigan and Arlo's conversation when he'd first arrived, she heard Darius and Jayden shift into a discussion of the day's work and how hard the dive was. Since she recognized there was a lot to discuss and she'd monopolized Darius up to now, she gave them their privacy.

Which left Gavin on the other side of her.

The security blanket of conversation with her new friend—all while diligently avoiding too deep of a conversation with Gavin—had vanished and she had to figure out how to control the increasing irritation they weren't a couple.

Or maybe better said, why they hadn't discussed being a couple up to now.

They'd discussed the baby. And their work. And even danced around the edges of what had happened back at New Year's. But they hadn't discussed the concept of what *they* were to each other. And suddenly, without any warning at all, that seemed to matter.

More, she had to admit she didn't like the feeling of not knowing.

"I think I'm going to go," Sera said, suddenly wishing she'd have thought of it earlier when they were in the midst of rejuggling their positions at the table.

"We just got here. Why are you leaving?"

"It was a long day and—" She stopped. It was tempting

to make up reasons or, worse, use her pregnancy as an excuse, and she stopped herself.

She wanted to leave.

In fact, it suddenly felt extremely important to remove herself from the social construct that was Gavin and his friends and their significant others.

"I'm going home."

"Then I'll take you."

"You don't need to take me." She gave a pointed glance around the table. "Please stay with your friends."

"You're not walking home alone."

She already knew they were being loud enough to be overheard, and the last thing she wanted to do was create a scene. So she tried once more to soften the situation, only this time without excusing herself.

"You're here with your friends. Enjoy the decompression time. I think they need it. You all do. This has been a tough week."

She believed the conversation done and, with a bright smile, made her excuses to Jayden and Darius and Kerrigan and Arlo. She even promised to follow up with Kerrigan on her big case and the evidence tour they'd discussed. It was mature, kind and congenial. A lovely way to end a long day.

Which made Gavin's determination to walk her out another frustration.

They had no claims on each other. And she knew how to come and go where she pleased. Hell, she was rather good at it, considering she'd been doing it since she was fourteen.

Sera traversed through the crowded bar, unwilling to make a scene inside.

Why was Gavin pushing this? They'd made no commitment to each other, and it was early enough. It wasn't like she was in any danger taking the subway a few stops to home. She often worked later than this and navigated her trip without incident.

Finally past the throng, Sera slammed through the door, stepping out into the street. The air was cold, a testament to the fact that winter still wasn't quite ready to relinquish its grip, especially once the sun went down.

"Sera! Would you stop?"

She came to a halt about halfway down the sidewalk, the sounds of the bar heavy and throbbing through the frosted windows. Whirling, she turned to face Gavin. "What is the matter with you? I'm going home. I told you that you don't need to follow me."

"I want to know what's wrong. One minute we're all having a good time, and the next you're running out like the hounds of hell are on you. What happened?"

"Nothing happened."

"Then why are you leaving?"

The urge to make an excuse hit her once more, but Sera ruthlessly pushed it back and went for the truth. "No, Gavin. That's my point. Nothing happened. We were in there with two couples, both of whom were supportive and loving of one another. Both of whom had quiet moments of intimacy talking about their day. And it made me realize—"

She stopped, aware this sudden burst of honesty was tied to a stressful day that capped off a stressful week. Gavin was back in her life. She was pregnant. And, based on her conversation with Kerrigan, she wasn't hiding that fact particularly well.

And then Kerrigan went and said that incredible thing about how Gavin looked at her like she was precious, and somewhere after that she'd managed to lose her equilibrium.

Did she even want that?

A small voice whispered very loudly in the back of her mind that yes, she most certainly did. Even as another one wanted to shut it up with copious amounts of ice cream and cake.

"It made you realize what?"

"We're not a couple. We had amazing sex, and we're having a baby, and we're not a couple. And I have no idea what to do about that."

She didn't. For someone who usually had an answer for every challenge she faced, this was a new experience. She was fresh out of answers. Worse, she was so confused she didn't even make sense to herself, let alone to anyone else.

Which made her next move that much more puzzling.

Right there in the middle of the sidewalk, she moved straight into his arms and wrapped hers around his neck, dragging his mouth down to hers.

White-hot need electrified his body as Gavin quickly caught up to the woman who'd wrapped herself up in his body. He sank into the warm welcome of her and the even warmer welcome of her mouth, desperate to convey all he felt, even as he knew there were so many emotions he hadn't fully figured out yet.

The confusion that had carried him through the past few minutes—all while trying to understand her abrupt change of heart—wasn't any closer to abating, but he had to admit he definitely preferred this version of Sera to the one storming out of a bar and leaving him in her wake.

Even if the question behind all of it was *why*. A point his body was presently ignoring as the kiss spun out between them, wanting and needy and even a little bit sad.

It was the sad that had him lifting his head, his gaze never leaving hers. "It'd be my greatest pleasure to kiss you straight through to next week, but what's this about? Talk to me."

Sera slipped from his arms, and while he was loath to have her pull away, he recognized the dangerous emotional ground they were both treading. Heavy emotional territory that included a new life they still hadn't spent all that much time discussing.

Was that what had her upset?

"Oh, Sera, I'm sorry. I know we need to talk about the baby. Really talk, about their future and how we're going to parent. Maybe a night out wasn't what either of us needed."

"We do need to talk about the baby." She nodded her head, her gaze distracted as she focused on something across the street. "But that's not why I wanted to leave."

"Then what has you upset?"

"I'm not upset. I'm emotionally all over the place. And it should be about the baby, but, I don't know. We'll work it out. I want what's best for our child, and I might not know you well, but I do know you well enough to understand that you want the same. We'll figure it out together."

"Then what's wrong?"

She stared across the street once more before turning back to him, the warm woman in his arms vanishing beneath all those emotions.

"It's us, Gavin! I'm trying to figure out *us*. What we are to each other. We have attraction, that's for sure, and we have from the first. But we don't have a relationship. We're not beholden to one another. We don't *know* each other!" That last piece seemed practically torn from her lips, almost like a plea.

But before he could respond, she pressed on, "I stood there at a table with two couples who not only know each other, but are so intimately involved with each other's lives that they read each other. Effortlessly. And I'm having a baby with a man I don't know. Not you or your moods or even what you like for breakfast."

Her gaze drifted off again at the end, and Gavin finally turned to follow her line of sight before turning back to her.

"We'll get there. This is all new, but I'm committed to getting to know you, Sera. To letting you know me."

"You mean that?"

"Of course I do."

"Then why did you clam up when I said you were part of a family with the Harbor team? And why haven't you mentioned any family member at all to me? Not once, even a casual reference?"

Her gaze drifted once more, and Gavin felt rising anger at how Sera had seemingly split her focus. "What the hell is so important over there? All while you're accusing me of not sharing things with you."

She shook her head, her attention snapping back to him. "Something over there keeps moving. And I saw something flash in the light of the streetlamp."

Her split focus kept distracting him, especially since he'd wanted to ask her the exact same questions she was pressing on him.

Where was *her* family? Beyond Enzo and Robin, she hadn't said a word. Had she told her parents she was pregnant? Had she told anyone? Because nothing they'd spoken of to date suggested she had.

Yet despite all that and what was possibly the most important conversation of his life, his cop instincts had kicked in and he couldn't let her comments go. "Flash how?"

"I don't know. It was probably somebody's bag or shoes or who knows. But something keeps catching my eye."

Gavin shifted his own attention across the street, trying to see anything that might be in the shadows, but all he could see were a row of storefronts and a small alcove to a doorway that led to the stairwell for the apartments built above the stores. Nothing flashed, nor could he even make out a shadow of anyone, even as something nagged at him to walk over and see what had her so distracted.

He wasn't armed, and he should grab Arlo if he was going to investigate anything. Gavin nearly said as much, asking Sera to follow him back inside to wait until they could take a look at whatever was over there, when Darius walked past them.

The man had his phone shoved to his ear and a steady stream of instructions crossing his lips about keeping a client happy, all while encouraging whomever he was speaking with to not get caught up in said client's problems. It was good, sound advice, delivered in a measured, confident, managerial tone that belied the man's expertise and professionalism.

If the man wasn't so focused on work he'd have asked him to stay with Sera while Gavin went to investigate. But he wasn't going to interrupt him now.

"The way something over there keeps distracting you, I need to go check it out."

"Why would you do that?"

"Because I'm a cop, and something has set your instincts off. I just need to go get Arlo to come with me."

"Look, it's fine. I'm just going to go—"

She hadn't even finished the sentence when the rapid clip of gunfire filled the air. Gavin moved on sheer instinct, throwing himself across her and tackling them both to the ground all while her screams filled the air. He cradled her against him and twisted at the last minute, cushioning the blow of hitting the sidewalk at a dead drop.

Before he could even catch a breath, everything seemed to move at once.

The few other people milling around on the sidewalk screamed and all raced toward the opposite corner, away from the gunfire. Gavin held tight to Sera, unwilling to let go for fear another round would start.

But it was the heavy shouts and familiar faces that he recognized as he looked up from where they lay on the ground that finally had him moving.

Arlo, Kerrigan and Jayden had barreled out of the bar at the distinctive sound of gunfire. All three now stood over him and Sera, yelling orders for information.

What had happened?

Gavin kept replaying it all in his mind as his three colleagues frantically looked around, assessing the situation.

But it was Jayden's scream that rent the air, agony layered in every syllable as he raced away from them.

"Darius!"

Chapter 9

Sera rubbed the soft material of her hospital gown and stared down at her feet. She'd been poked, prodded, given a sonogram and a physical exam and was just waiting to be cleared to go back to the waiting room and the vigil being kept by the entire Harbor team.

One of their own had been targeted. Another of their own was sitting with family and praying for the life of his husband. And no one was any closer to knowing why.

Gavin was pushed into an exam room himself, and Kerrigan had kept up a steady stream of visits to Sera when she had information to pass along, but Sera had spent much of the past hour alone. With her thoughts and a sort of liquefied, bone-deep fear that vacillated between the baby's safety and the fact that she and Gavin had been targeted and Darius had been collateral damage.

The doctor had assured her after the sonogram that the baby was fine, which was a deep relief. But it had left the other end of the fear spectrum to consume her thoughts.

Why had someone shot at them?

"Sera!" Gavin came into her hospital room, quickly rushing to her side. "I'm sorry I wasn't here. I kept at them to let me in, but no one would let me out of observation. I just kept getting the runaround."

"The baby's fine. I'm fine. It's all—" Whatever else she was about to say sort of petered out against his chest as he pulled her close.

"The baby's really okay?"

"Safe and sound." The words were garbled against his shirt, but the sheer relief she felt shimmering off his body went a long way toward calming her own tension. She clung to him, taking solace in the comfort.

He loosened his hold, but kept contact as he settled himself on the bed beside her.

"Is there any news about Darius? Kerrigan's been in to update me a few times, but all she knows is that he's in surgery."

"Nothing yet. I came straight here, but Kerr's been texting me. Jayden's family is here and with him, and they're all praying in the waiting room."

"What happened?"

"Arlo's trying to find out. He stayed on scene and has called in half the uniforms at the 86th to help him canvass the area."

"Anything yet?"

"Nothing. Not even a shell casing. It's like whoever was there was a ghost."

"Ghosts don't leave flashes in the light. I saw him, Gavin. That had to be what kept catching my attention across the street."

Even if *saw him* was a bit of a stretch. She'd seen that weird flashing and the form across the street, but she'd never seen an actual face. In fact, the more she thought about it, that had been part of what had caught her attention.

"The person was in a mask."

"You remember something?"

"That's just it. I kept seeing that flash under the lights in my mind, and I wasn't paying as much attention to the person, but there *was* someone there. I never saw a face, but I've been trying to remember. And then I thought maybe I didn't see a face because of the big hoodie they were wearing, but I realize now I never actually saw the person's face."

Gavin held tight to her hands, his thumbs stroking her flesh. It was such a simple gesture, but it brought so much comfort, and she didn't feel alone anymore.

"I should have gone after him."

"No, Gavin. No, you shouldn't have. He'd have hurt you."

"So instead, he hurt Darius? I could have disarmed him or unmasked him or stopped this from happening."

He needed to say it. For his own healing and peace of mind, he needed to get it all out. But the thought of Gavin walking across that street and confronting a masked stranger with a gun had her entire body going cold.

Especially because she was convinced they were the targets.

"That's not what I meant. He shouldn't have hurt anyone. But we were out there first. We were in his crosshairs. It's an awful, terrible mistake that he shot Darius, but we were the targets. I'm convinced of it."

"Why? What possible reason would anyone want to shoot at us?"

"That's what we need to find out. But I had to have seen the flash of his gun in the lights. And I knew whomever it was had been focused on us. That's why I kept looking over."

"So someone was just there, waiting for us to come out of the bar?"

The question stopped her, and she realized it was a valid question. Some gunman was waiting around on the off chance they might walk out?

What she'd seemed so certain of only moments before grew fuzzy at the edges.

Was tonight just some random attack? One that could have tilted in a bad direction toward anyone? And Darius had just happened to come out of the bar at the wrong time?

Or was it something more?

"Miss Forte?" The doctor tapped lightly on the door frame before walking in. "I'm Dr. Monroe. I'm the attending on call, and I've looked at all the tests my resident ran earlier."

Gavin stood, giving room for the woman to look her over. Sera answered the same questions she'd given the resident and the nurse before him, before being given the all clear.

"Um, Doctor," Sera started in, gesturing Gavin back to her side. "Our friend is here, in surgery for a gunshot wound."

The doctor nodded, her expression grave. "He's still in surgery now, but I can get you an update."

"Thank you. But, well, I want to be there. To be part of the group waiting on news." Sera glanced down and laid a hand over her belly, a gesture she'd done on repeat for the past hour. "But is it safe for the baby?"

"The baby's fine. Your fall was cushioned, and your tests all indicate there's nothing to be concerned about. I'm sorry for the stress and the trauma, but please take that particular worry out of the mix. Your baby is progressing right on schedule."

Sera nodded before glancing at Gavin. "Our baby. It's ours."

The doctor turned toward Gavin, gesturing him forward before laying a hand on his shoulder. "Your quick thinking kept them both safe. I know there's not much to take solace in this evening, but take comfort from that."

Gavin nodded, and once again, that quivering sense of relief was nearly palpable.

Their small family was safe.

She might not know what their future held as a couple, but tonight had proven that she, Gavin and their baby *were* a family and would be for the rest of her life.

Tears and prayers.

They would be the two things he remembered about this night, Gavin thought as he sat vigil in the emergency room waiting area. Except of everyone here, he was the only one who'd been through this before.

The only one who knew the horror.

And the only one who remembered. The fear and hope, fused so tightly together they were one emotion. One deep, throbbing need.

Jayden's family was assembled around the room, his mother, brothers and sisters and their spouses. Their faces all wore perpetually shell-shocked expressions, and their voices had descended into monotone whispers as they spoke quietly to each other.

He'd learned that Darius was an only child from Connecticut, with deceased parents. He also learned that he was a graduate of Yale, summa cum laude. And he also learned that he might have come into the Houston family by marriage, but he was as much one of them as every one of the children Mama Houston raised in that house with the cookery in the back.

Although Gavin had wanted to take Sera home and come back, she wouldn't hear of it. So after she was formally discharged, she took the seat next to him as they waited.

Kerrigan had kept up a steady string of texts with Arlo as he worked the crime scene, sharing the minimal news as she had it. No one they'd questioned so far had seen anything suspicious around the neighborhood. Nor had they come up with any security camera footage, since all the establishments on the block were closed. They did manage to get the feed from the bar, but other than more flashes glinting off the man in the shadows, similar to what had aroused Sera's suspicions in the first place, there was nothing usable.

Like a ghost.

"Do you have a minute?" Kerrigan came over to sit beside him, her movements casual even as her eyes said anything but.

"Of course. I actually need some coffee."

Sera was lightly dozing against his shoulder, but woke instantly with Kerrigan's arrival. She seemed to innately understand the need to stay put and quietly sent them on.

Although Gavin expected they'd be waylaid by Mama Houston's all-knowing stare, she was entirely focused on Jayden, holding him close and murmuring words of encouragement to him as Gavin and Kerrigan passed out of the waiting room.

"Bastards." Kerrigan might have whispered the word, but it held a world of fierce disdain and deep, frustrated anger as they hit the privacy of the hallway.

"What's going on? Did Arlo find something?"

"Not yet, but one of his informants reached out. Said he might know something."

Although Gavin recognized Arlo's connections in Sunset Bay ran deep—and solid information was gold, after all—he couldn't help but wonder if there was a better way. A world where people didn't turn on each other, and criminals didn't exist at all.

A rather silly thought for a cop, he acknowledged, but one that seemed more fervent somehow.

Was it the fact that he was going to be a father?

"Is the informant reliable?"

"She's a working woman in the know. She's got sharp eyes and is highly selective about who she shares her information with. And she knows all there is to know about the block where the shots came from."

"Keeps her eyes peeled for customers?"

"Among other things."

Although most of the women who worked the streets in Brooklyn steered clear of cops, it didn't surprise Gavin at all that one of Arlo's trusted informants was a prostitute. The man could charm the devil to give him ice, so it made sense he'd made friends with a woman who was both in a position to know things and whose vulnerability would be something Arlo Prescott was bound and determined to protect.

The fact he'd managed to make friends with the woman who worked the block outside a cop bar was another level entirely.

"Jade's a sharp cookie. Knows how to protect herself and the girls around her. So the fact she came forward with this so quickly is indicative of how much she respects Arlo. And she likes his ass."

If Gavin had already gotten his coffee, he'd have likely choked on it. "What?"

Kerrigan shrugged. "The man does have an exceedingly nice ass. I can hardly blame her for noticing. And it's those powers of observation that got us a break so quickly."

It was an odd sort of logic, but if Kerrigan didn't mind women ogling her boyfriend, who was he to argue?

"What did she tell him?"

"There have been rumors floating around for a while. Some important people have found a way to get rid of their evidence. They pay through the nose, but after they're done, they walk away basically scot-free from a crime."

"The cache of weapons we found." Gavin exhaled. Hard. "There were so many because they've accumulated over time. They weren't dumped all at once."

"Likely part of it. And a discovery like that, when your hidey-hole for all your bad deeds is suddenly discovered? Well, that's bad for business."

He thought about Sera's upset earlier: the fear that the two of them had actually been the intended target. He'd dismissed it, but was she right? Were the two of them the end game, and Darius had simply gotten in the way?

It didn't make sense. Especially since all those guns had just been discovered. Why put any plan of attack in place so quickly?

They walked up to the coffee machines in the hallway, and Gavin dug out some cash for their coffees. Kerrigan put her order into the machine next to his while he picked his blend, the machine whirling to life in time with his thoughts.

"I'm just not getting this. Someone decides to start shooting cops over a routine evidence discovery? That's a pretty bold choice when no one's done any digging on those weapons yet."

"Preemptive strike?" Kerrigan asked, pulling her cup from the machine. "Bold assertion of dominance? Who knows why criminals do what they do? All I do know is you need to watch your back. We all do. Sera, too."

"Sera, too." Gavin turned that over, her earlier fears that she'd been the target opening up yet another avenue. "She thought she was the target earlier. That Darius was shot because of her. Wrong place, wrong time sort of thing."

"Is she working any big cases?"

"I don't think so. Her schedule was shifted, like mine, to focus on the task force."

Kerrigan took a sip of her coffee. "Let's talk to her. See if she's made any enemies recently. Arlo got the sense this was a cop problem, but when criminals start a war it's not necessarily for a predictable reason."

"But why go to war at all? Those weapons were only just discovered. I still don't get why you'd draw this sort of attention."

"I don't have the reasons, Gav. I just have a new line for us to tug."

As he followed his friend and colleague back down the hall, Gavin wondered about that. It was an awfully flimsy line, with very few facts attached to it. What if they tugged too hard and unraveled something far deeper than they ever expected?

Yet as he thought about the deadly weapons laid out on the boat deck earlier, Gavin had to admit that they'd already started to tug that line. And maybe there was more in motion than any of them realized.

Sera had never considered herself someone comfortable with grief. She had her own, of course, but she kept it carefully buried. And she regularly came up against grieving families in her work. People decimated by the loss of their loved ones at the hands of another.

She'd found a way, through the years, to compartmentalize those tearstained, distressed faces. They were a part of her work, and that same work was what would give them some measure of closure. It didn't bring their loved one back, but she remained hopeful they found peace in the fact that justice had been done for them.

But now? Watching the entire Houston family rally around Jayden as he waited for news of his husband? Sera understood something else.

Just how clearly grief was an expression of love.

With that sudden understanding so present in her mind, when Sera saw an empty seat beside Jayden's mother, she moved over to offer whatever comfort she could.

"Mrs. Houston?"

The woman looked up, her expression still welcoming even in the midst of her sadness. "Sera, sweetie. Come take a seat."

They'd been introduced earlier after Sera had been released from her hospital room, and the kind woman had peppered her with questions about how she was feeling and how the baby was.

Sera hadn't even questioned how Mrs. Houston knew. She simply accepted that she did.

Weathered hands took her own, cradling them. Sera stared down to where they held on to each other, the seamless blend of youth and age wrapped together, and she wondered what it must be like to have such warmth and encouragement. Such care and love. Even before her mother's fall into apathy and recreational drug use, she'd never been a warm woman. Her parenting style was tepid at best and flat-out cold much of the time. For as much as she hated the reason she'd been given a peek into the Houston family dynamics, clearly led by their matriarch, Sera was touched and awed by how present they were for each other.

"This is a terrible time." Mrs. Houston shook her head, her dark eyes solemn.

"I only just met Darius and Jayden today. There's such love there. Such a deep bond."

"There was from the start." Mama Houston smiled, even through her sadness. "My boy thought I didn't know. Kept him and Darius a secret when they first started going out."

Although Sera didn't want to assume, not every family welcomed gay children and their significant others. While it flew in the face of what she'd expect from this family, you never could fully know what someone went through.

Which made the continued explanation that much more special, Sera realized.

"I know my children, and I've always given them all my love and told them to share that love with others. To be careful with others' hearts and ensure others were careful with theirs. But my Jayden was scared. Of the relationship. Of his feelings. Of the fact that this might actually be real."

And as the woman wove her story, Sera was astute enough to see a reflection of her own behavior in Jayden's all those years ago.

Even more, she recognized the fear Mama Houston spoke of with bone-deep understanding.

She'd recognized it after the night she'd spent with Gavin all those months ago.

Their night had been extraordinary, their connection

even more so. And instead of staying and, at minimum, seeing if he wanted to continue talking, she'd fled.

"Did you convince him?"

Mama Houston smiled at that, one that reached all the way to her eyes and broke through that haze of sadness. "It took longer than it should have, but he got in line quick enough. Love has a way of doing that, you know." Mama patted her knee. "You'll see. And you and Gavin will figure it out, too."

"Oh, I don't—"

There was another gentle pat to her knee. "You don't have to have it all figured out tonight. Or tomorrow. Or the day after. But that baby's going to have a way of solidifying all the things you're not quite ready to talk about. And then the two of you can figure out where you go from there."

Gavin walked back into the waiting room with Kerrigan, and their eyes caught and met.

Then the two of you can figure out where you go from there.

It was good advice. Wise, even. But she wasn't sure she and Gavin had the same base of love and understanding as Jayden and Darius had. Or if they were destined for the same.

Oh, they had attraction. And something that could blossom into a real friendship, which would be important toward building a stable future for their child.

But love?

"Thank you for that. Especially given all that's happening."

Mama Houston reached over and squeezed her hand once more. "It'll all work out, sweet girl. It will."

Sera nearly responded when a doctor came into the waiting room, her expression grim. Her gaze was unerring as it found Jayden and was full of a compassion that left Sera with a distinct sinking in her stomach. "Mr. Houston?"

Jayden stood, his attention on the doctor as he crossed to the entrance of the waiting room.

Sera watched it all play out, even as there was an odd awareness already filling her mind.

That grim look.

The compassionate yet resigned expression in the doctor's eyes.

And the seeming lack of air in the room.

"Mr. Houston. I'm sorry to tell you that there were complications. Your husband succumbed to his injuries."

Sera felt the collective wail of grief wash over the room. And without thinking, she wrapped her arms around Mama Houston and pulled her close, the grief that was an expression of love rising up around her in an overwhelming wave of pain.

Chapter 10

Numb.

Gavin had felt it once before—this absolute base functioning and little else—and had believed he'd never go
through it again, but he'd been wrong.

So very wrong.

Because this evening he'd gone to have drinks with his
good friends, and now he was taking Sera home in the
knowledge he'd never speak to one of them again, all while
another would be broken beyond repair.

Sera had been more than willing to stay at the hospital as long as was needed, but it had become evident that
while he, Sera, Kerrigan and the rest of the department
who'd gone to sit vigil were welcome, the family needed
to be alone.

Jayden would have need of them in the coming days,
weeks and months, but for the moment, he needed privacy and his family. So as a unit, his brothers and sisters
in arms, they'd stood before him, paying their respects before leaving him to the open maw of grief.

Sera had gently fussed when they'd first come in, asking
Gavin if he needed anything, but he just shook his head,
taking a seat on her couch after asking if he could stay for
a few minutes. She'd been quick to let him know he could

stay as long as he needed before disappearing into the kitchen and returning a bit later with a steaming mug of tea that smelled fruity for herself and a bottled water for him.

"Can I get you anything else?"

He shook his head, trying to find the words that were rolling around inside of him. The ones tied to big emotions he normally kept hidden.

Which was why what came out next was as much a surprise to him as it was to her.

"My father was murdered when I was fourteen."

He kept his expression neutral—a skill he'd honed over the years for the rare occasion this subject came up—and studied her face from where she sat on the opposite end of the couch, her knees drawn up.

Would she be shocked?

Horrified?

Angry he hadn't spoken of it before?

Only she was none of those things.

Instead, she unfolded her legs, laid her tea down on the coffee table and moved in closer, reaching for his hand. "Tell me about him."

Not *it*, Gavin thought. The murder. Or *what happened?*

But *him*.

His father.

"Robert Sinclair Hayes the Fourth. Of the Fifth Avenue Hayeses, a bastion of Manhattan society since the turn of the twentieth century."

When she only nodded, encouraging him to keep going, Gavin recognized the gift of simple understanding. And while it didn't make it easier to get through the story, it did make a difference that she was holding his hand.

He wasn't alone.

"My parents had a love match, which was a bit of a surprise for their upbringings, his especially, where duty was still somewhat expected. My mother wasn't from society, so that made waves for a while. But they got together in the '80s at college, and my grandmother ultimately stepped in with Bobby Three, as she called my grandfather. Told him to get with the times."

"Bobby Three?" Sera smiled. "As in Robert Sinclair the Third?"

"Yep."

"I like that."

"She coined it at their first meeting, and it's stuck for almost seventy years."

And it had stuck. Because while his grandparents had started out with a marriage of duty and social station, love had grown in its place through the years. Love and a heck of a lot of fondness and understanding.

Recognizing he was stalling, Gavin kept on with his story.

"My father had been through a difficult stretch at work. Late nights and, what we later found out, threatening phone calls almost daily."

"Who threatened him?"

"My father was a lawyer." He smiled as the recognition dawned, oddly, for the first time. "Like you."

Her smile was gentle, a sweet counterpoint to their dark conversation. "Clearly ensuring our child will have a balanced and measured legal mind."

"Obviously."

"Please tell me more, Gavin. I'd like to know."

Why did this never get easier?

He'd have thought, after nearly twenty years, talking

about that terrible day and all the terrible days that followed would be easier. Or, if not easier, something he could dispassionately recount, the emotion of it all shoved down so deep he could find his way through to the other side.

Only as the tears welled up, shaking his shoulders with wracking sobs, he knew an irrevocable certainty.

It would never truly be better.

And now his friend would live with the same.

Sera moved in, wrapping her arms around Gavin and pulling him close. He was a large man, and the embrace should have been awkward, but somehow they found a way.

They fit.

Hard sobs echoed through him, and Sera couldn't help but wonder how a person moved on past that sort of shock and grief. And then she realized it wasn't about moving past. Perhaps it wasn't even about accepting. It was simply about getting through to the other side.

Although she wouldn't compare her own life to this sort of devastating, shocking act by another, she did know what it was like to push through. To force yourself to keep going, even when the acts were small, destructive ones that added up over time until a person was simply numb from them. Until you finally accepted that the place you had to get to in order to survive wasn't like anything you'd ever imagined.

"I'm sorry." Gavin shifted to pull away, but she held firm.

"It's a terrible experience to live with. And it made all the horrors of tonight even more present. You're entitled to your emotions, Gavin. It's right you should feel them."

"Feeling them doesn't change a damn thing about the outcome. Not for my father and certainly not for Darius."

"But it does for you."

Of course, the reality was that his father and Darius were no longer in pain. There was no suffering for wherever they'd moved on to. It was those left behind who had to deal with the unbearable grief of their loss.

He didn't answer, but she got the distinct sense that while he acknowledged what she was saying, he wasn't ready to accept it. That he'd somehow convinced himself if he didn't feel his way through the loss of his father, he could simply hold it at bay.

Seem familiar, Forte?

Since the internal shot of honesty hit a bit too close to home, Sera refocused on Gavin. She did owe him the same honesty about her past, but now wasn't the time.

"Are you ready to tell me the rest?"

"It's not especially surprising. A disgruntled criminal he prosecuted found a way to strike back. His record was already much too long by the time my father came into his life, but somehow my dad became the scapegoat for all his anger and discontent with life. He'd gotten it in his head that someone had to pay and was already orchestrating things from inside prison. Two weeks after he got out on parole for good behavior, he shot my father coming out of his office in Midtown."

It was a risk lawyers lived with—the justice system was nothing if not public—but the actual number of lawyers who faced threats to their lives wasn't nearly as high as TV and movies made it out to be.

But it did happen.

And it was a risk.

One Gavin's father had paid a terrible price for.

"I'm sorry."

He turned to look at her, his dark brown eyes still grief-filled, even if some of it had dimmed slightly with the telling. "Thank you, but it was a long time ago."

"I'm still sorry. For your father. And I'm also sorry about earlier. About rushing out of the bar. I wish I could change that." She pulled away from him, suddenly unable to touch him as she faced the reality of what her impulse and anger had wrought.

All that upset and anger and weird reaction she'd had to the other couples had sent her out into the street, desperate to go home and be alone. Wrapped in her cocoon of isolation where she felt safe and warm and in control.

"I brought this on. By leaving the bar. By putting us outside. By putting Darius in the crosshairs."

"You didn't do this."

"How can you say that?" And suddenly, the whole night crashed in on her, the terrible truth of it all. "And how could I have blocked it out up to now? I was the reason we were outside."

"You didn't aim the gun, Sera. Nor did you pull the trigger." He reached for her, but she'd already stood, moving away from him and whatever comfort he thought to offer.

"I let my emotions carry me outside like a child. How can you say I'm not responsible?"

"Because you didn't pull the trigger!"

The outburst was a surprise, Gavin's words sort of echoing through the sudden quiet of the room.

And in its wake, she simply crumpled. "That wonderful man is gone."

Gavin was by her side immediately, pulling her into his arms and holding her upright. His voice was soft in her ear, and any lingering harshness in his tone vanished as he crooned softly to her. "I know he is. I know."

"I—"

"Shhh. You didn't. This wasn't you, Sera. You didn't do this."

The fierce urgency in his tone and the deep conviction that she wasn't at fault echoed through her mind, a discordant counterpart to what she already thought.

Nay, what she already *knew*.

They were targeted this evening. She didn't know how or why, but she and Gavin were the target of the shooter. The way she'd seen that flash under the lights. And the fact that there was such a focus on the two of them as they stood there, having their argument.

Yet why had the shooter missed, hitting Darius instead? He wasn't all that far from them, but he wasn't so close that she believed the shooter had simply had bad aim.

Which circled her back around to the why of it all.

And how much could have been avoided if she'd just remained inside.

The text had come late confirming the early morning meeting at the 86th, but Gavin had expected it. He'd already spoken to Wyatt and Arlo the night before and had been anxious to get in and get going with whatever information Arlo managed to uncover on scene outside the bar.

What he didn't expect was the full turnout at the 86th.

Officers spilled out of every doorway and filled the bullpen near to bursting as everyone gathered around to hear Captain Reed speak, updating the precinct on the events at Case Closed. After he spoke, Arlo was on deck to present his findings.

"Everyone really turned out for Jayden," Kerrigan whispered where she stood beside Gavin. "He'd be so touched."

"Somehow I think he'd prefer there wasn't any reason for us all to be assembled in the first place."

Kerrigan's mouth dropped in shock as she turned to him. "Well, yes, of course."

It was all so close, and his emotions were all jumbled up, simmering at the surface and just waiting to erupt. Or find a convenient victim.

"Kerr—" He broke off, running his hand through his short-cropped hair and tugging. "I'm sorry. I know what you meant. Honest, I do know. I just— Truly." He hung his head. "I'm so, so sorry."

It was a testament to her goodness and the friendship they'd forged over long shifts together that she was quick to forgive. "I get it. I bit Arlo's head off this morning, and he basically hasn't slept in thirty-six hours." She reached for his hand, squeezing tight. "So yeah, I know."

"It sucks, Kerr. It sucks so bad." He could only nod as she laid her head on his shoulder just as Captain Reed got up to speak.

Everyone quieted, and Gavin couldn't help but think of his time with Sera the night before. He never spoke of his father's death. It was something he'd gone to grief counseling for, addressed and then moved on. It never went away, and he wasn't trying to fool himself that it would, but he deliberately kept that part of his life separate. And instead, chose to honor his father in a way that was both meaningful to him *and* filled him with purpose.

Yet he had told Sera.

Was it because they were having a baby? Or because she'd experienced the horror of Darius's death, too?

He'd considered all those reasons, but it was only as he walked into his apartment around three that morning that he'd finally accepted the truth. He had wanted Sera to know. He wanted her to understand that part of himself.

It was only after he'd told her that the real panic had set in.

Would she pity him? Or worse, would she think less of his police work, believing it was a vendetta of some sort instead of his calling in life?

Only she hadn't reacted that way at all.

She'd said please. And she'd told him she'd like to know more.

It was a level of compassion and understanding he'd never felt before. And, perhaps, he admitted to himself, he might have felt it more often if he let people into that area of his life. If he shared who he was with the people who cared about him the most.

Jayden certainly was going to need that understanding in the coming weeks and months. And Kerrigan, Wyatt and the whole rest of the Harbor team had shown themselves to be his brothers and sisters in arms from the first.

Would telling them be so bad?

He considered it as he took in those same faces he trusted implicitly, all solemn as they stood before their captain. And he vowed to think about how he could be different. How he could show up differently for all of them.

Captain Reed's assured voice complemented that thought as he began to speak.

"As you all know, one of our own lost a loved one last night to an as-yet-still unknown shooter."

Captain Reed caught everyone up on the investigation to date, and even though most everyone knew the basics of what had happened the night before, the room was eerily silent.

"The team has already put calls into every business on the block to secure street cameras as soon as everyone opens. The bar has cooperated and already provided footage from their sidewalk cams."

"Which proved to be a dead end," Arlo said dryly from where he stood beside the captain. "The shooter stayed in the shadows, and as far as we can tell from some vague footage at a distance, they were masked to avoid easy detection."

When Captain Reed only nodded and turned the room over to Arlo, the detective shared all he'd managed to uncover.

Gavin looked at his friend—Kerrigan's comments about thirty-six hours without sleep looked pretty spot-on. Arlo's face was wan, his normal robust look drawn and pinched with fatigue. If he also knew his friend, the man wasn't going to rest until he had a suspect in custody. It was then that Gavin hatched a plan.

He and Sera had made considerable progress on their task force work. There was no reason he couldn't devote more time to the investigation, supporting Arlo and figuring out what the shooter was after.

Because he was increasingly certain Sera was right. They were the object of the shooter's attention.

He had no idea why. Nor did he have any clue why Darius ended up being the target.

He hadn't had a chance to run it past Arlo yet, but Gavin wanted to share his ideas with their smaller group and see what everyone thought. At minimum, he wanted to get these jumbled, roiling emotions out and see if anyone else could make sense of what he felt much too close to.

Because with the exception of Wyatt, they'd all been together last night.

So what was the motive for killing Darius?

Around 5:00 a.m., after tossing and turning all night, Sera decided to spend the day in the office. It would give Gavin some much-needed space with his fellow officers, all while burying herself in work. She was still processing what had happened the night before and knew that she'd be climbing the walls by ten if she attempted to work from home.

Which made Gavin's text message asking her to come over to the precinct and meet in "their conference room" about fifteen minutes after she got to her desk something of a surprise.

Had they had a break in the case this soon?

Anxious to know the answer and desperately hoping that they had, in fact, caught the monster who'd killed Darius, she'd quickly packed up what she'd just unpacked at her desk to head out.

And came face-to-face with David.

"Where's the fire?" Her DA smiled, his impeccable bearing practically regal even this early in the morning.

"Oh, David! Hello! I'm sorry to rush out, but I have to run to a quick meeting—" She nearly fumbled over her words, stopping herself at the last minute before giving the explanation for where she was going.

His smile was indulgent, and Sera had no idea why she'd had the weird premonition to say nothing. Yet even now, with a few beats to consider it, she still wasn't inclined to tell him where she was going.

"A meeting? Why'd you even bother coming in?"

"I thought I'd get ahead of a bit of work before going to my meeting. The task force is amazing, but I'm definitely juggling a few things."

His eyebrows slashed hard over brown eyes so dark they were nearly black. "It's not too much, is it?"

"No, no, of course not."

If she hadn't had such a strange reaction to the whole conversation, she'd have likely been a bit more eloquent, but finally she landed on something that wasn't a fabrication. "I've been a little under the weather these past few weeks, and I've fallen a bit behind on some of my case reading I typically catch up on in the evenings. I figured I'd try powering through with fresh eyes."

"If you're sure?"

"Of course." She nearly had the urge to push past him before stopping herself. A few extra minutes wasn't going to make or break her meeting with Gavin, and her boss did deserve her time.

Even if she was struggling with this antsy feeling she couldn't define.

A feeling that had come in steady waves since the night before. Gavin had stayed a bit longer after their discussion about his father and her guilt over Darius. While they had no difficulties talking with each other, they'd both acknowledged there wasn't a lot to say.

After he'd gotten a text from Arlo letting him know about the early morning meeting scheduled at the precinct, she'd encouraged him to head home and get whatever sleep he could.

It was more of those vacillating emotions that had sent her out into the street at the bar in the first place. She and Gavin had been thrust into a level of intimacy that at moments felt right and at other times…left her struggling to find her footing.

"I do apologize for rushing out on you."

"Of course," David waved her on, his smile benevolent. "Please get to your meeting. And let's plan some time to catch up before end of week on your caseload."

"I'd like that." She smiled, trying to diffuse her impatience. "I'll bring the coffee."

"You're on."

Her impressions of the brief conversation lingered as she headed out of the office and toward the 86th. It was an odd, unsettling feeling, and she couldn't quite pinpoint the reason for it.

Yet David's attention had seemed…sharper, somehow. Did he sense she was pregnant?

It hadn't been a secret she'd had a few difficult mornings in the bathroom throwing up. And a suspected pregnancy was the sort of news people loved to gossip about.

Whether someone had overheard her and deduced the truth or David figured it out on his own, it was the push in the direction she needed. Because what had originally felt like maintaining her privacy and taking the time she needed to ensure her pregnancy was progressing well had passed.

The time had come to share her news. With her family, as Aunt Robin and Uncle Enzo had every right to know. And once she shared the wonderful news with them, it was time to share with her boss and her office mates.

Putting the awkwardness behind her and resolving to think on how she'd give David the news as well, Sera walked into the precinct. She quickly moved through the security check-in and went on up to the conference room, where she found Gavin, Kerrigan, Arlo and Wyatt assembled inside.

"Is there news?" The question came out in a rush before she'd even said her hellos, her anxiety over discovering Darius's killer more pressing than she even realized.

"Not yet," Gavin said as he stood to give her his seat. "But we wanted you here for Arlo's briefing. He took the department through his findings, but he's got a few more ideas for how we might crack this."

She took the seat Gavin had vacated, briefly touching his hand as he held the seat for her. It was more outwardly affectionate than she was normally comfortable with, but it felt good to offer that small shot of reassurance.

To feel the warmth of his skin beneath her fingertips.

To connect.

Arlo started in quickly, his delivery succinct and pointed. "While we haven't found any details that give us a name or a gang to follow up with, the video we have gotten so far corroborates your instincts, Sera."

"Someone set up across the street from the bar, and they were lingering there," Gavin said, before adding, "planning something."

"That's what doesn't make sense, though." Sera considered the steady stream of thoughts, memories and random theories she'd cycled through on her way to the 86th. "What I can't wrap my head around."

"Around what?" Kerrigan prompted.

"How would they know we were there? That any of us would be there? It was an impulse decision, made on the boat coming back into Sunset Bay. Targeted implies advance knowledge and planning. *We* didn't even know our plans."

Arlo took a seat next to her, his attention laser-focused. "Walk me through it."

It was the question she'd turned over and over in her mind. The one, when she got past the sharp grief over Darius and that horrific feeling of responsibility, that she couldn't stop thinking about.

"The shots felt distinctly personal. The fact that Gavin and I were in the crosshairs from across the street. It was noticeable, for lack of a better word. The guy was there, and despite trying to hide, it was obvious he was watching us." A small shiver raced down her spine in remembrance of that flash of reflection under the lights across the street. "But then Darius's murder doesn't feel like an accident."

"The gunshots seemed to reinforce that," Kerrigan said, her expression pained. "A shooter might have one bullet that went wild. But three?"

Which was what had Sera pressing on. "Yet Gavin and I were the people being watched."

Arlo just nodded throughout her telling, taking in her impressions. "Go on."

"What I'm trying to put together is how would someone, obviously watching us and lining up a shot, shift gears and hit Darius? It wasn't like he was in the middle of my and Gavin's conversation. He was on the phone near us but having his own call."

"You think it was deliberate?" Wyatt said. "Like he was the real target?"

"No. Yes." Sera shook her head, trying to find the words to explain what she only felt. "I have nothing to go on with this. Nothing that's proof or even a solid image. All I do know is I kept being distracted by this reflection across the street. Gavin even remarked on it, that I was distracted from our conversation and kept looking away."

She heard Gavin's small laugh before he spoke. "I was sort of pissed about it, to be honest. We were having a serious conversation, and she kept looking away."

"It was distracting. But it was *us*. We were the object of this guy's attention."

"And you never saw a face?" Wyatt pressed.

"No. Nothing." She shook her head, remembering those weird moments of awareness. "Which added to my unease. But then Darius comes out, and he's the one who's deliberately shot. Why?"

"Could he have been the target?" Kerrigan turned toward Arlo, obviously testing it out. "We keep looking at this like it's a cop shooting, but Darius had an important job. He runs with some big players. Is it possible he was the target all along?"

"I've got Cormac and Sanjay looking into that angle," Arlo confirmed, naming what she assumed were two officers in the precinct. "They're heading straight to Darius's office this morning to talk to the staff as well as his boss. Anything's possible, and we're going to turn over all the stones. But based on everything Sera's describing, it still sounds a bit like wrong place, wrong time."

"Yet not," Gavin said, his voice grim.

He'd been solemn since she walked in, allowing her the space to share her impressions and thoughts. But now… Now she heard the anger and the grief, mixed together in a powder keg of emotion.

"Not how?" Arlo pressed.

"I heard those gunshots. I protected Sera myself, also convinced we were the target. But Darius was the intended victim. Three bullets, precisely delivered, with deadly intention."

"Forensics aren't back yet," Kerrigan argued. "I know I already went there, but it's still a leap, Gavin."

Despite the sound arguments from his colleagues, Sera saw clearly that Gavin wasn't buying any of it.

"Come on, Kerr. We both saw it. Forensics can have the time to do their work, but you know as well as I do. That was a sharpshooter with perfect aim. And Darius paid the price."

Chapter 11

Gavin could see Kerrigan wanted to argue, if for no other reason than they were all fixed on the idea that last night was meant to be a cop shooting.

And it *felt* that way.

He kept circling around that point, over and over in his mind. But Darius was the obvious victim, too. Those gunshots were too precise, not shots that went wild, missing their intended target.

Forensics report be damned.

What was going on?

"Deliberate. That's what you mean." Sera's blue eyes were hazed with that same layer of guilt he'd seen last night, but beneath it he was pleased to see the determination shining through.

"It's exactly what he means," Arlo added, stepping in. "If that's the case, and I'll take a cop's gut instinct as a lead to tug any day, then what it also means is that there's some larger orchestration behind this."

"But no one thought we'd be there." Sera turned to Kerrigan. "I'm not wrong about that, am I? When it came up on the police boat, it had seemed like a last-minute decision."

"It was," Kerrigan agreed. "But that bar's known as a cop hangout. And even without preplanning, it wouldn't

be that hard to follow a group of us if someone was determined enough to do so."

It fit, Gavin had to admit. The bar wasn't far from the
precinct. Their police boats came in and out of the dock
area every day. If someone wanted to do harm, he and his
fellow cops weren't too difficult to find.

So now the real question was why.

"Son of a bitch." Gavin exhaled on a hard sigh. "The
guns."

Wyatt and Kerrigan caught up just behind him, their
expressions grim as everyone started talking at once.

"Someone's covering it up," Kerrigan said.

"Was Darius a diversion, like the kayakers last fall?"
Wyatt asked.

"What sort of diversion?" Sera interrupted them, and
Gavin felt a distinct shot of pride at how easily she fit in
and how quickly she was able to go toe-to-toe with the entire room.

"I went through it on a case last year." Wyatt quickly
filled her in on the investigation involving the father and
grandfather of his new wife, Marlowe, and the dead kayakers who were set up by a local crime group to divert the
cops' attention from what they were really doing with the
drug trade. "The initial approach was to keep us so busy
chasing our tails that we wouldn't put as much focus on
the real crime."

"Which didn't last long." Arlo grinned at his friend
before he shifted the conversation. "But something about
this feels different."

"Different how?"

"Yours was a diversion, Wyatt. A very deliberate one
that used Anderson's reputation at the 86th and his history

with his son to keep things quiet. But this has the marks of a vendetta."

Gavin turned it over in his mind, and he had to admit, it checked a lot of boxes. That feeling that he and Sera were the targets, inducing his fear for her safety. *And* the fact that Darius was shot with evidence that pointed to him being a very deliberate target.

"So now we have a new problem," Gavin said, a level of certainty he'd rarely felt on a case slamming into him with all the force of an Atlantic hurricane. "Who's in a position to know what Harbor was doing up at Hell Gate?"

Kerrigan shook her head. "A lot of people know a lot of things, Gav. Why would this be different?"

"Yes, but how would anyone know this fast? The discovery hasn't been publicized. The local reporters haven't even caught wind, and Captain Reed's gotten agreement from the chief to hold on any press for another few days."

"So whoever's doing this figured out their hidey-hole is compromised?" Kerrigan might press him, challenging him as she always did, but he also saw her gaze light up in agreement as she processed his point.

"Exactly."

They still didn't have a lot to go on, but it was a direction. And the sooner they figured out if it was the right one, the sooner they could get justice for Darius. It mattered, Gavin realized. For Darius and Jayden. For that bone-deep, aching fear that had rushed him the moment he believed Sera was in danger.

And for their unborn child she carried.

The protection of that life mattered to him in ways so profound he hadn't even realized it until this moment. But now that he knew—now that he *felt* it clear through each

and every cell of his body—he also knew what needed to
be done.

They had a killer to catch. And he'd be damned if he
was giving the bastard an opportunity to touch anyone else.

Four days.

Four long, lonely days, Sera thought as she finished the
last layer of noodles on the lasagna she was prepping for
dinner.

Other than a few text messages each day, email ex-
changes on their task force work and one brief call to update her on the funeral arrangements for Darius, Sera had
had minimal contact with Gavin.

She understood why. She'd even encouraged it, the clear-
eyed focus Gavin and his colleagues needed to hunt down
the culprit up at Hell Gate something she supported.

The time apart had given her the space to work through
her own thoughts and the overwhelming grief over Darius
as well. Sera knew that she wasn't at fault—Gavin, the rest
of the Harbor team and pretty much the entire 86th were
hunting the one responsible—but the terrible sorrow continued to batter her in waves.

And none of it, no matter how levelheaded she sought
to be, changed the fact that she missed Gavin.

It was an odd sort of ache, she'd finally admitted to herself late last night as she tossed and turned. One that had
actually developed after their night together and had only
grown stronger with his reemergence into her life. What
did it mean, to want someone this much after so short a
time? And how was it possible she could feel this wide
range of emotions for someone she didn't really know?

Even if she had begun to know him better, seeing various sides of him with each hour they spent together. His dedication and devotion to his work, tied so intimately with his dedication and devotion to the people he worked with. It was fascinating to watch and something she really didn't understand in her own life.

Yes, she supported her fellow ADAs, but their lives weren't intertwined in the same way.

Yet the men and women of the 86th? Their lives depended on each other. Each dive together. Each day out on patrol. It was appealing in a way she never would have expected, Sera admitted to herself as she thought about her outing on the boat up to Hell Gate. There had been collaboration and a sort of coordination that spoke of deep training and shared responsibility.

It had been obvious later, too. The way the Harbor team had rallied around Jayden. And then the next day, the way Gavin, Arlo, Kerrigan and Wyatt had shared ideas in the precinct conference room. That shared risk created a bond that was as resolute as it was absolute.

And it gave her the inward courage she needed for what lay ahead that evening.

Aunt Robin and Uncle Enzo were coming to dinner to spend some time with Gavin, whom they only knew as a tenant and to learn about the baby. Her aunt and uncle were the closest thing she had to parents, and she'd owed them an update far sooner than now.

"But you're doing it now," she whispered to herself, breathing in for a shot of courage. They were her family, but she was still entitled to manage the personal details of her life as she saw fit. And, well…today she was managing those details by sharing her good news.

And introducing her aunt and uncle to Gavin.

Which was why, she told herself later, her heart leaped in her chest when the knock came at her front door at precisely seven. And why it positively melted as she took in the sight of him, in a dress shirt and slacks, two bouquets in hand.

"Gavin. They're beautiful."

"One for you." He extended a handful of spring tulips in a riot of colors before leaning in to press a kiss on her cheek. "And one for your aunt."

"She's going to love them."

"I hope so."

Sera gestured him into her apartment, and as she did, she caught sight of the set of his lips, the tight wall of his shoulders and the way he kept clearing his throat.

He was nervous, too.

Whether it was the four days apart or her own nerves or the simple happiness at seeing him, it probably didn't matter. But she laid a hand on his arm to stop his forward motion and, with her free hand settled her fingers against his shoulder and pulled him close.

Their lips met in a rush, a mix of need for one another and the most lovely sense of comfort at the end of the day. It was heady, she realized, to be able to find both with one person.

Desire and comfort.

Security and a needy sort of heat that scorched the blood.

Gavin wrapped an arm behind her waist, pulling her so close she worried she might crush the flowers between them.

And then she didn't care as his lips ravished hers, his tongue sweeping against hers in promise.

They'd done a good job up to now of keeping a tight leash on the attraction that had driven them in their first meeting. It was never far from her thoughts—that exquisite night they spent together—but it wasn't something she'd expected they could act on again, either.

Only now…

Now it seemed a bit inevitable, really. That there was some laughable shortsightedness she'd carried, thinking she could resist this man.

Why would she even want to?

Gavin lifted his head and stared down at her. His dark eyes held a wealth of emotions, but it was the gentle smile that struck a chord deep in her heart. "Your aunt and uncle will be here soon."

"They will."

"And we have a lot to tell them."

She nodded, the seriousness of the evening coming back to her. "We do."

"There are going to be questions about us. About what we mean to each other."

She tried to pull away, the sudden dash of cold water on an otherwise heated moment harsh. Jarring.

And it was altogether a surprise when he held firm, gently keeping her in place in his embrace.

"Beyond the baby, I don't know what our future holds, Sera."

Wasn't that part of what she struggled with, too? She cared for him, yet she didn't really know what he wanted.

Or, if she were honest, exactly what *she* wanted.

Which made his next words a wonderful balm to those roiling thoughts that never seemed to fully land.

"But the part that's just about you and me? I do know I want to find out."

"Me, too."

The knock at the door had them pulling apart, a reminder there was still a lot in their present they needed to work out.

But as she opened the door to her smiling aunt and uncle, gesturing them in and watching as Gavin exchanged respectful, warm pleasantries with them both, she had the first real assurance that things would be all right.

She'd already found that months ago for her future with the baby. From those very first moments, she'd known things would work out. She was going to be a mother, and the deepest part of her embraced that from the start.

But this time with Gavin? It had given her hope for their future, too. Hope that no matter where they ended up, they'd find a path forward.

Romance? Friendship? Co-parenting?

Who knew?

Maybe she didn't need to have all the answers right now. Maybe, Sera thought as she left Uncle Enzo and Gavin to talk in the living room and she and Aunt Robin crossed to the kitchen to check on the lasagna, it was enough for right now to simply know that he'd be there.

The news out of the 86th was encouraging.

Slow, like a drip feed, but encouraging all the same.

No leads. No suspects. And not one single witness. Which meant no one, not even a crew led by the biggest hotshot detective in the department, had made a dent in discovering the sniper across from the bar.

Nor had anyone actually figured out how Darius St. Germaine fit into the equation.

But it *had* given him an idea.

It was so pedestrian to target cops. Going after their families was far more effective. It did maximum destruction and damage, all while inciting panic and fear. Two traits that made even the most stalwart professional lose their ability to think clearly.

And it was a fitting punishment while he hunted for a new dumping ground for the weapons.

Which, despite the satisfaction he got from sowing these seeds of unrest, was his real problem in all this.

That dumping ground up at Hell Gate had been perfect. Easy to get to, isolated enough to be ignored during the dump itself and not on the beaten path of Harbor's normal routines. That miserable confluence of water patterns had been his saving grace. Literally, the perfect hiding place for his crimes.

Only now, all he needed was for the NYPD to put one weapon together with a former case out of his office, and they had a problem on their hands. The chances were slim, but possible all the same.

And he preferred his odds absolutely stacked in his favor.

It was why he'd put Sera on the task force, effectively removing her from an upcoming case that might require… disposal of evidence. It was also why her appearance on that harbor boat was a concern.

He kept close tabs on all his ADAs, and she'd never given a whiff of anything improper or outside of team norms. Nor would he have pegged her for fraternizing within the task force.

But she'd been on that boat.

And his sniper, Bart Alonzo, had described her to a T.

Even more interesting, he'd described her *with* one of the Harbor team members. Even after considerable probing on that front, Bart had maintained his belief they were a couple.

So he'd keep an eye out. And he'd see if there was something going on with her and one of the Harbor guys. He'd use that knowledge to probe a bit further when they were together, gently coaxing whatever he could get out of her.

In the meantime, he had a follow-up assignment to plan for Bart.

Harbor was targeted first. He'd considered going after another one of theirs—that safecracker was a hot number and had a lot of name recognition in the borough—but that was awfully high-profile, too. Maybe too high-profile. Besides, the scare tactics would likely work better across a broader swath of the department.

He considered all the work underway on the cache of weapons and knew he had his next target.

Forensics.

Give the brave and honorable science geeks something to really worry about. They weren't used to the danger on the streets or under the water. Which would only ratchet up the fear factor tenfold.

The plan had merit. A hell of a lot of it, as a matter of fact. And he had all the resources he needed, right here at his fingertips. Case notes. Discovery files with reams of data. All underpinned with the name of every man or woman who'd ever worked forensics out of the 86th.

It really was good to be king, David Esposito thought as he tapped in a few commands into his computer.

Very, very good.

* * *

The stink eye he'd expected from Robin and Enzo when he and Sera shared their news was, thankfully, short-lived.

Gavin had braced for it, well aware Sera's aunt and uncle were a test run for their meeting with his own mother.

Sera's aunt and uncle had certainly sized him up, asking several pointed questions about his intentions. But it was a testament to their love for Sera that they quickly shifted gears to excitement over the baby and all the plans to welcome him or her to the family.

Of marked interest was the lack of mention of her parents.

No reference to them or the standard question of *what do they think?* Not even a subtle nod to them if they'd passed away.

Nothing at all, as if they didn't exist.

He'd thought to ask Sera about her mother and father more than a few times, but the flow of their conversation would shift, and he'd file it away and vow to ask later. And she certainly hadn't mentioned them beyond that vague dismissal during their first real conversation after getting reacquainted.

Which he supposed hadn't been all that strange, the actual number of hours they'd spent in each other's company having been somewhat limited. Their time alone even more so. It had been less than two weeks since that first day of the task force, and they had spent several days apart since that first meeting. So, really, it shouldn't be a surprise that the subject of her parents hadn't come up.

Only he was beginning to suspect that was on purpose and *that* stung a bit. Especially since he had shared the details of his father's death.

Which was dumb, Gavin thought as he picked up a small plate to select a few items from the charcuterie board Sera had laid out. This wasn't a tit-for-tat situation, and if he wanted to know something, he could damn well ask.

But it would have been nicer to learn the information voluntarily.

A fact that he'd have to ponder later as Robin came up beside him and laid a hand on his arm. "The flowers are beautiful."

"I'm glad you like them."

"It's big news," Robin said as she began fixing a plate for herself. "Happy news, but very big."

"It is. And while unexpected," he launched in, more than willing to set the stage succinctly with his intentions, "it's happy *and* welcome news."

"It most certainly is."

"Sera and I haven't known each other all that long, but—" He left the thought trail off because, really, how did you talk to a woman about how sexy and attractive you thought her niece was?

Even if Robin's knowing smile came winging back at him, whip-quick, her gaze doing a quick flight to Enzo before returning to him. "When you know, you know."

"We're still trying to figure that part out."

"Figure it out or just go with the feeling." She winked at him. "Since you started with feelings, maybe you should just stay on that path. Keep the brain out of it altogether."

"Aunt Robin!" Sera came up behind her, wrapping an arm around the woman's shoulders. "Discretion."

"I'm only speaking the truth."

Sera shot him a helpless look, and for the first time since that explosive kiss when he walked in, Gavin felt something unclench in his stomach. He wanted her, that had been clear from the first. But he'd struggled with whatever his brain kept tossing at him.

Statistics on their likely success rate as a couple.

The pressures of both their jobs.

Starting a family without that rock-solid, get-to-know-you time together before as a couple.

All fair points. And all equally relevant to living a life he took responsibility for, but maybe there was something to be said for not allowing those thoughts to take over.

Raw attraction had brought them together. It had been quick and electric, unlike anything he'd ever felt before in his life. And maybe—just maybe, Gavin admitted to himself—he wasn't giving that base connection enough credit.

Especially since there was no way he could think his way out of this one. He and Sera had shared something extraordinary, and it had momentous, life-changing results. Whoever he was last year, he'd become someone else entirely different as the page turned on a new year.

Wasn't that the real truth underneath all of this? His life had changed exceptionally quickly. The last time that happened, it had brought immeasurable grief.

But this time?

This time it brought a tremendous power for change and opportunity and *need*. Bone-deep and soul-defining.

He needed her.

Sera.

And as he kept imagining the child who would be here in a few short months, Gavin realized he needed the family they would become.

"Your aunt's right, you know," Gavin said, the words

springing to his lips with ease. "Feelings and gut instinct are never to be underestimated."

"I knew I liked you." Robin patted Sera's hand where it rested on her shoulder. "Listen to the man, my dear. He's got something there."

"Are you two in cahoots?"

Although she voiced the question with serious tones, Gavin didn't miss the light in Sera's eyes or the quick wink, so like her aunt's, that she shot him before turning to Robin. "And don't let her fool you, Gavin. This is the same woman who made Uncle Enzo propose three times before she said yes."

"Four!" Enzo hollered from his perch on the couch in front of a basketball game.

Robin shushed her husband before pursing her lips. "I needed time to figure myself out."

Unwilling to be dismissed, Enzo kept pace. "Took you long enough."

"A woman shouldn't be rushed."

"But what about all those feelings, Aunt Robin?" Sera pressed her point, and in the insistence—even one based in humor—Gavin had a sense of Sera's dogged pursuit of justice in the courtroom.

Robin simply laughed in the face of the pressure. "How do you think I got so smart about it all? I hemmed and hawed with all those ideas in my head. They were just getting in the way of what my heart already knew."

She lifted her face to press a kiss to Sera's cheek before slipping from beneath her niece's arm and crossing to Gavin. With a gentle smile, she pressed a matched kiss to his cheek.

"Don't repeat my mistakes. If it's what you both want,

take the joy of the moment. Don't let all those pesky thoughts get in the way."

The kitchen timer went off, effectively snapping everyone's attention away from Robin's words. And as he watched Sera and her aunt move into the kitchen, Gavin had to admit he was deeply comforted and, oddly, more confused at what should come next.

So when Enzo waved him over to the couch after complaining about a bad ref call, Gavin went willingly. If he was going to feel his way through it all, he could at least holler some smack talk at the TV with his child's great-uncle while they waited for the lasagna to cool.

It wasn't an answer, but it sure felt like a solid start toward the future.

Chapter 12

Sera had her feet up on the couch, her eyes drooping, when she heard the distinct sound of a dropped dish in her kitchen.

"Are you okay?" she hollered in the direction of the noise, well aware she should get up and help. Even if her body felt like it was weighed down with lead.

The morning sickness had continued to improve along with her energy levels, but something about the worry over the past few days, prepping for the dinner, had taken more out of her than she'd realized. But after an absolutely outstanding dinner with Gavin and her aunt and uncle—with the pressure suddenly gone—she'd crashed hard after Aunt Robin and Uncle Enzo left.

It felt a bit silly now, with things having gone so well, but she could acknowledge that she'd been anxious about the dinner.

Would they like Gavin? Would Gavin like them? How would they take the news of the baby?

She certainly had the maturity and lifestyle to handle an unplanned pregnancy, but that lingering sense of…well, not shame but *old-world values*, she finally settled on, had weighed a bit. Maybe more than she'd realized, if the exhaustion dragging at her was any indication.

"I got it!" Gavin's voice rang out from the kitchen. "Nothing broke."

She supposed she should leave him to it, and really, who even cared if he broke every dish she owned? It would be worth it not to have to scrub that lasagna pan. After Robin and Enzo headed out, Gavin had ordered her to the couch with a cup of fruity tea and said he'd handle the dishes.

She settled in for the indulgence, sipping her tea and letting the evening float through her mind on a hazy loop.

He'd been charming. In a way that had been so deeply genuine and caring. Her aunt had been enamored from the first, and in a small way, it had helped that her family already knew him as one of their tenants. Her uncle had been stern at first, but he'd warmed quickly, that preexisting knowledge of Gavin enough to smooth out a few rough moments.

After all, she was a grown woman. One who'd seen her fair share of life and was excited to bring a baby into this world in spite of that. Robin and Enzo were the only ones who truly understood that.

And it was time Gavin understood it, too.

She stood to go in and help him with drying the dishes when he walked into the room, a fresh mug of tea in his hand and a cup of coffee for himself. "The lasagna pan's soaking and also happens to be the only thing left."

The sight of him—standing there with two mugs in hand and a soft smile—nearly undid her, but she held on. She'd resolved to tell him about her past, and there was no chickening out now. "Let it soak overnight, and I can get it tomorrow."

He waved a hand. "I'm all-in. It'll be a quick cleanup before I leave. In the meantime, I'm going to enjoy my coffee and not think about having a second piece of that pie your aunt brought for dessert."

"Since Aunt Robin's apple pie is widely known throughout Brooklyn as being the best, I might join you."

"Watch out. Lucille might bar you from entering her shop if she hears you spreading that one."

He spoke of one of Sunset Bay's most well-loved proprietors, the ageless Lucille, who ran one of the shops on Main Street. Her pies were excellent, and even Robin would give the woman the edge on her peach pie and on her coconut-custard. But when it came to apple, Sera's aunt owned the ribbon.

"Then it's a good thing they're fierce friends," Sera said, unable to hold back the smile.

"Fierce?"

"They would fight to the death not to reveal their respective pie crust recipes, but trash talk either of them in earshot of the other and prepare yourself for a rant and then, as I believe it's called, 'the cut direct.'"

"So noted." He took a seat on the chair that sat beside the couch where she'd been dozing, his dark gaze appreciative as he looked at her over the top of his mug. "That went well, all things considered."

"It did. It definitely helped that they already liked you *and* have checked your credit score." At Gavin's easy laugh, she kept on with the truth. "But you're also easy to like. Charming and earnest, and your words about being all-in as a father went a long way."

"I am. All-in. And getting more and more excited every day. I'd like—" He stopped, but she was more than curious to press for more details.

"You'd like what?"

"If it's not too much to ask, I'd like to come with you to your next appointment."

Sera didn't consider herself someone easily rattled. She had to be firm and think through all the angles in her job, a trait that had carried over to the rest of life. Or perhaps she'd found a job that accommodated the traits she already had.

No matter, she mentally shook her head.

What mattered, she realized as she stared into those deep brown eyes, was that he was *in* this with her. They might not have a relationship, but they would co-parent together. It meant a lot.

It meant everything, she amended to herself. And because it mattered, she owed him all the rest.

"I'd like that. It'll be at the end of the month. I'm having an ultrasound, so you'll get to see the baby, too."

"Have you had one before?"

"Just once, at around eight weeks. Actually—" She glanced toward the small treasure box she kept on the coffee table. Opening it up, she pulled out the small stack of black-and-white images. "I have a few copies. Please take one."

Gavin set down his coffee, his gaze unmoving from the photos in her hands. Gently, almost reverently, he took the small stack and flipped through them, one by one.

The photos were mostly the same, Sera knew. The baby was so small, almost little more than a blob in the center of the picture, sort of like a bean. Even with the vague outline, there were a few telltale signs including the clear shape of his or her head.

"We should be able to see the arms and legs in the next one. And more definition of his or her head. Who knows, we may even get a little wave at the technician taking the ultrasound."

"That would be amazing." Gavin traced the outline of

the baby with the tip of his finger before lifting his head. "This is amazing."

"I'll give you all the details for the next appointment."

He nodded, his gaze returning to the photos, and in that split second of time, she felt an easing of an anxiety she hadn't even realized she'd carried. She had a partner and ally in raising a child, and until that moment, she hadn't fully comprehended just how much weight she'd carried at the idea of raising a tiny human all on her own.

"Gavin. There's something I'd like to tell you."

He set the photos on the end table, his focus fully on her.

"Actually, I don't normally talk about it, but it's something I think you should know."

"What is it?"

"My mother abandoned me when I was fourteen. She didn't love me." Sera shrugged, the truth of that still able to sting nearly two decades later. "Or maybe said another way, she didn't love me enough."

Gavin was still reeling from staring at images of his child, so he'd later consider the fact that he might have handled Sera's words with more finesse. More understanding. But at the moment, the social subtlety his mother had drilled into him since birth was nowhere in evidence.

"That's the most ridiculous thing I've ever heard."

"Ridiculous? Excuse me?"

"You're wildly lovable and perfect. Your mother's the unlovable one."

He watched as that shot landed, her mouth briefly scrunching up in confusion before she parried back. "How would you know?"

"Because I have eyes. Because I talk to you. And because any parent who would walk away from their child has something deeply, irretrievably wrong with them."

"Way to toss the judgment, Gavin."

Was it judgment?

In the strictest sense of the word, yes. But in a broader sense, he wasn't going to apologize for his ready defense of her. A point that was only reinforced by the fact that Sera's words didn't hold censure so much as resignation. Wasn't she entitled to anger at being left? By her mother, of all people?

"Yeah, well, I'm not apologizing for it, either."

"You don't know someone's situation."

"No, I don't. And I do recognize no one can understand every circumstance, so my attitude may seem harsh. But my first instinct will always be to defend the child. I'm certainly not apologizing for that."

It would have been his reaction before, but now? With photos of his own child sitting in his direct line of sight? He simply couldn't take back the words or feel badly about them.

People had reasons for lots of things, and he'd never understand or know the hearts that beat behind those decisions.

But he did know Sera Forte.

He knew *her* heart. And there was nothing that would convince him her mother's reasons were good enough or strong enough or reasonable enough to excuse her actions.

But that sort of dogged stubbornness wasn't what Sera needed, either. So he shifted gears and focused on what *she* needed. Because that was really all that mattered.

"Why don't you tell me about it?"

"My mother and Robin are sisters. I think Robin had a sense things weren't okay, but she was almost twelve years older than my mom and was out of the house when my mom was still pretty young."

He'd hit fairly hard with his initial comments, so Gavin only nodded, giving her the space to tell him the rest.

"My dad wasn't really in the picture. He was older than my mom. He got her pregnant a few weeks after she graduated high school, and they sort of tried to make a go of it for a while."

If the similarities to their own relationship reared up at him, Gavin fought to tamp them down. Other than the way they were starting their parenting journey together, it wasn't the same. He'd make sure of it because he absolutely intended to *be in the picture*.

Only he said none of that, opting for that continued calm, easy understanding. "Do you remember him?"

"A bit. He'd leave for a time when things got bad between them, and then he'd show up again a few years later. I don't remember the first time he came back because I was too young, but he did it again when I was five and then again when I was eight."

"Any reentry into your life would be difficult, but those are impressionable ages."

"I suppose."

Since Sera had shifted into a sort of robotic telling of her childhood, he stopped interjecting. It was time to let her get through this.

"Anyway, my mom wasn't the most attentive mother. She spent a lot of time in her head and forgot me a lot. That improved during those short bursts when my dad was around, but it got worse each time he left. I was sort of relieved when he never came back after that last time."

Once again, he fought to hold back what she'd termed judgment, but which he could only consider basic decency. To abandon your family? To go into some sort of ignorant state where your child—a small child by Sera's own admission—was left to fend for themselves?

He couldn't find a way to justify that simply to make her feel better.

But since he hadn't lived those years and she had, he also recognized pushing her on it was hardly fair. Even if a small part of him broke at the thought of her fending for herself at such a young age.

"I'm sorry for all of that. Most of all I'm sorry that the people who should have made you feel the safest in this world took no responsibility for that."

Something flashed in her eyes. Memory? Hurt? A lingering anger she was fully entitled to?

It was hard to decipher and perhaps that was the point, Gavin acknowledged to himself. Emotions were complex and rarely black-and-white. All he could do was reinforce that he was there for her. For their child.

"Where is your mother now?"

"She died about a year after she left. Robin always worried it was suicide, but I looked into it a few times with the access I have at work." She shrugged, the move anything but careless. "She was driving around late one night out in the small town she'd settled in on the end of Long Island. A drunk driver came at her the wrong way, and she was killed in the accident."

"What was she doing out?"

"That was core to Robin's concerns. That she'd gone looking for trouble. But she had nothing in her system, nor was she the one in the wrong lane. And while I'd agree she lived an aimless life, I don't believe she made a deliberate choice to end it."

Again, he recognized his job in this moment was to listen, but Gavin would hardly agree her mother's choices weren't deliberate. *Not* engaging in her daughter's life was a choice, no matter how you cut it.

"My father was long gone by then. I don't know if he even knew. Or if he even cares."

In the end, it was those words that broke his heart. Because everything about Sera made him care.

Her heart.

Her ideas.

Her warmth.

There were so many facets to her, and he knew—positively *knew*—he'd only skimmed the surface so far.

And all he could really do, Gavin recognized, was prove to her that he wasn't walking away.

A strong breeze kicked up, the wind carrying that bite early spring was capable of. Sera marveled at the turnout all around her as various members of the NYPD and what looked like nearly all the Harbor team stood in their dress uniforms outside the church deep in the heart of Sunset Bay.

They were burying Darius today.

She'd anticipated finding a quiet spot alone in the church, but Gavin had arrived bright and early at her apartment, ready to escort her for the day's sad events. It was one more show of warmth that she was coming to learn was so like him.

They hadn't seen each other since the dinner with her aunt and uncle and all the family information she'd shared after.

The conversation had left her rattled, but also glad she'd finally gone there. Told the tale. But maybe best of all, that she'd told Gavin and he'd…understood.

Oh, he'd pressed her, too. Given her quite a few things to think about, actually, in the two days since. She *had* taken on the abandonment of her parents as something wrong with her. And while the calm, rational, adult part of her knew the responsibility didn't rest with her, the child inside struggled to find that truth.

But Gavin's ready defense had gone a long way toward opening her adult eyes and shuttering the ones of her inner child a bit.

Especially now that she was going to be a mother.

The fierce protection she already felt for the life she carried had given her an additional perspective she'd never had before. There was nothing she wouldn't do for her child. And the mere thought of abandoning him or her left her feeling bereft inside.

"Sera?"

With that lingering shot of conviction still roaring through her mind, Sera turned to find an elegant blonde woman who'd moved up next to her in the crowd. "Marlowe, right?"

"Yes. I'm married to Wyatt." Despite the somber mood, a small smile tilted the woman's lips at that statement. "I'm still getting used to saying that."

"I hear you got married recently. Congratulations."

"Thank you."

They kept their voices low as they spoke of the service and the outpouring of love to Jayden and his family.

"I can't stop thinking about Jayden. About the senseless loss. As a cop's partner, you understand the risks to them." Marlowe shook her head. "But when that risk is turned back on their partner? It's got everyone upside down."

Sera knew the description fit. Gavin's obvious frustrations with the situation since the night of the shooting had been clear. It was like the order of things was wrong. *Off.* And it had all of them on edge.

"Do they have any additional leads?"

"Nothing. Arlo has put together a small team, and they've scoured whatever they can get their hands on, from doorbell cams to a full canvass of the neighborhood in a five-block radius around the bar. Nothing's turned up. Not even a hint of the shooter."

"Which makes it feel even more ominous. And deliberate," Sera added, piecing it together.

Gavin had let her know they were still short of any real leads, but the additional information from Marlowe added an important dimension. That absolute lack of details meant they were dealing with someone more crafty and cunning than originally thought. To be that deft in avoiding detection meant someone was determined not to be identified or even seen.

Like a ghost.

"That's Wyatt's take, too. He's not sure what they're dealing with, but the entire team has ruled out anything random." Marlowe glanced around at the assembled men and women in uniform. "My grandfather is a veteran cop, and I married one. I've been around the 86th precinct my entire life. When the force turns out like this, you know it's important."

Sera had sensed the same, but hearing the words— *seeing* it for herself—made it tangible somehow.

It reinforced those same thoughts she'd had the week before about her own work. Although she considered herself part of a unit with the rest of her fellow ADAs, their work didn't carry the same camaraderie. Did that come from putting your life on the line?

Or was it something more?

Were the people determined to live with honor and sac-
rifice and protection more able to feel these things, so they
were drawn to police work? Or did it embrace you the moment you became a member?

"That's what will get Jayden through," Sera said, conviction and certainty coursing through her. For the first time,
she felt a small shot of hope that the smiling, happy man
she'd met out on a sunny spring day would find a way to
piece his life together. He'd never be the same, but someday he *would* feel the sun again. More important, he'd have
support to keep the dark at bay.

His biological family and his work family would ensure it.

It didn't change the reality of what he faced, Sera knew,
but it was assurance that he wouldn't face it alone.

The sense of motion had them both quieting, and Sera
and Marlowe turned their attention to the front doors of
the church. Jayden stepped through the doors, holding his
mother's arm as he helped her down the marble steps.

The casket followed, carried by six officers in their finest dress. Wyatt and Gavin were at the front, with Arlo directly behind Gavin and three others she didn't recognize
making up the rest of the pallbearers.

Each moved with purpose, their steps heavy with the
solemn duty they carried.

And as she brushed away tears, Sera prayed for the man
she barely knew. For the family who held him up. For the
lovely, vibrant man who would never grow old.

Chapter 13

Gavin stared at the heaping table of food that ran along the wall of the large hall in the basement of the church where they'd honored Darius's life. The delicious fixings were designed to be comfort food on an impossibly hard day, but as he took in the tables generously laden with food, he found it anything but consoling.

Instead, his need to rant and rail—to *break* something—only increased moment by moment as they moved closer in the receiving line. Nothing could distract him for long from staring at Jayden's positively destroyed visage. From bristling at the sheer anger of an absolute waste of a life.

Or from how vividly he still remembered those days.

Although the loss of a parent was different than a spouse, the pain of such sudden and explosive loss after a murder was unfathomable. No matter how much living prepared a person for death entering their world, such a cruel, deliberate action added a layer of heartbreak that simply shattered the soul.

The soft hand that touched his shoulder pulled him back into the moment, and Gavin looked over to see Sera, her gaze gentle. "Are you okay?"

He only nodded and was grateful as she took his hand

in hers, holding tight as they waited their turn to speak to Jayden and his family.

The Houstons' church family had turned out as magnificently as the NYPD, preparing a feast in honor of the family's loss. They'd extended the food services to three other locations in the neighborhood to feed every single person who came to the funeral.

But it had been at Mrs. Houston's insistence that he and Sera had come to the church seating.

It was an honor neither of them had taken lightly. It was also one that she'd handled beautifully up to now, seeking out Jayden's brothers and sisters, sharing her condolences.

Although he wasn't surprised, he had been deeply touched to see how much warmth and kindness she'd extended to each person by name. In return, so many had asked after her own well-being since the shooting, a warm, embracing circle that could still provide care even in the midst of such grief.

It gave him hope, that circle. It was one of the few things today that managed to push its way past that need to break things. The other was Sera's unwavering support. Of him. Of his friends. And of the entire Houston family.

She might have carried her own grief over Darius, but she'd set it aside to focus on Jayden and his family. And she'd done it with an effortless grace that simply awed him.

He wanted to tell her all of that, but the line that had seemed interminable suddenly felt much too short as he and Sera stood before Jayden. His friend's dark eyes were red-rimmed, a layer of exhaustion Gavin had never seen before in their depths. Their work ensured that they regularly pushed themselves to the physical limit, but what Gavin saw now was a soul-deep exhaustion that wouldn't be erased with rest.

"Jayden. I am so very sorry." Sera leaned in and pulled Jayden close in a hug, the move so easy and natural it stunned him. That this warm, caring woman had ever had a stray thought—even once—that she wasn't lovable or deserving of her parents' warmth and affection...

Especially when her innate kindness welled up and spilled over with such care and compassion for others. She murmured something to Jayden, the words themselves far less meaningful than the warmth of her touch and the obvious outpouring of support.

And then she moved on to Mama Houston, leaving Gavin to his friend.

To the stark reality that nothing he could ever say would bring Darius back. That he and Sera had been the object of the shooter before they'd somehow shifted their attention to Darius. And that forevermore, the time in his life when he learned he'd be a father would be wrapped around his friend's dead husband.

It hit him in a wave, even as Gavin also knew he was one of the few people in this room who understood the grief and loss and sheer anger at the senseless killing of a loved one.

How did he reconcile that?

And how did they navigate through it?

The weight of it all had been far heavier than he'd realized, until Jayden reached out and pulled him close. Tears laced the man's words, the hard echo of a sob vibrating against Gavin's chest.

"Thank you for being here."

"I'm so sorry." The words were a croaked whisper, but they held all the interminable grief he couldn't wash away. "We were there. On the sidewalk. I'm so damn sor—"

Jayden's arms tightened once more before he shifted back,

his broad, capable hands never leaving Gavin's shoulders. "Be sorry he's gone, but don't, for one damn minute, think you're the reason this happened."

"But we were…"

"There. You were there, Gavin, that's all. And you stayed and cared for him and did everything you could. We're going to find the bastard who did this. I will never stop searching for answers, and there's no distance they can run I won't follow."

"You're not going to chase him alone. We'll make sure of it. None of us will rest, you have to know that."

Whatever carried him through the hug and the conviction of his words winked out, Jayden's eyes shuttering with the weight of it all. And somewhere down deep, Gavin knew, the inner vow the man had made to himself had become his north star above all else.

There was no way Jayden was going to rest until Darius's killer was found. Which meant Gavin and his fellow cops just needed to be sure they found the killer with him.

Because he had every idea what Jayden was capable of.

And he had no desire to lose the man to the darkness that waited him on the other side of it.

Sera filled a plate, the heaping platters of food ensuring no one would go hungry. It would have helped if she had an appetite, she admitted to herself as she took a napkin-rolled set of utensils. But appetite or not, she'd eat for the baby, and she'd eat in gratitude for all that had been prepared to comfort the Houston family.

Her skin still bore the imprint of Mama Houston's warm hug, her soft, whispered words a mix of grief for her family's loss and an innate well of care, asking after Sera's pregnancy and how she was feeling.

It was amazing, to have someone who should have no thought or care for anyone else's need in that moment still so firmly in control of their own ability to think of others.

You're wildly lovable and perfect...

Your mother's the unlovable one...

And because any parent who would walk away from their child has something deeply, irretrievably wrong with them...

Gavin's impatient arguments from the other night had rolled through her mind more than once, forcing her to question herself and her long-held assumptions.

She'd accused him of judgment, but as she'd stilled and really listened to all he said, it had ignited a change inside of her. A new way of seeing her situation and her place in the world.

But something about speaking with Mama Houston had made it real. As if Gavin had built a bonfire, but Mama Houston had tossed the match.

She wove her way to the table where Gavin, Wyatt and Marlowe had settled, making additional room for Arlo and Kerrigan and a man she remembered from the day on the boat up at Hell Gate, along with his wife.

Sera went to reintroduce herself, but the man with the kind eyes beat her to it. "You're Sera. I'm Mack, part of the forensics team." He turned to the pretty Latina woman beside him. "This is my wife, Valencia."

Although everyone carried the proper notes of somber reverence, it was good to sit with others. And over the next hour, she learned more about Jayden and Darius. How they met. Their funny quirks that somehow made it not only possible, but *right* that a cop and a businessman found each other. And then there were the silly stories that made each of them smile around the table.

It was Kerrigan who'd laughed the longest, even when a hard sob punctuated her dying laughter. Arlo pulled her close, his arm solid and reassuring around her shoulders.

All of it, Sera admitted as they began the process of saying their goodbyes and heading back for the street, mattered. And if it weren't for the task force, she'd have missed all of it. Would have missed getting to know these people.

But maybe she and Gavin wouldn't have been on that sidewalk. And Darius wouldn't have been outside. And none of these horrible events would ever have come to pass.

"Sera?" Valencia's smile was kind as she worked her purse strap up over the arm of her coat. They stood in the small lobby at the back of the church basement while everyone had gone to say their goodbyes to Jayden. "You look lost, sweetie. Are you okay?"

"I—" The pragmatism she fought to keep in check all day fell away, the harsh reality of having been so close to Darius's death taking over. "We were there. Gavin and I. On the same sidewalk where Darius was shot."

"Shhh." Valencia moved in close, her arm a solid support as Sera fought for air. "Deep breaths now."

During the course of their lunch, she'd come to learn Valencia was a nurse, and Sera did as she was told, desperately seeking some calm in the big, steady breaths.

Small hands rubbed circles over her back, and even through her coat Sera felt the firm strokes and tactile efforts to calm her down.

"If only we hadn't been there. If only…" The words died

on her lips, the endless string of what-ifs and if-onlys so endless they'd become maddening.

"You can't take ownership of an evil act, Sera. You didn't do this. Your presence didn't do this."

"I know. I—" Sera took one more of those deep breaths, willing herself to not only calm, but to also breathe in the truth of what Valencia was saying. "I know this. I prosecute crime for a living, and I know to the depths of my toes the person who perpetrated the act is the guilty one. I just can't stop going over it in my mind. The senseless act. Being so close to it."

"It's a weight. I'm not suggesting it isn't, but you must separate the sadness from guilt that isn't yours to own."

Sera nodded. "Thank you."

It was all so new, so recent, and it was going to take time to get the proper perspective back. A day immersed in the loss of Darius was, by its nature, the opposite of getting perspective, and Sera knew that.

But in the coming days and months?

She had to work on this heavy weight that seemed determined to drag on her, twisting her emotions toward places she didn't own. She deserved it, but more than that, her child deserved it. Their lives had been spared at the hands of someone who could have decided differently. Negating that grace and the work of a deadly moment was not only dismissing the future for both of them, but it meant Darius had died in vain, and she refused to allow that.

Her if-onlys be damned.

Gavin, Wyatt and Marlowe, Arlo and Kerrigan and Mack had returned, everyone with coats in hand. The time had come to leave the family to their grief, and they all understood it as they ascended the basement steps to the street.

The sea of uniformed officers that had filled the blocks around the church had dispersed, traffic having returned to normal.

It was still a bit lighter than Sera usually saw, the midafternoon crowds still in offices and the kids still about twenty minutes from school dismissal.

Maybe it was that lack of traffic—one she rarely saw—that heightened her awareness of the moment. Or perhaps it was just that lingering sense of sadness over being so close to a murder victim that had her on high alert. But as each couple started off in their own direction for home, she saw Mack head for the corner where someone had gestured him over to talk.

Valencia waved him on as she dug her phone out of her coat pocket, lifting it to her ear.

Kerrigan and Arlo, then Wyatt and Marlowe had already stepped onto the crosswalk when Sera heard the squeal of tires and a distinctive image visible through an open window.

She turned away from Gavin and toward the woman on her phone as a heavy scream filled her throat, leaving her lips in an agonized shout.

"Valencia! Watch out! There's a gun!"

Sera's scream still echoed in his ears, along with the heavy, rat-a-tat-tat sound of rapid gunfire.

Gavin didn't even think, he simply reacted, wrapping himself around her body and moving her deftly toward the ground, cushioning her every bit of the way.

Shouts filled the air even as the thick squeal of tires indicated the car was already racing away from the scene. Arlo and Wyatt ran after it, picking up a few other cops along the way, more shouts indicating the shooting was already called in.

Satisfied the immediate threat was over, Gavin shifted off Sera, her screams gone, replaced with steady, cool-eyed anger.

"She needs help. Now."

Before he could stop her, Sera was on her way to Valencia, kneeling down on the sidewalk, on the opposite side of where Mack cradled his wife.

He wanted to stay with her, but Kerrigan was already at his side, urging him on toward the chase through downtown Sunset Bay.

Sera must have seen his indecision because she was already waving him on. "Go! Go help them. I'll stay here."

Everything in him wanted to stay by her side and keep her safe, but Gavin recognized where they were both needed, and it wasn't watching what went down together. They each needed to act, and Sera already had a towel out of her purse, pressed to Valencia's wound.

He'd ask her later where the towel had come from. Just like he'd check her out head to toe for himself to ensure she was okay. But right now, he was a cop, and every officer was needed on the chase.

He and Kerrigan ran in the same direction as Arlo and Wyatt.

But it was Kerrigan's shout that had them switching course. "Gav! There!"

Their late start gave them a different perspective on the fast-moving getaway car, and even at this distance he could see far down the block that there was enough of a police presence that the driver had abandoned ship and was trying to flee on foot.

Random, wild shots flew into the air as the driver fired off a gun, and the already-considerable risk to civilians suddenly ratcheted up.

"You wearing your ballistics armor?" Kerrigan said, even as she kept rushing toward the shooter.

"Yeah. You?"

"Yep."

The confirmation they were both armed with some measure of protection pushed them both harder, racing toward the fleeing perp.

He'd briefly considered the armor to be overkill as he'd dressed that morning, but now, with a threat still lingering, Gavin recognized it would have been the height of stupidity to have gone without. They still didn't know who shot Darius, and now, he'd bet every dollar he'd ever earn the shots directed at Mack's wife were done by the same perpetrator.

Or group of perpetrators.

What the ever-loving hell was going on?

Resolved to worry about it later, he put on another burst of speed, narrowing the gap with the fleeing gunman. The man had picked up his pace since he'd stopped the random shooting, likely needing to reload. But as they got that small reprieve, Gavin and Kerrigan let out twin curses when his next move became evident.

"Damn it! He's headed into that shop." Kerrigan dragged her phone out, hitting the face of the screen.

Arlo's voice, winded from running, flowed out of Kerrigan's speaker, barking out whatever he could remember from chasing the perp from the opposite direction. "One gun we can account for, no idea how well armed he is beyond that."

"We're assuming to the teeth," Kerrigan said as the two of them came to a halt about twenty yards from the shop, out of immediate view from the inside.

"Perp entered the sub shop on Ninth," Gavin reported as he scanned the area around them.

"Do you have a visual?"

"Not yet," Kerrigan said as the two of them crept closer to the shop.

"Civilian risk?"

"School's not out yet, and we're past the lunch rush." Gavin quickly listed out risks as they moved closer to the storefront. "No visual through the front windows yet."

Sirens filled the air, their whiny shrieks indicating they were getting closer as Arlo and Wyatt rounded the corner. Both slowed, careful not to move within viewing range of the window. They stood on the opposite end of the store from Gavin and Kerrigan, Arlo remaining on the phone to avoid shouting and possibly being overheard from inside.

They continued an assessment of the location and possible risks to rushing the building when the door opened, and a petite older woman was pushed out. She stumbled before catching herself, her eyes flashing with terror as she ran from the building.

"Ma'am!" Gavin intercepted her, gently moving her out of the sight line of the sub shop windows. "I'm an officer. What happened in there?"

"A man! He has a gun! He ran in and started screaming at us."

"How many people are inside?"

"Three now."

"Patrons?"

"No, four total including me. I worked a few extra hours

on my shift and stopped in to grab a late lunch. Two workers behind the counter and one other person inside besides me."

Gavin had to give her credit—she was shaken, but she was sharp.

"The man with the gun sent me out. Said I was to tell all the cops outside the other three are hostages because he 'don't kill old ladies.'" She sneered at that, her fear over the situation not enough to remain unaffected by the insult. "Those other people don't deserve this."

No one deserved it, but Gavin directed her toward the pair of uniforms who'd arrived on scene as he discussed the details with Kerrigan. Arlo had heard most of what was shared on the connection and confirmed that SWAT was on its way.

With the instruction everyone needed to remain in place, Gavin could only wonder about Mack's wife, Valencia, and how she was doing. Had the ambulance arrived? Was she alive? Or would they repeat today's tragic sadness in a matter of days?

The rush of activity had slowed to a crawl as they waited for SWAT's arrival, and that sudden hush gave him far too much time to consider what was really going on here.

Civilian targets both married to cops.

High-profile shootings in public places full of NYPD personnel. First at a known cop bar and now at a funeral riddled with cops paying their respects.

It wasn't coincidence. Just like he'd have bet everything on the two incidents being related, Gavin sensed the targeting of loved ones was by design.

What would instill maximum fear in a group who already willingly put their lives on the line for their work? Go after their families.

It played. Way too well, it played.

SWAT arrived on scene, and a perimeter was quickly set up, keeping direct view from the restaurant to a minimum. Their training collectively kicked in, and Gavin and Kerrigan outlined what they knew as they helped with the setup: blocked perimeter; shields to minimize onlooker views while also limiting the view from inside the sub shop; and a relay of the woman who'd been taken hostage and her step-by-step recounting of what had happened.

Gavin stepped back, giving them the room to work as he marked steps around the building, stopping every ten feet to turn in a full circle and consider his surroundings. Unlike the incident in front of Case Closed when Darius had been shot, the street opposite carried no hiding places. Instead, a large storefront took up the majority of the block. Other than heading inside a store, which their perp had done, there was nowhere to hide.

Which meant they were now dealing with a cornered predator.

He continued his mapping of the street, taking in the small, aged smoke shop beside the sandwich shop that was the center of their focus. The few people lingering inside had already come out based on the commotion on the street and had been quickly herded away from the storefront.

Beside that was a small alley. It was small, barely wide enough to fit the width of a truck. It was one of those weird quirks of the way the street had built up that the squat structure housing the smoke shop didn't fully touch its neighbor, a six-story building with a dance studio on the first floor.

Gavin cataloged it all, waving Kerrigan over. "We need to get down that alley."

"SWAT has part of the team on the street a block over, coming in from behind. They'll cover it."

"Do they know about—"

The words vanished as he caught sight of a body running through the alley behind, the form visible through the tunnel made between the buildings.

He took off and paid no heed to Kerrigan's shouts behind him telling him to stop.

There was no way the runner wasn't related to this.

Was it the shooter?

His limited visuals earlier suggested that man was tall and slim, and this figure was smaller but more solid.

Accomplice?

A partn—

The thought died in his mind as his entire world tilted on its axis. Heat like the opening of an oven consumed him in a huge roar before everything went silent. Just before he was bodily lifted by the swirling inferno of violent power and sheer force.

He slammed into something hard, his head hitting the ground the last thing he felt before the world went black.

Chapter 14

Sera paced the hospital waiting room, the four walls fading around her as her mind still only processed an open street in Brooklyn, full of madness and terror and someone determined to mete out death.

The ambulance had arrived shortly after Gavin and Kerrigan took off to chase the shooter, and she'd stood with Mack, his arms empty and his bearing bereft as the EMTs worked over his wife as a team before rushing her away. She'd been in the midst of trying to figure out what to do for someone she'd only just met when one of Jayden's brothers, Tariq, came to them, his voice warm, caring and his touch easy as he showed them toward his car parked across the street.

I'll take you to her.

Over and over, those words had thrummed through her mind as Tariq drove them to the hospital.

Would Valencia meet the same end as Darius?

Would there be another funeral?

Would she—

"Sera?"

Kerrigan stood on the opposite side of the waiting room, Arlo and Wyatt flanking either side of her. All three still wore their dress uniforms, but each was covered in a fine white dust, and Kerrigan even had a cut along the side of her cheek.

"Kerrigan!" She rushed toward her. "What happened?"

"Sera, I'm sorry. I have to tell you—"

Sera heard the words, but they sounded like they were coming from very far away. It was only Wyatt stepping forward and taking her elbow, leading her toward an empty row of seats that kept her grounded.

Kept her somehow in her body.

In the moment.

"What's wrong?" She stared up at Wyatt, his eyes bleak with whatever news they'd come to share.

But it was Arlo who finally spoke. "It's Gavin, Sera. There was an explosion. The ambulance brought him in, and he's in with the emergency team right now."

"An explosion?"

How had she missed it? Yes, she'd been focused on Valencia and then on Mack, but how could she have missed an explosion?

"Where?"

Arlo quickly gave her the updates of what had happened since she and Gavin had separated at the church. How they'd given chase to the gunman who'd fired on Valencia. The way Gavin and Kerrigan had gone one way and Arlo and Wyatt had closed in from the other side. Then the stakeout while they all waited for instructions from the cornered gunman.

And then the blast.

"Gavin saw something, Sera," Kerrigan added. "And he took off after the person."

Questions bubbled up in her mind, a witch's cauldron of dark thoughts and even darker images, but she put none of them to words. Instead, she let it all flow over her.

She'd watched death come for Darius. She stood vigil even now to know if it waited for Valencia. And now Gavin faced the same. The need to run—to move and rant and rail to *someone* on Gavin's behalf—filled her, but Sera stayed in place.

What right did she have?

She wasn't his wife. They barely knew each other. She could hardly go chasing everyone at the nurse's station for updates.

And yet, they had a connection. Something so deep and intimate between them her life had irrevocably changed. They had a child together.

"We need to let his family know," was all she finally said. All she could say when faced with the very real truth that she had no claims on Gavin Hayes. Certainly none the hospital would or could acknowledge.

"They're getting that information from the office. I'm sorry to say none of us know how to reach his mom," Kerrigan said, her mouth thinning with obvious chagrin at the fact that, even as Gavin's friends, they didn't have that knowledge.

Sera let that sink in, the truth that Gavin kept his personal life so private even his friends had been kept at a distance. It didn't comfort her, exactly, but it did galvanize her in ways her and Gavin's conversations up to now hadn't been able to.

Hadn't she been living the same way? If something happened to her at work, would anyone know how to help her? How to reach Aunt Robin and Uncle Enzo for her? How to find her family? That number might be counted on one hand, but they were her family. And she'd held them and everyone else in her life at arm's length.

That had to stop.

For herself, yes. But for the child she carried? She had to break the pattern of choosing a life kept separate from the people around her.

Her child deserved more.

Just like her child deserved to grow up with a father. It was that need—one so deeply felt—that had her pushing all the rest away. She'd focus on it later and she *would* make changes. Starting with introducing herself to Gavin's mother when the woman arrived and letting her know she wanted her to have a place in her grandchild's life.

But for now, they had to get through whatever was going on around them.

Whatever had decided to make the 86th a target.

"Mrs. Hayes?"

A doctor came into the waiting room, pulling their collective attention toward the door. It was Arlo who spoke first, wrapping an arm around Sera's shoulders. "She's here."

Mrs. Hayes?

Sera shot Arlo a side-eye, but he didn't say a word, just kept his attention focused forward.

"What can you tell us, sir?"

"He's going to be okay. Took a solid hit to the body when the blast knocked him down, but his ballistics armor did its job. It's not going to feel like it when he's sore for the next few days, but nothing's broken. His exceptional conditioning is going to go a long way toward a quick recovery, as well."

The doctor eyed Arlo, Wyatt and Kerrigan. "I understand you all were at the site with Officer Hayes. I'd like each of you to get checked out, too."

"Why don't we get Sera back to Gavin first?" Arlo slid

in smoothly, pulling her forward across the waiting room lobby. "She's been beside herself waiting for news."

The doctor looked unconvinced, but he did extend a hand, gesturing Sera from the room. "Please come with me, Mrs. Hayes."

Sera's head was spinning, the adrenaline rush from hearing that Gavin had been hurt to the second spike when the doctor had asked for her as *Mrs. Hayes*.

Where did he get that idea?

It was only as she passed Kerrigan, the woman's strong arms coming around her in a hug, that Sera got her first clue. "I wanted to make sure you could see Gav as soon as possible. Don't be mad."

Sera hugged back. Hard. "Thank you."

How could she fault the woman for giving her exactly what she wanted and what she feared she could never have?

Gavin listened to the steady hum of machines and the air conditioning system and the comings and goings in the hallway and tried to remain steady. Calm. And with his mind *off* the thrumming pain in his body, rippling out in great waves each time he so much as lifted a hand.

God, he felt like he'd been run over.

In a way, he supposed it was an apt description since whatever had detonated at the sub shop had an effect equivalent to an oncoming truck.

He'd been disoriented when he came to in the ambulance, drifting in and out of sleep, but the EMTs had been determined to keep him awake. The fact they kept the back of the emergency vehicle meat-locker-cold had likely helped, as well.

They'd talked him through the ride to the hospital, ask-

ing questions and keeping him talking on any number of
subjects including the Mets' chances that season. The doctor who took over when he came in had continued the idle
chatter, checking him out and peppering medical requests
with odd questions obviously designed to make him think.

"Mr. Hayes? I have someone here who'd like to see you."
The nurse who stood in the doorway had a smile on her
face. "Your wife's been so worried."

Wife?

How hard *had* he hit his head?

And then Sera peeked around the corner, a wry smile
on her face that suggested she was in on the joke, even if
the nurse was completely serious.

"Hi." He waved her forward, and Sera came straight to
him, leaning down and wrapping her arms around him.

If this was a dream, he wasn't going to argue, but when
he saw the nurse's indulgent smile from the doorway, he figured he'd better play along and worry about the truth later.

Or just keep flowing with a dream that had suddenly
gotten way better than his aches and pains. He had Sera in
his arms and all that pain seemed to fade away.

When the nurse was gone, Sera pulled back from the hug.
His reflexes weren't at maximum capacity, and he nearly
let her before thinking better of it. Lifting a hand to the
back of her neck, he tugged her back down for a real kiss.

If she was surprised by the move, she didn't show it. Nor
did she even offer a token protest, instead sinking in and
kissing him back with a fervor and urgency that matched
his own.

He reveled in the moment, unable to believe she was
here. He wasn't going to question his good fortune. Instead,
he drank her in, savoring everything about her and des-

perately trying to forget how close he had come to never touching her again.

She finally lifted her head, resettling herself beside him. "Those very hot lips aside, how are you feeling?"

He grinned at that, even as the movement had him wincing slightly at the pain that insisted on going head-to-head with his hormones. "Mrs. Hayes, huh?"

"Kerrigan's doing."

"I'll make sure to thank her later."

"What if we get caught?"

Pain aside, he couldn't stop the bark of laughter at that one.

"What's so funny?"

If he didn't have Sera's hands held tight in his, Gavin suspected she'd have crossed her arms over her chest. "Do you think they ask for marriage licenses at check-in?"

"It was a lie."

"One delivered by a cop. I think you can put your worries aside. Besides——" he lifted a hand out, tracing the curve of her cheek "——I want you here. The patient's always right, you know."

"The patient took a hit to the head if those bruises are any indication." The vivid blue of her eyes clouded over. "What happened to you? Kerrigan said there was an explosion."

"We chased the perp into Archer's sub shop off Bay Street. He took hostages."

"Oh, Gavin. No."

"We got lucky timing-wise. School wasn't out and the big lunch rush was over." He pictured the older woman who'd been pushed out of the restaurant. "But there were still innocent people inside."

"You went into the restaurant?"

He recounted the wait for SWAT and his review of the building and his surroundings.

"Was it like last time?" she asked. "At the bar?"

"No, and that was what got me. The bastard who shot Darius was able to hide in darkness and the various doorways on the opposite side of the street. He also had some sort of exit strategy that got him out of the way quickly. But this time?" Hazy images refilled his mind, and Gavin realized he'd forgotten those last few seconds before the blast.

"What is it?"

"An alleyway. Between the buildings. I had my attention there and told Kerrigan we needed to make sure no one could escape that way. But she said we needed to wait for SWAT."

"She was right." He must have looked ready to argue because Sera barreled right on, cutting him off. "You're lucky you had armor on, but you weren't in full gear. How would you have gone up against someone back there determined to do harm?"

"Which I did have the sense to listen to when Kerrigan made the same basic argument. And I would have stayed put."

"Would have?"

"The moment I saw someone running back there, someone who didn't look like the perp? All bets were off."

"This is your life, Gavin."

"And it was Darius's life. It might be Valencia's life. You think I could let the person responsible get away?"

"No." Sera shook her head. "I know you couldn't."

"Whoever it was, they had other ideas."

"You think there are two killers?"

"It plays. I didn't have a close look at the gunman, but

he had a long leanness about him. Whoever ran down the alley was shorter. More solid. And the guy in the alley wasn't dressed like the perp we chased."

"He could have changed inside. Maybe taken clothes from someone there?"

"Sure." Gavin considered it but dismissed it. "Lead the witness all you want, Counselor, but even with my head addled, I'd swear they were two different people."

The small tease was enough to draw a smile out of her, and Gavin had the overwhelming desire to kiss her again. But he held back, also fascinated to see how she worked the puzzle with him. Because while he might prefer kissing her, the increasing sense they had a ticking clock over their heads had become evident with the panicked gunman abandoning his car and making a run through the streets of Brooklyn.

"So you think they're partners, then?" Sera finally said, aligning to his belief there were two perps.

"'Partner' suggests some sort of collaboration. Not one leaving the other for dead."

"It's an oldie but goodie for a reason. There's minimal, if any, honor among thieves."

"Maybe, but—"

He broke off at the high-pitched wail echoing from the hallway, before a very recognizable figure burst into his room.

"Gavin! My baby!" She kept moving, heading straight for the bed where Sera sat beside him, her hands still firmly in his.

He could already feel Sera trying to pull away and off the bed, but he hung on tight. There was no way he was facing this new threat alone.

"The nurse said your wife was with you! Wife! What wife, I said!"

Gavin knew his head wasn't functioning at optimal capacity, and the headache he'd diligently ignored was equally unprepared for the shrieks that hit his skull like the repeated stab of an ice pick.

But pushing it all aside, Gavin still recognized he had a duty. And if he ever hoped to have sex with Sera Forte again, he'd best get to it.

"Mother. Let me introduce you to Sera."

Sera had always recognized that if she were lucky enough to find someone to be in a long-term relationship with, they were going to come with parents. Her personal circumstance—basically orphaned by her early teens—wasn't the norm, and most individuals in the dating pool still had at minimum one parent. It was the reality of modern life, and she was happy for it. She'd even dated a guy a few years back who had both parents, two stepparents and three other former stepparents, all of whom had remained in his life.

That one had been…a lot. A sweet sort of *a lot*, but somewhat overwhelming all the same.

But even that expansive set of parental figures hadn't prepared her for Evelyn Hayes.

Gavin had determinedly hung on to her hands, but the moment his grip loosened as his mother crossed the room, Sera took her shot and slipped away, getting off the bed. How awkward would it be to meet his mother practically draped over her son?

It was awkward enough the rumor of his "marriage" had reached her before anyone had the chance to do damage control.

Although Sera stepped away from the bed, she didn't go far. It was time to see this through *and* explain how the hospital staff had come to call her Gavin's wife. Wasn't that what she'd vowed to herself a short while ago, awaiting details in the waiting room with the others? That she wanted her child to know their grandmother? To have a family to lean on and depend on?

"Mrs. Hayes?" Sera addressed the woman, oddly aware she'd been addressed similarly not that long ago.

Evelyn Hayes turned from her son, her face settled in soft, albeit confused, lines.

"I'm Sera."

"Mom, I'm sorry that the two of you are meeting under these circumstances, but Sera's someone very special to me."

"Your wife?"

Although she couldn't be entirely sure, the question sounded more intrigued and excited than angry or upset, and Sera wasn't quite sure what to make of it.

Gavin, however, seemed far less confused. "No." Gavin smiled as Sera fought the grimace. "There was, ah, some miscommunication with the nurse's station about that."

"I see."

Again, Sera searched for something dismissive in the woman, but she was fast catching on that Evelyn Hayes had a bit more fortitude than her initial shrieks entering Gavin's room might suggest. A point she proved as she turned toward Sera and extended her arms for a hug. "I'm Gavin's mom, Evelyn. It's lovely to meet you, dear."

Sera went into those open arms, shocked to realize just how badly she needed the hug. And how worried she'd been about this meeting. "It's so nice to meet you, too."

Evelyn squeezed her once more before pulling back.

"Now. Why don't you two tell me what's going on here? Because you might not be married, but I'm a woman of a certain age who has had plenty of years to read any number of signs as well as social cues."

"Mom—"

Evelyn waved a hand at Gavin, ignoring the urgency in his tone. "Hush. It's not every day a woman's son is nearly blown to bits by a bomb, *and* she finds out she's going to be a grandmother. I'd much rather focus on the latter so I don't fall to pieces over the former."

"How'd… I mean, how do you know I'm pregnant?"

"A mother knows, dear. And since this will be my first grandchild, I can't say I'm sorry about it in the least."

"But we're not—" Sera stopped abruptly, suddenly uncomfortable painting a picture for Gavin's mother of exactly what she and the woman's son were to each other.

It had been convenient to categorize them as a *one-night-stand with consequences*, but that no longer seemed to fit very well. Neither did *two people in a steady relationship*, though, so she was sort of at a loss for how to categorize them.

Evelyn reached out and grabbed her hand. "You don't need to define anything for me. That's for the two of you to decide." With the matter seemingly all figured out, she turned back to Gavin. "How are you feeling?"

"Good."

Sera was close enough to see the exasperation on Evelyn's face before she spoke. "Want to try that again?"

"I am good, all things considered. I thought I'd cracked a few ribs, but the body armor did its job, and they're just bruised. I did hit my head, but the doctor said it's a mild concussion."

"It's a wonder you escaped something far worse."

"Yeah, well, it's a good thing I have a hard head."

Evelyn leaned in, maneuvering through the wires and the tubes to wrap him in a hug. Although her words were whispered, Sera managed to catch most of them. "It's an even better thing you had on protection."

Sera stepped back, giving the woman a few moments to talk to her son. If it also gave her a few minutes to collect herself, well then, she'd take it. It wasn't every day you met the future grandmother of your child, after all. Nor was it every day you got a hug that felt a lot like welcome, not a whiff of censure anywhere to be found.

She was still reeling and not quite sure what to do about it all.

"It's okay, Mom. Really. I'm fine. I promise."

"What exactly happened?" Evelyn's gaze skipped to the machines, IVs and the two large bandages visible, one on his shoulder, the edges clear beneath his gown, and the other along his jaw.

"We were chasing a suspect, and someone rigged the sandwich shop he ducked into."

"Rigged? What does that mean?" his mother asked.

"Someone blew it up. With a bomb."

"With people inside?"

"I'm afraid so. I've been waiting for updates, but they just released me to have visitors and haven't talked to anyone yet."

She'd watched the tennis match of a conversation between Gavin and his mother and finally realized she had something to contribute. "Kerrigan, Arlo and Wyatt didn't have any details before I came in here, either."

"How did you get here?"

"Darius's brother, Tariq, drove Mack and me over."

"Valencia!" Gavin's eyes widened. "How is she?"

"Unfortunately, there hasn't been any news there, either. She was still in surgery, and none of us had any more details down in the waiting room."

Sera quickly got Evelyn up to speed on what had happened to Valencia outside the church.

"Two shootings? Of family members?" Evelyn shuddered. "Just like your father."

She murmured the words, and Sera saw the way Gavin's expression went cold and bleak. A match for his mother's.

"It's been a long time since Gavin's father died, and that horror is still something I live with every day. This feels similar. Deliberate, even."

"But why?" Gavin asked. "Why would anyone even know who Darius and Valencia were? Or care that one was married to a member of the Harbor team and another on forensics?"

"Fear doesn't need a reason, Gavin. It just needs a target."

David Esposito walked into his office and closed the door. He had a slim briefcase with him, but it was big enough to hold a spare change of clothes. He'd changed into that extra suit after leaving the back of Archer's sub shop.

The store had been a good front for him for a long time, Dex Archer more than willing to share the secrets of the neighborhood in exchange for payments and protection.

David had always delivered both. He'd made it his business early on to understand who he could use in each of Brooklyn's neighborhoods and who had the loyalty to remain silent.

Only now Dex was dead, along with his son, another patron in the shop and the shooter who couldn't handle a damn assignment.

An assignment, David considered as he pulled his soiled clothing out of his briefcase, that he'd planned down to the most minute detail. He'd set it all up perfectly. He'd given the shooter a target, the exact timing to take her out and the perfect place to create maximum chaos with others so he could avoid detection and get away.

And instead, the ass had screwed around, been late to the funeral, hadn't set up well with his long-range scope and had been scattered with his overall focus on the job.

So what had he done?

Instead of ending the job and picking another time to make the hit, he'd rushed it, then proceeded to race through the streets of Sunset Bay waving a gun and shooting into the air.

Come the hell on.

David caught himself just before he rested his clothing on the top of his desk, the distinct odors of bomb materials and the dust of the building emanating from the material.

Damn it. Now he was the one who was scattered, making idiot, amateur mistakes.

He'd brought the clothing here to hide it in a legal box on his shelf. No one touched his files, and he'd leave it here, disposing of it at a later time. It always amazed him how little people paid attention to the files at work and how easy it was to use innocuous cardboard boxes people ignored every day as a parking lot for things he wanted to go unnoticed. He'd collect the soiled clothes in a few weeks and dump them, no one the wiser.

Right now, he had a bigger problem.

Because his shooter had botched the job, there was no way of knowing if the lovely wife he'd targeted was dead or not. And he needed her dead for this all to work.

Mack Phillips was leading the Hell Gate forensics work and had been lead on several other cases David's team had prosecuted. The man was thorough and often caught things others missed.

It was why he required this distraction from the Hell Gate work. And it was why David had required the man's wife pay the price for that dedication.

With the clothes safely stowed at the bottom of a brown file box, David finagled a few folders on top of it, then closed the lid. With a deep breath, he considered his next moves and then repeated them in his mind.

He was in control, and he would see this through, exactly as he'd planned. No case was perfect. No trial flawless. Realistically, he knew that. Hell, he'd made a damn career out of it. And always—*always*—he managed to come out on top. Just like he'd do here.

He'd deal with the clothes later.

Pending the wife's surgery outcome, he'd figure out how he wanted to handle Mack Phillips.

And he'd line up the next target.

Because David had learned the most important lesson early in his career as a young lawyer: when the momentum was building, you didn't let up off the gas.

You pushed and pushed until you got the verdict you were aiming for.

Chapter 15

Gavin would have preferred to be in the emergency waiting room with the rest of the team, supporting Mack however he could, but the doctors refused to let him go without overnight observation.

They had moved him out of the emergency ward into a regular room, and it had become something of a war room for the team, people coming in groups, two by two, as they got information throughout the evening.

Gavin had caught the frustration of one of the nurses after Arlo had brought burgers in, but the head nurse on duty had addressed the situation with him.

"Give the cops the space to do their work," she'd admonished before giving Arlo a wink.

That was all it had taken. She'd even given the man he was sharing a room with his own private one down the hall to allow for more space to work. And Arlo had called out and ordered up more burgers for the nurse's station to smooth over any ruffled feathers.

It wasn't a conference room at the 86th, but it would have to do.

Which made the quiet moment, with no one in the room except for Sera, a reprieve he hadn't known he needed.

"How are you holding up?"

She glanced up from writing in a small notebook, a gentle smile on her face. "I could ask the same of you."

"I'm..." He stopped, realizing he could only give her honesty. "I'm tired."

"Would I be a traitor to the cause to say same?"

They'd reduced the number of attachments running in and out of his body down to a lone IV, and he used the additional freedom to extend a hand. "Come sit with me."

She nodded and tucked the notebook in her bag. When she made to sit on the edge of the mattress, he shifted, pulling her closer. "I'd really like to hold you."

It was a bold ask, one that he wasn't necessarily entitled to, but when her blue eyes went hazy and slightly unfocused, he realized he'd asked just right.

"I'd really like that, too."

She slipped out of her shoes—heels he had no idea how she'd managed in all day—before climbing in next to him and stretching out.

"Are you o—"

He had his lips on hers before she could finish the sentence, sheer relief washing through him at having her close. The soft sigh that escaped the back of her throat made him wish for different circumstances. For a different place to see this through to completion.

Because whatever else had happened over the past few weeks, the two of them drawing closer to one another had been the most important.

The heat and desire and overwhelming *need* he'd felt at the New Year had only grown stronger, with the added dimensions of their journey to parenthood as well as the opportunity to see her passion for her work.

Her deep commitment and belief in what she was doing.

Her determination to seek justice.

And her deep, deep feelings and care for others.

All had touched him, reinforcing that initial attraction with the realities of what made a life with someone.

Of what made two people fall in love.

She was so responsive to him, her kiss as warm and welcoming as the rest of her. And as Gavin lifted his head, laying his forehead against hers, the things he'd only been able to *feel* up to now suddenly had words.

He loved her.

He loved Sera.

And he wanted to make a life with her.

He was as sure of those things as his next breath, but he wasn't as positive she felt the same. So he'd give her a bit of space. Give them a few days to get to the other side of this latest eruption of violence and hate, and then he'd tell her. They had her appointment with the ultrasound coming up, and he could already picture drawing her close after and telling her how he felt.

In the meantime, he was going to revel in the moment. And he was going to take these few minutes of peace.

Which made the stirring in his arms and whispered "I'm sorry" a jarring counterpoint to the quiet he floated on.

"Sera?"

"I'm sorry. Really, Gavin, I am. I just…" She disengaged from his arms and ran back to her purse, grabbing the notebook she'd stuffed in the side. "It's just that I think I put something together."

Sera had contributed throughout the evening, just like she had a few days before back at the precinct, so it was no surprise she was set on something. Her lack of police procedural knowledge was offset by one of the keenest minds he'd ever seen, and she caught on quickly when there was a topic she wasn't fully versed on. She also wasn't afraid to ask questions, no matter how small or specific.

In fact, Gavin had to admit it was that focus on the specifics that had led to a few key discussion points, namely how the shooter had gotten so close to the funeral and why Mack's wife, Valencia, was targeted.

"What are you thinking?"

"It's what your mom said. Before. About fear not needing a reason. Just a target."

"You think someone's trying to incite fear."

"Yes, but for a very specific reason. Darius. Valencia. They were specifically chosen targets."

"Targeted why?" Gavin watched as the connections lit up inside of her, the past few weeks seeming to coalesce in a flash.

"It's the guns, Gavin. Up at Hell Gate." She paced back toward him, rattling the hints off as she saw them. "That's the start. Of all of this."

"Which is why they should be coming after cops. Instead, Darius and Valencia are collateral damage?"

The words practically burned his lips, the raw anger something he hadn't felt in a long time.

Not since his father…

But it was Sera who had the calm logic to see past it all. "Darius is married to one of the divers who worked the guns. Valencia is married to one of the forensics team members who handled them. It's fear by association."

Gavin felt the way the room seemed to electrify, her idea taking root and bringing him to a sitting position. He winced at the movement, but there was no way he could lie down for this.

"Here." She was by his side in an instant, fiddling with the electric riser function. "This will be easier."

With his bed set into a sitting position, Gavin pieced it together along with her, poking and prodding, adding and subtracting along the way.

"Okay, but let's pressure test this. I get the connection you're making, but Darius was murdered the day the team brought up the rest of the guns. That's awfully fast between Jayden working the dump site and his husband being shot."

Sera stilled, turning it over. "You've all said it, but in different ways. The guns were a sophisticated operation, not some random find. The dump location. The missing serial numbers. Someone planning like that would have to have an exit strategy."

"Okay, then next point. Why Darius specifically? Why Valencia? There are other divers. Other forensics team members." He knew he was playing devil's advocate, but they needed to ask the questions.

If the Hell Gate guns were the root of all this, then they'd been looking in the wrong place, just trying to find a shooter. It was a necessity, but if the gunman was nothing more than a tool, catching him stopped the violence, but it didn't stop the underlying problem.

And like a hydra, it would only regrow a head somewhere else.

"Jayden brought the guns up. Mack was on the team processing the evidence." Sera's mouth fell as that last piece clicked. "Spouses. Partners for life. Maybe there was some selection process, but it has to be tied to the NYPD members who worked the site."

"You go after the cop, you get a lot of cops riled. Go after their loved ones, get them scared," Arlo said, stepping into the room. "Kerrigan's been saying that all along. And sorry if I'm interrupting, but I couldn't miss overhearing it all outside the door."

"It's a horrible strategy," Gavin considered. "But it's effective."

"It's also a perfect way to hide." Arlo took a seat in one of the small folding chairs the nurse had brought in for him and the others earlier. "And it gives even more credence to the angle I've been running down on a well-run, organized offering to those who can pay for it to dispose of their guns, essentially making their crimes go away."

"Your informant," Gavin remembered. "Kerrigan mentioned her."

"Jade's rock-solid with the intel, and I think she's onto something. Unfortunately, I haven't been able to find a single line to tug on that one. Whispers and rumors aren't evidence, no matter how telling they really are."

Sera had remained quiet in Arlo's overview, but finally spoke, adding one more dimension to the problem. "The chain of evidence. Remove the gun, and it's awfully hard for someone like me to prosecute you."

Arlo nodded. "Damn hard."

It made sense. And more than that, it gave support to why someone would create a fear campaign to protect their interests.

Fear doesn't need a reason. It just needs a target.

"The loved ones *are* the target," Gavin said, seeing it all in his mind's eye. Remembering those tense moments out in front of the bar and that feeling of being watched. Because they had been. But they weren't the end game. "We thought it was us, but we were the diversion. It was Darius all along."

Even as the reality of it all hit him, Gavin felt that anger and fury riling him up, just like Arlo said.

And as fast as it came on, it quickly shifted in a new direction.

Because if the loved ones of cops were now the target, he'd just put a bull's-eye on Sera.

And he was wholly, desperately, irrevocably in love with the mother of his child.

Wyatt and Kerrigan rejoined them, fresh bottles of water in hand for her and Gavin, coffees for the rest of them as they swept through the door of Gavin's room.

And they brought good news. The best news, Sera thought, as Kerrigan recounted all she'd learned in the past half hour.

"Valencia came through surgery. She's got a long recovery ahead of her, but the doctors have every confidence she's going to be fine. She'll spend the night in intensive care, but they're already talking about possibly moving her tomorrow."

"That's amazing." Sera swallowed hard around the distinct tightening of her throat, the prick of tears behind her eyes hot as they spilled over.

Kerrigan came to stand with her, her support absolute as she wrapped an arm around her shoulders. "Now fill me in on what I missed."

Gavin caught everyone up on all they'd discussed.

"Weaponizing our fear," Wyatt practically spit out the words.

"And preying on cops' families," Arlo added.

Although the tears still threatened, the renewed round of anger as Wyatt, Arlo and Kerrigan got on the same page as she and Gavin went a long way toward reigniting her own fury. And with it, Sera considered all she knew from her job. All the cases she'd prosecuted and all that she understood about the inner workings of the city she'd served for nearly a decade.

At the heart of it all was data.

Human beings were the victims, but they were targeted via databases. And someone with access and motive.

"Everything since Darius was shot has been focused on the gunman. We need to look at the data. The forensics on the guns. Who would have access to HR data. And how to trace any comings and goings at Hell Gate."

Gavin added, "It's like the work for the task force. What are the systems in place? Where are the gaps? And if you can find those, you can find the points of risk."

"I can clearly see all you've laid out," Kerrigan started in, "But I'm not making the connection with the gun recovery. Where's anyone getting the details on our work? It's not like they can get up there and see what we're doing."

"Cameras?" Arlo asked.

Kerrigan shook her head. "That bridge isn't easily navigated. It's not a pedestrian bridge. It just carries the Amtrak trains."

"Via electrified train lines," Wyatt added. "You'd have to be a fool to try to walk up there. Even if you knew how to skip the lines, trains run through there all day."

"You can bike and run the Hell Gate Pathway to Randall's Island," Kerrigan said, considering. "If someone found a way there, they could try watching what's going on. It's been a while since I've been up there, but I don't remember a lot of easy water access, though, to get a good lookout."

"The guns weren't directly under the bridge, though."

Sera brought up a clear picture in her mind of the area where the Harbor team had brought up the cache. "It was a bit of a ways down the shoreline, on the Manhattan side just below Randall's Island. Maybe they're not watching from the bridge at all."

"All true." Kerrigan nodded.

"Very true, Kerr," Wyatt said. "Remember how bad the water was? We'd scoped several quadrants north and south from the dump point off the RFK. It was sheer dumb luck we found that cache. And we only found it because the water was running so hard, we had to expand our search."

"I'm not sure your work was dumb luck, Wyatt." Gavin was quick to support his friend and dive partner.

"But it sort of was," Wyatt pressed. "We'd never have been that close to the shoreline if we'd found what we were diving for. Those guns could have stayed there for who knows how much longer, and we'd never have been the wiser."

"But you did find it. And someone's awfully upset their dumping ground is gone." Arlo three-pointed his empty coffee cup into a nearby trash can. "So now we need to figure out who."

Sera might not have a physical component to her job, nor was she trained in cop work, but she did know research. Forward, backward and upside down if needed. She knew how to dig into the most obscure points until she had an answer. She'd done it in law school and had spent the better part of her professional life doing the same.

"Those guns are evidence, Arlo. If you can get me descriptions, I can look at recent cases. See if anything pops there."

It felt ridiculous to be talking about teeing up her work

databases in the middle of a hospital room, but she needed to do *something*. And this was something she was very, very good at.

Through a cop's eyes, the goal was to find physical evidence. But for her? The evidence was just the place to start. She was on the hunt for motive.

One strong enough and desperate enough to kill without compunction.

A week.

It had been a damn week, and she had nearly made her eyes bleed she'd hunted through so many files. Haunted every database she could find to search for details. She'd even gone to the file storage facility they housed in Red Hook to get her hands on a few old files that had seemed promising.

And still, nothing.

Not one damn thing.

Sera threw her pencil on top of her desk, about ready to call it a day. She still had a brief to write, and she wanted to get to Gavin's for dinner.

And to surreptitiously see how he was doing.

She hadn't made a big deal of it, but she suspected he had downplayed the pain from his injuries. That, along with the worry for his concussion, had her working hard to avoid the mother hen routine. She hadn't fully succeeded, but had usually been able to subdue his suspicions with a well-placed kiss.

Since they turned heated quickly, it was enough to distract him.

Even if she was paying for it with a raging case of hormones—amplified even further by her pregnancy—

and a healing man who wasn't fit yet for sex. No matter how much he tried to convince her otherwise.

Even with her hormones on overdrive, she refused to be swayed. The doctor had discharged Gavin the day after the explosion, but he'd been put on medical leave from active duty for a week, with a required appointment to be cleared to return.

His checkup was tomorrow, so there was that, at least, Sera admitted to herself. It would hopefully confirm he'd healed, it would get him back to work and, if she were lucky, distracted enough for her to figure out what she was going to do.

Because with every day she spent with him, she was forgetting all the reasons she'd believed she needed to hold her heart separate. In fact, each day had brought them closer, the kissing only a portion of the growing intimacy between them. They spoke of everything, from the case to their task force to their overarching career ambitions. Places they liked in Brooklyn, favorite restaurants and a rather heated debate over the best slice of pizza.

He also wasn't afraid to keep pushing on her lingering feelings over her parents, gently drawing her down the path of accepting their responsibilities and shortcomings in raising children by contrasting it to how the two of them wanted to raise their own child. And in return, she ensured they invited his mother to dinner one night and gave her one of those ultrasound photos, too.

But it had been the day he'd brought up names for their child when Sera finally admitted that the careful wall she'd built to keep her heart intact was crumbling, brick by brick.

Which only further reinforced why she had to focus on

the work and off Gavin's body. Or the way she felt when they were together. And definitely off parts farther south.

It's not like you can get more pregnant...

That little voice had grown stronger, popping up with that argument at inopportune times.

Like when she was kissing him.

Or brushing her teeth.

Or pouring a cup of coffee.

Pretty much every hour no matter what task she was engaged in.

It was why she'd started a nightly visit with his team to keep them all mentally engaged.

Each night Gavin, Kerrigan, Arlo and Wyatt would re-group. Arlo outlined whatever he'd discovered in the course of the investigation while Kerrigan and Wyatt provided updates on the harbor work and feedback from the forensics team on the guns. Sera and Marlowe would then apply their non-cop brains to alternative theories. So far, they'd run the gamut from another crime leader trying for the top spot in town to a new drug node making a go of it to a murder-for-hire group.

Even as each one netted out as a dead end.

Through it all, Sera couldn't stop thinking there was something they were missing. Something that would explain the erased serial numbers of the guns. No matter how many times she considered the woefully small set of details they knew, that was the one she kept circling back to.

Even the cleanup from the burned-out sub shop hadn't given them a lot to go on, although they did find out the name of the gunman. He'd been a careful criminal who tended to operate alone, with a relatively short rap sheet after a lifetime of crime. He hadn't been high on Arlo's list of local suspects to investigate, but when a search of his home produced ballistics evidence that matched the shots that killed Darius and also shot Valencia, it had given them some measure of reassurance they'd caught the right guy.

It wasn't much, but it was the one bright spot they'd had in the case, and she knew they were all clinging to it.

"Sera, do you have a minute?"

The interruption was welcome from the endless maze of her thoughts, and she jumped at the opportunity for a diversion. "David! Of course."

They hadn't seen much of each other with her task force work keeping her out of the office, and she was surprised, as he took a seat on the other side of her desk, to see that he was looking tired. Even more, he looked *worn*. While she fully recognized everyone went through periods of difficulty, she had to admit it was a shock to see him looking less than the dapper figure he cut in the courtroom and around town.

It was hardly a fair assessment. The pressure on him was immense, the responsibility for ensuring justice for a borough filled with more than two million people unrelenting.

With her smile firmly intact, she wondered how she could provide support. "Is there anything I can help you with?"

"I came to ask you the same. The news of what's been happening out of the 86th is concerning. Especially when it came to my attention that you were involved."

"Oh, well, I—" She wasn't sure what to say. His tone was conciliatory, with a clear layer of concern. But it was overlaid with…well, *censure*, Sera admitted to herself. "I wouldn't say I was involved."

"You weren't there?"

"Yes, I was. But thankfully, I wasn't the target. I was able to help."

"These are terrible risks, Sera. I put you up for the task force because I wanted to see you advance. But I can't afford to lose you."

"I hardly think—" She'd barely worked up a head of steam when she stopped at the strange twist of his lips.

What was going on with him?

David Esposito hadn't become one of the city's top legal minds—*or* the district attorney of New York's largest borough—because he was easily swayed. But she also wasn't comfortable sitting by letting him think she was going to kowtow to some ridiculous order to stand down when someone needed help.

Or was this simply a different side of him?

She'd worked for him for years and had believed she knew him, but it was entirely possible she'd only seen a side of him that he wanted her to see. And since she'd cultivated a reputation of quiet acceptance of the endless workload all while driving impeccable results, he'd had no reason to show her displeasure.

But now?

I put you up for the task force because I wanted to see you advance. But I can't afford to lose you.

Lose her?

Well, he'd shown his true colors that every action—every opportunity given—was only to advance his own standing. It was sad, but really, why should her boss be any different from anyone else?

"You hardly think what, Sera? That you're not at physical risk from the madman prowling the streets? You're fraternizing with the same people who are being targeted. How does that make you safe?"

Whatever else she might have said, it all died away. David actually thought she might be at risk of being killed?

"David, it was two incredibly unfortunate incidents. The gunman for both crimes has been caught, and the case has been closed. I'm fine."

"Until you become a target."

Something distinctly cold uncoiled in her gut at his insistence.

"It's a risk we all carry working in this office," he pressed on. "One that you're now flaunting by traipsing around town with a killer on the loose."

What was wrong with him? And using words like *flaunt* and *traipse*? As if she were flouncing around town in a ball gown and heels, taunting a killer?

One who'd been caught in a trap of his own making.

None of it made sense, coming from someone she respected.

And it was only because of those long years of working together, on top of that worn-out look that stretched his normally smooth veneer, that Sera tried to find some sort of common ground in the midst of his put-downs.

"David, if you're concerned about my work, please tell me. Otherwise, I'm afraid I need to stress that I'm hardly flaunting anything. I may be a public defender, but I'm also free to live my life as I see fit."

"I care about you, Sera. About your well-being."

"I care about my well-being, too. In fact—" She hesitated briefly, almost thinking better of saying anything during this odd and inappropriate debate between the two of them. But her body was changing by the day, and she wasn't interested in hiding the truth any longer, either. "I have some happy news."

"Oh?"

"I'm pregnant."

"You're—" It was his turn to catch himself, more of those strange emotions crossing his face. "That's wonderful news, Sera. Babies are a celebration. A wonderful affirmation of life."

"I think so."

She got the distinct sense he was about to ask her about her personal life, especially since he knew she wasn't married or in a relationship, when he seemed to think better of it.

In fact...

If she wasn't sitting right opposite him, watching for his reaction, she had no doubt she'd have missed it. But with a brief flash of awareness, she saw it.

A sort of knowing in his dark brown eyes.

And quite without knowing why, Sera fought off the wash of cold that gripped her bones with fierce fingers and refused to let go.

Although he technically wouldn't be cleared for work until tomorrow, Gavin had refused to sit home when he'd heard that Captain Reed was going to honor Mack and Valencia with a small reception at the hospital.

Valencia had made incredible progress, her own determination to leave the hospital matched with the incredible good fortune that the gunman had missed several major organs when he'd shot her. And this evening she was going home.

It was just like Captain Reed, his focus and care for his people the endless proof of how strong a leader he was and why they all had such unswerving loyalty for the man. And because of it, Gavin had headed out to the hospital, pleased to be there for something hopeful instead of the reasons for the past few weeks' visits.

He'd also gone to visit Jayden on his way over. He was finishing up his bereavement leave and would be back on Harbor the following week. Gavin had extended an invite to join him for the small party, but Jayden had declined, using a dinner at his mother's house as his excuse for missing it.

Gavin gave him the space, well aware the man could have done both, but recognized why this was too big a leap right now. And why, no matter how positively Jayden felt that Valencia was heading home, it couldn't erase the fact that his husband would never do the same.

But his parting words still stuck in Gavin's chest.

Thanks for being there for me, man. At the hospital and in all the time since. And thanks for inviting me tonight. Keep asking. One of these days I'll be ready.

He'd lived years with that lack of readiness. Probably too long, if he were honest with himself. And it made the reality of the changes Sera had brought to his life deeply affirming.

It was also proof that people could not only heal, but they could find their way back to something good.

Oh, how he wanted that someday for Jayden.

His text notification went off, and he pulled his phone out as he walked the last block to the hospital.

Almost there. You won't believe the day I had.

He stopped to text her back, stalling on the sidewalk so he could greet her and walk in with her.

Can't wait to see you. You can tell me all about it.

As he hit Send, Gavin couldn't hold back the smile. The fact they could share things at the end of the day had very quickly become one of the best parts of his evening, and he couldn't wait to put an arm around her and pull her close.

It was that steadily growing need to be with her, to talk to her, to *touch* her that drove him. Where before he had found that solace in a job well done and in pushing himself to be the best physically and mentally, all that energy had shifted.

Not that the work was less important or that he wanted to cut back on his conditioning, but it…consumed less. And instead, he was consumed with Sera. With their talk of the baby that would be here in a few short months. With the future he envisioned for the three of them.

What had begun as intense sexual desire had combined with the deepest sort of intimacy and interest in another person. And the more time he spent with her, the less he could see his life without her in it.

It had his heart catching in his throat as he saw her walking toward him from the opposite direction. And even though she was so close, he couldn't stand still, waiting for her. He caught her up halfway down the block, pulling her close and nearly off her feet.

"Gavin!" The breeze caught strands of her dark red hair whipping around her face, carrying her laughter up on the air.

"I missed you."

She stilled, her smile dimming as it moved to her eyes while her arms lifted to wrap around his neck. "I missed you, too."

Their mouths met, an affirmation of all he'd anticipated while waiting for her. And as he sank into her, taking her lips with his own and spinning them on a wild ride of yearning and fulfillment, he knew it was time to tell her how he felt.

Later. When they were alone and could talk. It was time to tell her how he felt. How much he wanted her and a future with her. And how determined he was to show her every day what she meant to him.

"Well, I think I know why all my days used to drag." Her arm was still around his neck, her smile flashing in the dying light of the day.

"Drag how?"

"They didn't include welcome kisses at the end of the day like that. I like it."

He nipped her lips for one more quick kiss. "Me, too."

They turned to head into the hospital complex hand in hand when he heard his name from across the street. Captain Reed's wife, Miranda, and their youngest daughter, Zuri, waved at him from the crosswalk, and he waved back, indicating they'd wait for them.

The early evening was quiet, the steady hum of traffic moving through the light at a sedate pace. It was only as it turned yellow, the various cars slowing, that Gavin heard it. The crazy, out-of-control swerving that indicated someone wasn't stopping.

He shouted to Miranda and Zuri, who were already stepping off the sidewalk. And then he took off at a run, determined to reach them before whoever was bearing down could get to them first.

Determined that one more loved one of a cop wasn't going to end up in the building behind him.

Chapter 16

Sera distributed the small pieces of cake even though she had no interest in eating. Gavin was still outside with Captain Reed, Arlo, Wyatt and Kerrigan as well as several other uniforms on patrol in the neighborhood, viewing the crime scene and taking pictures.

Captain Reed hadn't been able to stop touching his wife and child as they'd stood out on the street corner, recovering from the shock of the oncoming car and Gavin's race across the street that had tackled them both to the ground.

She'd wanted to do the same for Gavin, but had given him the space to focus on what happened, relaying each detail to the captain including what little he'd seen of the driver.

When the initial shock faded, Captain Reed had finally brought Miranda and Zuri into the hospital cafeteria where they'd set up the cake for Valencia and asked them stay there.

"I still don't know what to say." Miranda had moved up beside her to cut the cake after Valencia had done the honors on the first piece. Sera suspected the busy movements were keeping the woman from mentally reviewing each and every moment of the attack, and she'd avoided suggesting she sit down.

Sometimes action was the best medicine, and right now

she could console herself that she was taking care of her husband's team.

"You're sure you're okay?"

"We are because of Gavin." Miranda's hand shook as she picked up a few more plates to move them to the end of a long table where people were helping themselves to the cut squares. Her gaze unerringly found her daughter, where Zuri played with Mack and Valencia's daughter, Gia, across the room. "I can't stop going over it in my mind."

"It's so fresh it's hard to digest. But it will fade in time." Sera tried to offer as much consolation as she could. "Become less urgent."

"I know." Miranda nodded, grief filling her deep brown eyes. "And I know there will come a day I don't want to latch myself onto my child and never let her go. Which I promise I won't do." The woman smiled. "Or won't after I give myself a solid week of overcompensating."

Miranda took a deep breath. "But we will get through this. Because I'm a cop's wife, and I know the risks. What I won't get over is why some monster has decided my family and Mack's family and Jayden's family are disposable targets, used to meet some sick end."

Miranda's use of the word *target* had Sera's mind shifting back to that odd conversation with David earlier.

David, it was two incredibly unfortunate incidents. The gunman of both crimes has been caught and the case has been closed. I'm fine.

Until you become a target.

He'd used that word, too. Target.

And now there was a third incident, in such a short period of time. The risks had expanded, the inclusion of a child in this attack a dark sign of escalation. How did they fight this? Because if random street-level attacks were suddenly the norm, no one was safe.

Which made the large hand that covered her shaking one as she picked up a few more small plates of cake a welcome relief.

"Hey there."

She looked up to find Gavin, his expression soft as he gently took the plates from her, setting them back on the table before pulling her close.

There wasn't even a heartbeat of hesitation as she went into his arms.

And as that same heartbeat thrummed against his, she tried to calm her racing thoughts. Who was doing this? And if they'd escalated their fear-based targeting to children, how much more appealing would it be to go after a pregnant woman?

In his nearly ten years at the 86th, Gavin had seen their captain mad—even furious on occasion—but nothing had prepared him for the blind rage that had cloaked the man this evening.

Someone had come after his family.

That reality would always have been upsetting, but now that he was facing fatherhood, Gavin understood the rage in a whole new dimension. All-consuming, with a desperate need to protect that refused to be sated.

He still struggled with it as he took Sera home, hypervigilant to any possible threat. It was only when they finally reached her door, both of them safely inside the apartment, that he let out his first easy breath.

"Why don't you come in and sit down for a bit?" Her voice was gentle as she gestured him toward the couch. "I know you keep telling me you're fine, but you're still recovering from bruised ribs and a mild concussion. Today was another difficult day."

He tried to process Sera's words, but all he heard—all he really understood—was that his family was in danger. He'd lived with that outcome once, and there was no way he could go back there. No way he'd survive it again.

"I can't lose you."

"Gavin, I—"

Her words vanished as his arms came around her, burying his head in her neck. Breathing her in. Wanting desperately to build a life with this woman and the child they'd created.

"You're not going to lose me," she whispered against the side of his head. "We're here, and we're not going anywhere."

He wanted to believe it. Even now, with all the strife and uncertainty, he could see that future he wanted. Could see the life he wanted to create for his child.

"But, Gavin. Right here. Right now. It's just us."

He felt her meaning before it registered, the kiss she pressed to the side of his head followed by featherlight kisses over his forehead, his eyebrows, his cheekbone. She continued that miraculous exploration, on down over the day's worth of stubble on his cheeks to his lips.

Only then did she take his mouth fully with her own, the warmest welcome he'd ever known.

"Come all the way inside with me."

She took his hand and without waiting for him to say anything, drew him into her apartment and back toward the bedroom.

The work bag she'd carried home fell somewhere along the way, as did the raincoat she'd worn.

He vaguely felt her stop their movement to discard her shoes and insist he do the same.

Halfway down the hall to her bedroom, she slipped off the blazer she wore. His shirt ended up floating to the floor beside it.

And by the time they stepped into her bedroom, he had her slim figure in his arms, clad in nothing but a thin blouse and skirt, pressed to his bare chest. With her hands on him and his deftly removing what little remained, in a matter of moments Gavin was laying her down on the bed, naked and gorgeous beneath him.

"You're even more beautiful than I remembered." He ran a trail of kisses over her throat. "And I remember really—" he pressed a kiss "—really—" and then another "—really well."

She sighed under his mouth, and he continued his exploration, on over her pretty expanse of cleavage before trailing his tongue over her breast. Soft moans filled the air, her body growing more restless beneath him as he took a nipple between his teeth. Her throaty response grew deeper, huskier, and he was gratified to know he gave her pleasure.

The signs of her pregnancy were everywhere, and as Gavin sat back and looked his fill, he had to admit the changes were gorgeous on her. Her breasts had an additional roundness that wasn't there before, her hips, too. But it was the light swell of her stomach that captivated him.

Their child was there, nestled safe inside of her.

Sheer awe coursed through him as he bent and pressed his lips to that slight mound, imagining the small, perfect little form growing just beyond. Once again, that fierce need to protect rose up and swamped him, practically stealing his breath with its intensity.

His. They were his, and he'd give his life for them. Without thinking. Without hesitation.

Even with those feral thoughts raging through him, he felt the gentleness surround them. But it was the soft light in Sera's eyes, as he lifted his gaze to hers, that nearly did him in. Whatever had brought them to this moment— whatever trials they'd faced so far and whatever they'd face in future—he knew he wanted to face them with her.

As partners.

As protectors.

And, with the miracle growing between them, as parents.

"Gavin."

Her voice was whisper-soft, even as he heard the distinct notes of a demand beneath the quiet. Had his name ever sounded so sweet? So perfect?

And had he ever been more ready for a woman than he was at this moment? That insistent hum in the blood that could only be sated by making her his had ratcheted up so that he could hear nothing else. So that he could only *feel*.

He removed his slacks and underwear, the last barrier between them, and gave himself up to her.

It had been more than three months since they'd been together, but the pleasure arcing between them felt as familiar as breathing. And as new as a sunrise.

He positioned himself at the entrance to her body and stared down into her eyes. The woman he'd believed he would never see again—never touch again—had somehow found her way back to him.

It was a miracle mixed with a beautiful twist of fate.

And he would never take any of it for granted. Would never take what they had between them for granted.

There was still so much to figure out, but what had seemed unconquerable only a few weeks ago now seemed like an open road ahead. One they'd navigate together.

And as he felt her deft touch take him in hand, teasing his flesh as she guided him to her core, Gavin knew another truth. There was no other woman in the world for him. No other woman who could be so utterly perfect for him. No other woman who felt like home.

Home, he thought as their bodies joined, quickly finding a rhythm that worked for them both.

Whatever life had thrown at them both up to now, none of it mattered. Instead, the winding path to each other had provided perspective, wisdom and an understanding of why no one else had been right before. Why this time and this place was finally, perfectly, right.

When he felt the tell-tale signs of her release, his quickly followed.

And he let her welcome him home.

Was it possible to live on sex alone?

Sera knew the realities of her body suggested she'd have to move sooner or later for food and water, but in that instant, wrapped up in Gavin, she'd be content to stay here forever.

"Are you awake?" She whispered the words into the air, unable to move for the heavy sprawl of man who lay over her. It was a magical sensation, even if it limited mobility. Or, she hated to admit, a bit of her breath.

She didn't have to wait long for an answer, his smile wide when he lifted himself up onto his elbows to look down on her. "Sorry. You made me forget my own name there for a while."

Sheer delight coursed through her at his compliment. "Aren't you sweet?"

"Actually, I'm a bit brain-dead, but who really needs the ability to balance a checkbook?"

"Those are the brain cells you gave up?"

"I wasn't all that good at it anyway, so you've given me an outstanding excuse."

She laughed at the silliness of it all, even as she had to admit his thoughts weren't too far off the mark. "I was trying to calculate how long a person could stay in bed having sex without needing food or water."

"And miss out on the decadence of having food in bed after sex?"

"You're hungry?"

"For you, always." He bent down and pressed a kiss to her shoulder. "For pizza?" A wry smile lit his face. "Always."

Sera laughed again, pure, simple joy roaring through her in a flood. For the magic of being together again. And the warm, wonderful reassurance of his body covering hers.

"Now that you mention pizza, I am a bit hungry." She tickled his side, the motion enough to have him moving slightly, giving her the opportunity to slide out from beneath him and neatly flip their position.

And while she was hungry for pizza—and would dial up her favorite neighborhood delivery in a bit—she was more interested in exploring the man in her bed a bit longer.

Or forever.

The thought whispered through her, beating in time with the heavy pumping of her blood.

Where that would have scared her even a week before, now...it didn't. And wasn't that a miracle in and of itself? The belief she wasn't worthy of something good and lasting—or worse, that she was incapable of it—had faded. What was actually fear, way down deep, that she'd held to so tightly for so long had been upended by this man.

By his patience. His insistence. And by the amazing fact that he showed up, fully present. Hadn't that been something of a revelation? From the first moments of knowing about the pregnancy, he'd made it clear he wasn't going anywhere. He was a part of his child's life, and nothing about that had wavered, not for one single instant.

And maybe, if she took the leap and voiced what she wanted, he'd stay for her, too.

It was a risk, Sera knew. But the reward was so very great.

Bending down from where she straddled his hips, she kissed him. And in the sweetness of meeting lips and the responsive male beneath her, Sera finally knew what she needed.

To be happy.

To feel safe.

To find her future.

All of it was more important—even more than sex or food or the safe cocoon she locked herself in—if she wanted to find the pathway to a future for her and her child.

And it all rested with Gavin.

"I love you."

The words she'd never spoken as an adult felt right. *Perfect*, actually.

His dark eyes never wavered from hers, but the hands that had settled on her lower back while they'd kissed moved to gently cup her cheeks.

"I love you, Sera. I want to build a future with you. For

our child, yes, but with you. Somehow, someway, I sensed that from the very first moments."

"Me, too." She closed her eyes before allowing them to pop back open. Here. With him. There was nothing to hide from. "I ran out on New Year's Day because I didn't believe this could be real. That you couldn't actually feel this way about someone so quickly. But I was wrong."

He lifted to meet her halfway for a kiss, their love for each other wrapping around them. And as she sank into him, the two of them falling back to the bed, it was a long while later before either of them thought about anything but each other.

"I have to hand it to you, Gavin Hayes. Sex pizza is pretty great."

"Sex pizza?" Gavin asked, still floating on a satisfied mix of outrageously good sex, perfect pizza dough and the woman beside him in bed.

The woman he loved.

"I can't say I've had all that much sex pizza." She eyed him as she took a small bite of her cheese slice. "Or any sex pizza since I assume it requires sticking around and sharing a meal. But I have to say, it's an inspired choice."

If he were honest, he couldn't say he'd had all that much "sex pizza," either. He'd had pizza after sex, standing alone in his kitchen, and he'd had it before, grabbing a slice somewhere before going out. But never in his life could he remember eating it naked in bed with a woman. "Me, either."

"I wonder why that is. It's pretty great."

He leaned in and licked a small drop of sauce at the corner of her mouth she hadn't yet gotten with her napkin. "It's awesome with the right person. Which you most definitely are." He reached for another slice from the heavy cardboard box they'd laid out in the middle of the bed. "But I'm not sure I've ever wanted this sort of intimacy with another person."

"Sex is intimacy."

"So's eating food. And sharing stories. And talking. I never had that before you, Sera."

"I've never had that, either." The smile that filled her face dimmed, the carefree light seeming to fade from her eyes.

"What's wrong?"

"I can't help but think of Jayden. Of all he's lost. I found you over these past few weeks, and he's lost the same beautiful life."

"I know."

And he did know. The loss his friend was facing was the pain none of them could forget. The stark counterpoint to the sheer joy he felt in finding Sera again and preparing for their baby's arrival.

Sera set down her pizza and turned, laying a hand on his arm. "He's not alone. You, Kerrigan, all of you, really. You'll see to that. But for him now? The future must feel like an endless stretch in front of him. Something to be dreaded instead of embraced."

"It's the senselessness of it I still can't get my head around. And you see a lot of senseless waste as a cop. But to target loved ones to hide your crimes? To scare cops and divert them from the work?"

The hand on his forearm tightened, Sera's gaze going wide. "Gavin!"

"What's wr—"

"Me! How did I miss this? Arlo said he's not been able to

find any leads on that crime ring. That he can't get a handle on what amounts to rumor on disposing of weapons."

"What does that have to do with you?"

"I have access to the files. I've spent all week looking at prosecuted cases, but I can also see what's been thrown out. What never made it to trial. What has gaps in evidence." She scrambled out of bed, clearly unaware of her nakedness, as she raced to her dresser for one of her ever-present notepads. "All we need is to get the dates forensics has estimated on the guns. I can use that to set my date criteria in the databases and work backward from there."

It couldn't be that easy. There was no way it was that easy, Gavin thought.

But even as he tried to keep his excitement in check, he knew she was right.

"Cross-jurisdictional work at its finest."

She looked up from where she was making notes to grin before crossing over to him and laying a big smacking kiss on him. "And score for the local team. You and I, Mr. Hayes. We're going to kick task force ass!"

Chapter 17

Sera wasn't quite sure how she'd gone from the glories of an evening in Gavin's arms and the joys of sex pizza to an all-nighter at work, but she couldn't deny how right this felt.

Finally.

They had a lead. It was slim, and it was going to take a lot of digging, but it was something they could actually work with. He'd dropped her off at the DA's office before heading to the precinct to run down whatever he could on the forensics work, with Arlo, Kerrigan and Wyatt heading in to meet him.

They all exchanged texts throughout the night, with a steady drip feed of dates as they got the information off the guns, which she'd cross-reference with as many files as she could find in the same time frame.

She hunted through it all. The discovery process. Briefs. And then actual trial notes and transcripts. All of it filled page after page of her legal pad, but as of yet, she couldn't find a connection.

But she did find threads.

Sera sat back and stared at all she'd written down. There wasn't an exact pattern, but there was a consistency. Somewhere in the discovery process, she could see references to gun activity and crimes. But by the time she got to the actual trial notes, evidence wasn't available.

It was frustrating and slow and she'd nearly given up, vowing to come back at it tomorrow, when she saw movement outside her office door.

"Sera!" David's smile was broad as he peeked his head in the door. "You're here late."

"You, too. I didn't see you when I came in."

"I just got here."

At three in the morning? "Your work ethic's impressive, David, but that's an early start for anyone."

"The work's been on overdrive lately. I couldn't sleep and had some ideas on a few cases I wanted to get down. Figured I'd get ahead of my day."

"Of course. Justice might be blind, but she doesn't sleep." She made the joke, smooth and easy, just some of the simple banter she and David had shared for years.

Years.

It was the camaraderie of colleagues. Laced with the respect she'd always had for her boss.

Her boss whose name she'd seen at the bottom of each of the files she'd looked through. His bold, scrawling signature dismissing each case she'd flagged with a suspicious lack of evidence.

But it all hit her now, a vicious gut punch as dot after dot connected in her mind.

Seemingly oblivious, David waved at her from the door. "I'll leave you to it, then."

As he moved out of her line of sight, her phone rang, Gavin's name filling the screen. The ringer was on silent, and she opened the line, about to tap the speaker button, when David stepped back into view.

"What are you working on this late, Sera? I reduced

your casework so you could take full advantage of the task force."

"I know, David, and I appreciate the consideration." Her heart throbbed in her throat in a heavy pounding sensation and she forced herself to remain calm. To speak in as normal a voice as possible as she made a point to use his name. "I'm actually here because of the task force."

"Oh?"

"The work my partner and I have been doing. We're focused on the chain of evidence. How much it matters and how much can go wrong if any team mishandles a single bit of it."

"It's a good angle."

"It certainly is." She prayed Gavin got her message, well aware she was about to take the biggest gamble of her life. "And it's amazing to realize just how many facets of the police touch evidence. The cops first. Then the forensics team takes over. All under the captain's leadership."

She avoided even looking at her phone, afraid to tip David off to their audience, but she had her messaging app also open on her computer screen and saw Gavin's text come through.

I've got you.

He did have her. And it was that rock-solid knowledge that had her making the final leap. "But you already know this, David. Don't you?"

"You couldn't just stay out of it." David took a few steps into her office. "I put you on the task force to give you advancement. To give you opportunity."

"And I appreciate it."

"I had some selfish reasons for it, too. Namely to get you out of my hair. You've always been way too attentive, working long hours to make sure you're number one."

Before she even had time to be insulted, he had a gun out of his pocket, directed at her. It was an odd-looking piece, like something a person could assemble on their own.

And not for one minute did she believe it any less deadly.

"How'd you get a gun inside the building?"

"You'd be amazed what you can get in and out of here. Especially when you're the most favored man of the people."

And as he cocked the trigger, gesturing her up and out of her seat, Sera gave one last glance to her phone and prayed Gavin would get here soon. Because the man she'd respected—the one all of Brooklyn had voted to represent them—had betrayed them all.

Everything in him was cold.

Not like huddling in a jacket on a winter's day or trying to find warmth on a January dive, but bone-deep cold.

Soul-deep cold, actually.

It was all Gavin could think as he briefed Arlo, Wyatt and Kerrigan before Wyatt rushed out to call Captain Reed.

All he could feel as they strapped on Kevlar and collected their weapons to head to the DA's office.

All he knew as they drove the nearly deserted streets at 4:00 a.m.

David Esposito had proven he would kill for no more reason than to instill fear. With all her knowledge, did Sera have any hope of surviving his wrath?

Gavin willed those thoughts away, even as he went through each required step. He called in backup for a probable hostage situation while Kerrigan called in the orders to get SWAT in place.

Each step felt like a century, but they had everyone mobilized and heading toward the building that housed the DA in under five minutes. Along the way, they briefed the security team in the DA's office.

That team was instructed to quietly assess what they could and they quickly affirmed that all office cameras were off on the DA's floor. Add to that the tinted exterior windows, and they were effectively blind to the situation.

All they had to go on was the intel Sera had gleaned by keeping him on her phone line and the understanding of what risks David posed to his own discovery. Intel that had vanished when the DA had ordered Sera out of her office.

That was the lone thought that kept Gavin going as they raced through the night. If David hurt Sera in the building, he had no hope of ever covering up his crimes. The man still didn't know she'd had him on speaker, which meant he might still be under the illusion he could get away with it.

And if he thought that, he'd have to get Sera outside the building.

"We're going to get her, Gav." Arlo had said the same thing over and over as they navigated the neighborhood.

"He's a good guy, Arlo. Sera has talked several times about his leadership and how much she liked working for him."

Gavin tried to map that description—one from someone he respected—with the realities of what they were racing toward. "And now he's a messed-up human being in over his head. Which makes him dangerous and unpredictable."

The worst combination they faced as cops.

And as they got out of the car a block away from the

DA's office, Gavin realized he felt dangerous and unpredictable, too. He had to get a handle on it. Had to push it away
and remain focused only on getting Sera safely out of the
clutches of a madman.

It was the only way to save her and the baby.

The baby.

Sera couldn't stop thinking about the life growing inside of her. Couldn't stop thinking about the ultrasound
photos nestled in the treasure box on her coffee table and
the excitement she and Gavin both carried about the new
images they'd get at her upcoming appointment.

They might even find out the baby's gender.

They'd talked of both wanting to know, excitement hum-
ming between them as they talked about names.

The baby was their future. One they were building a
foundation for now.

And if all she knew of her boss was true, all of that was
now at risk.

David hadn't tied her up, but he kept the gun trained
on her, forcing her to stay seated in one of his plush office
chairs while he sat in the one beside her.

"Why are you doing this?"

"Why?" He looked up from where he flipped through
something on his phone. "Isn't it obvious?"

"Actually, it's not."

"Money, Sera. Please don't tell me you're also a naive
workaholic who doesn't actually understand it makes the
world go round."

Once again, she opted to ignore the insult. Was she really
going to get upset over the opinion of someone who was so
broken? So utterly, absolutely bereft of a soul?

With that firmly in her mind, she peppered him with questions instead.

"Then why go into law for the city? If you only cared about money, there are enough corporate legal jobs to have kept you in designer suits for ten lifetimes."

"And then you're stuck with partner politics and all the ridiculous BS that comes with getting along well with others."

Since the common wisdom at the big firms was "eat what you kill," Sera wasn't ready to give him the point on that one, but really, what did it matter? He'd created some story for himself that separated him from what he was doing. What she had to do was create enough of her own story to get her and the baby out and away.

Memories of that text message filled her thoughts, pushing her on.

I've got you.

Gavin would have put everything into motion by now, so her focus had to be on getting *out*. Because staying in was the worst thing she could do.

No one could help her inside.

And David had likely rigged everything to his benefit in here.

She needed out.

"I always respected your leadership. It's why I've stayed here. Why I choose to work for the city, each and every day."

He looked up from where he tapped on his phone, an overbright grin marring his features. "Glad to know the ol' act worked."

"If you won't consider letting me go for me, at least consider it for my child."

The grin fell, and in its place was a rapid set of calculations. "The cop. It's his baby. The one you were cozying up to on the police boat."

The police boat? "What—" The question was nearly out before she realized what he meant. "You have a watchman up at Hell Gate?"

"People get in the way, Sera. Modern tech is so much better. Removes too many sets of eyes and gives me all I need."

Somewhere down deep, Sera realized that was the final piece of the puzzle. A part of her—bigger than she'd realized—had kept hoping he had been dragged into this somehow. Influenced by darker forces who seduced him with money and promises of even more power.

But there was no one else.

"It really is you. Behind all of this."

"You seem surprised by that." The statement was said so clearly as to be almost academic. It nearly tripped her up, because it felt like so many other conversations they'd had through the years. Debating a legal point. Discussing motives. Reviewing various legal theory.

But it wasn't any of those things. It was just the horrible, terrible truth that one more person she trusted had betrayed her.

"It's time to go now."

"What?"

He'd already stood, the gun in hand unwavering as he pointed toward the door with his phone. "It's time to go."

"Go where?"

"Where I can get rid of you and still have a shot at keeping my little enterprise going."

* * *

They wanted David Esposito alive.

Arlo had run him through it. Captain Reed had added his requirements via a call before confirming he was on his way. SWAT had been given the same set of instructions.

Unless the risks were too great, the man was to be kept alive at all costs.

The fallout would be enormous, a betrayal on this scale from an elected official in the largest city in America. And the very highest echelons of the department wanted it all on record so they could make an example out of him.

Gavin understood the orders. He even had every intention of following them.

Unless there was a whisper of risk to Sera. Then all bets were off.

He and Arlo had set up with the SWAT team in front of the DA's office. The fact that Esposito had bombed the sub shop was enough to get the bomb squad in as well, and they were on point should anything suggest David had rigged the government building.

"Heat signature!"

Gavin moved closer to the SWAT team manning the equipment. "Two bodies, on the move."

He watched the movement on screen. Saw the awkward way the two people walked, like one was restraining the other in some way.

They moved through the third floor, from the back of the building toward its center to a stairwell. Step by step, he could see them walk, before they arrived on the second floor. He'd only been in the building once, but could still picture the large stairwell that ran up the middle of the structure. It had reminded him of high school, those stairs a sort of common meeting ground on the lobby and each ascending floor. Stairs that, once descended, would bring someone to the lobby where you could go out the front door to the main thoroughfare or out the back door to an alley and a small parking lot beyond.

"He's moving her. Getting her out of the building," Gavin said, certain they'd exit in the back. Even more certain no one on point in the back would take the needed shot.

With absolute conviction, he recognized the truth. David Esposito was too important. And that made Sera expendable.

He took a few steps back from the assembled SWAT team and the expert manning the heat signatures. He was the only one who had her best interests at heart.

One deep breath.

He stilled himself for one deep breath, but in the end that was all he needed.

His took in the screen SWAT had set up, his gaze never leaving the moving forms visible as heat signatures.

He watched as those two figures rounded the stairwell, just about to head down to the lobby.

Watched when one pushed the other.

And watched as a body fell down the stairs, the other one taking off at a run.

"Could you slow down? I am pregnant."

David kept a tight grip on her with one hand, the gun never wavering in the other. "You barely look any different."

"Yeah, well, I've been sitting for a few hours, and my ankles are swollen."

As lies went, it tripped off the tongue, and she gave mental thanks for the *What to Expect* book she'd been reading each night for the inspiration.

But she did feel him slow, whatever lingering chivalry the man possessed coming to the fore. It was what she'd banked on, and it gave her the slight advantage in position she needed.

Slow step. Down.

Slow step. Down.

Slow step…

Sera took a deep breath and pushed David as hard as she could.

Whether it was the years of trust they had built between them or his sheer underestimation of her, she didn't know, nor did she care. All she did know was she had the small space to get out.

Away.

And if she could get out, she'd find Gavin. She knew it.

Ignoring the shouts behind her, she ran as hard as she could down the rest of the stairs, zigzagging her way toward the front exit as soon as she hit the main level. She briefly debated the back alley and parking lot, but the front would give her access to the street and, if the cops were there, ready and waiting protection.

David continued to shout behind her, firing off a shot just as she got the heavy front doors open. They led into the main lobby and screening area, and she pushed through there, desperate for fresh air.

For the street.

For Gavin.

Shouts went up as she slammed through the main entrance door, lights so bright she thought it was daytime.

And still, she ran.

Away from the building.

Away from the oncoming threat.

And straight into Gavin's arms.

"Sera!"

He wrapped her up, turning so that his back was to the building and the threats that lay beyond.

"You're here." She clung to him, the shouts behind her fading away at the protection and warmth and safety that enveloped her.

"I'm here."

They stayed like that for long minutes, arms wrapped tight around each other, whatever tableau playing out behind them someone else's worry.

Someone else's problem.

"I can't believe it was David all along."

"I'm so sorry." He kept her tight against his chest, his words a thick murmur in her ear. "One more betrayal you don't deserve."

His concern was so caring—so deeply felt—and it caught her in the moment that she hadn't given that aspect of David's actions a single thought.

His betrayal of the people and the office he held? Absolutely?

But of her?

Not once.

She lifted her head from his chest, gazing deep into his eyes and willing him to understanad. "You came for me and our baby, Gavin. You. That's all I need."

The old part of her would have wanted to be in the thick of it all. Part of the action and excitement to hide all she was missing in the rest of her life.

But she didn't need that any longer. She no longer needed

work or cases or the perception she was number one from an external source. She still intended to strive for it, but she no longer *needed* it. And as she held Gavin close, murmuring over and over how much she loved him, Sera realized that made all the difference.

The things that had made up her days were important. Justice for the people of the city she loved would always matter.

But the life she and Gavin would make for themselves and their child?

Well, that was everything.

* * * * *

Dear Reader,

I shared these thoughts in the first book of this series, *Danger in the Depths*, but do feel it bears repeating.

While there is an expert team as part of the NYPD who manage all the police work of the harbor and the surrounding waters of New York City, their day-to-day activities are not widely publicized, nor is there much information available about them.

This series is born of my deep respect for what these brave men and women do, with representation of them and their duties coming from my own imagination. Any errors are my own.

Addison Fox

HARLEQUIN
Reader Service

Enjoyed your book?

Try the perfect subscription for Romance readers and get more great books like this delivered right to your door.

See why over 10+ million readers have tried Harlequin Reader Service.

Start with a Free Welcome Collection with free books and a gift—valued over $20.

Choose any series in print or ebook.
See website for details and order today:

TryReaderService.com/subscriptions